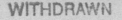
vas
the
me

her
out

fur

nd
ed.

rp

. . .

**Books by Peg Kehret**

Available from MINSTREL Books

# FRIGHTMARES™

## The Ghost Followed Us Home

**Peg Kehret**

A MINSTREL® BOOK

PUBLISHED BY POCKET BOOKS

New York   London   Toronto   Sydney   Tokyo   Singapore

This book is a work of fiction. Names, characters, places and incidents are products of the author's imagination or are used fictitiously. Any resemblance to actual events or locales or persons, living or dead, is entirely coincidental.

A MINSTREL PAPERBACK *Original*

A Minstrel Book published by
POCKET BOOKS, a division of Simon & Schuster Inc.
1230 Avenue of the Americas, New York, NY 10020

ISBN: 0-671-53522-6

First Minstrel Books paperback printing January 1996

10 9 8 7 6 5 4 3 2 1

Cover art by Dan Burr

Printed in the U.S.A.

*For Brett Konen*

The
Ghost
Followed
Us Home

# CARE CLUB
## We Care About Animals

I. Whereas we, the undersigned, care about our animal friends, we promise to groom them, play with them, and exercise them daily. We will do this for the following animals:

**WEBSTER** (Rosie's cat)
**BONE BREATH** (Rosie's dog)
**HOMER** (Kayo's cat)
**DIAMOND** (Kayo's cat)

II. Whereas we, the undersigned, care about the well-being of *all* creatures, we promise to do whatever we can to help homeless animals.

III. Care Club will hold official meetings every Thursday afternoon or whenever else there is important business. All Care Club projects will be for the good of the animals.

Signed:

*Rosie Saunders*

*Kayo Benton*

# *Prologue*

## Sedan, France
## August 1914

Chantal Dubail ignored the distant gunfire.

"Sing for the soldiers," Chantal said as she pushed on the sides of her new musical cat. She worked the bellows in and out, in and out, smiling as the gray mohair cat produced a brief tune.

"Good Kitty," Chantal said. "Your music makes the soldiers happy. Papa and Jacques and all the other brave French soldiers clap when they hear your song." She lifted the cat to her face and kissed its velvet ears.

"Chantal!" Mama's cry startled Chantal out of her daydream. "Hurry! We must hide in the barn."

Chantal frowned, not wanting to leave her game. She was tired of hiding, tired of hearing guns in the distance. Tired of war.

She pulled her blue kerchief farther down over

1

her ears, trying to block out the sound of Mama's voice.

This time, she decided, she would not hide with Mama. She and Kitty would stay here and finish their pretend concert for the French soldiers. Mama could hide in the barn by herself.

It was Chantal's sixth birthday, after all. On her birthday she should be allowed to play with her gift. She should not have to hide from the German army.

The Germans never came, anyway. Three times already this week Chantal had left her games to hide in the barn, only to emerge hours later, tired and cross and smelling of cow manure, when the threatened attack failed to happen.

"Chantal!" Mama's voice was urgent now. "Hurry! The Germans are coming this way. I hear shots."

Chantal pressed herself against the floor beside her bed and squeezed her eyes shut, pretending to be asleep.

She heard Mama run into the room. Chantal lay still.

Mama grabbed Chantal's arm, jerking her to her feet.

"Come, Chantal," Mama said. "We must hide. Quickly!"

Chantal reached back to get Kitty, but Mama was already dragging her toward the door.

"Wait!" Chantal said. "I want to take Kitty."

"There is no time for toys," Mama said. "Run, Chantal! Run!"

Mama raced across the dirt yard to the barn, pulling Chantal with her. Tears puddled in Chantal's eyes, and she stumbled over a rock.

Inside the barn, Mama pointed to the stall where Sylvie the cow chewed her cud. "Get in the stall with Sylvie," she said. "Pull hay over yourself and lie very, very still. Stay quiet until I come for you."

The tears spilled down Chantal's cheeks. "I want Kitty."

"Do as I say, Chantal! Now!" Mama turned and climbed up the ladder to the hayloft.

Chantal ran into the cow stall and crouched in the corner, near Sylvie's head. She listened to the noises outside. They came from the direction of the river.

Rifle shots. Voices.

The shouting was louder than it had been on previous days. As she listened, the gunfire grew louder still. Closer.

Chantal lay down and pulled hay over herself. The dry hay made her skin itch and she scratched at her cheek.

*Boom! Boom! Boom!* A series of shots echoed across the barnyard.

Sylvie swished her tail and mooed.

A shudder ran down Chantal's arms. The German soldiers were really coming this time. The horrible German soldiers, the men Papa and Jacques had gone away to fight, were coming here, to her farm. The soldiers were marching across Papa's wheat field, trampling the grain.

What would they do to Chantal's house?

Before Papa and Jacques went away to fight, Chantal had heard them talk about how the German soldiers plundered the buildings in their path, looting and burning. Would they set fires here? Would Chantal's house soon be rubble and ashes?

Kitty! The German soldiers will burn my Kitty, Chantal thought. I must save her!

Chantal flung the hay aside and sprang to her feet. She ran to the door of the barn and lifted the heavy wooden latch. When the door swung open, she dashed across the yard toward the house.

"Kitty!" she cried. "I'm coming! I'll save you!"

A single shot rang out, sharp and loud.

"Kitty!"

# Chapter

# 1

This is terrible," Kayo Benton said as she brought the *Oakwood Daily Herald* newspaper inside. "Someone broke into the doll museum."

Kayo's best friend, Rosie Saunders, leaned over Kayo's shoulder and they read the article together.

### DOLL MUSEUM BURGLARIZED

The Oakwood Doll Museum was broken into early this morning. The museum's burglar alarm went off at two A.M. When police arrived five minutes later, the thieves had left.

Police Chief Brian Stravinski said there were no clues to the identity of the burglars.

The door to a small office had been forced open and . . .

Kayo flung the newspaper down in disgust without finishing the article. "I am going to quit reading the news," she said. "It's too depressing to know what goes on in the world."

"That's why Mom does her U.K.s," Rosie said. "She says there are so many unexpected bad things that the rest of us have to do unexpected kindnesses, in order to balance it out."

"It will take a lot of U.K.s to make up for robbing the doll museum," Kayo said. "That's my favorite place in the whole world. Except for baseball fields, of course."

"Mine, too," Rosie said. "I hope the thief didn't steal the miniature dictionary."

"Or the Jackie Robinson doll," Kayo said. "That doll even has a tiny Ted Williams bat, and a little ball, and number twenty-four on his Dodger uniform."

"Remember the musical cat?" Rosie said.

"Oh, I hope the musical cat wasn't stolen. It was the best toy of all. Remember how we wished we could play it?"

Rosie nodded, remembering. The girls had gazed into the glass display case, admiring the gray mohair cat. With its black and yellow glass eyes, its embroidered toes, and its ears lined with light gray velvet, the cat looked almost lifelike. It even had a tiny pink tongue.

Rosie had read the information card aloud. " 'Made in France, circa 1900.' "

"What does *circa* mean?" Kayo asked.

"I don't know," Rosie replied. "The information cards on some of the other dolls also say *circa* before the date. I think it means 'approximately,' but I'll look it up when I get home. We need a vocabulary word for this week."

Rosie took her notebook and pencil from her hip pocket and wrote *circa*.

Kayo read the rest of the information on the cat's card. "Mohair. Maker unknown. Internal bellows play music when cat is squeezed."

"What a wonderful toy," Rosie said. "It looks brand-new, as if nobody ever played with it."

"If I had a musical cat," Kayo said, "I would play it all the time."

Now, only three days after they had visited the doll museum, Rosie gave the newspaper a kick, crumpling the pages. "What kind of lowlife person would break into the doll museum?" she said. "Why couldn't they steal computers or television sets or jewelry? It's like robbing Santa Claus."

Kayo sighed. "Remember how everyone at the doll museum was smiling?"

Rosie nodded. "It's such a happy place. Mom

7

and Dad said they were reminded of their childhood."

"I don't suppose it's a happy place today," Kayo said.

"Let's go there," Rosie said. "I want to know if our favorite toys were taken or not."

"All right," Kayo agreed. "But if the burglar took the musical cat and the Jackie Robinson doll, I won't be able to stand it."

Half an hour later Kayo and Rosie got off the bus and, sharing Rosie's umbrella, hurried through a light drizzle toward the doll museum.

Just inside the front door a doughnut-shaped reception counter was equipped like a small office. The woman in the center, a volunteer docent, collected admissions, answered the phone, and directed visitors.

"We're sorry about the robbery," Kayo said as the girls paid their admission. "I hope the thief didn't get your musical cat."

"Nothing was stolen," the woman said. "The burglars broke into the office. We know they found the keys to the displays because the keys had been moved, but no dolls were taken. We think the police arrived before the theft could be carried out. Or else the thieves were looking only for money."

Behind the reception counter was a large open area. Two stairways, one against the right wall and one against the left, led to the second floor. A sign directed visitors up the stairs on the right; the other stairs were used to exit the second-floor exhibits.

Rosie and Kayo walked slowly through the entire museum. They watched three videos and learned that dolls have been made for thousands of years. Some were even made of bone.

They looked at a doll stove with copper pans, and a dollhouse equipped like a pet store. Another display showed an old-fashioned hospital with little nurse dolls, beds, carts, tables, and even a doll wheelchair.

"The beds and other equipment were salesmen's samples," Rosie said. Rosie always read the information cards.

They were in a special temporary exhibit of angel dolls when a loudspeaker announced that the museum would close in fifteen minutes.

Surprised, Rosie looked at her watch. "We've been here almost two hours."

"I want to go in the museum store before we leave," Kayo said.

They looked at the paper dolls, teddy bears, and books in the store until the closing announcement was made.

"You're the last to leave," the woman at the circular counter said as the girls headed for the door. "You must have enjoyed the museum."

"We did," Kayo said. "We always do." She opened the door. "It's raining again," she said. "Hard."

Rosie stopped. "My umbrella," she said. "I left my umbrella upstairs, in the rest room."

"Go get it," the woman said as she put on her coat. "But hurry, please. The museum is closed."

Rosie and Kayo hurried up the righthand stairway. The women's rest room was at the top of the stairs.

When Rosie tried to go in, the door was locked. "Someone is in there," she told Kayo.

"That's odd," Kayo said. "If we're the last to leave, who's in the rest room?"

"It must be one of the museum staff," Rosie said.

Kayo looked at the closest exhibit while they waited for the person in the rest room to come out. The lights on the second floor were turned out. The dolls looked different with only the light that came from the open stairway.

Rosie tried the door again, just to be sure. "Still locked," she said.

Kayo wandered toward an exhibit of large French dolls. She moved slowly in the dim light, her footsteps silent on the thick carpet. As she looked at the French dolls, she heard faint music.

She stood still and listened. It was a strange tune, played on an instrument she did not recognize. The same few notes were repeated, over and over, as if someone were practicing a brief passage in a song, trying to get it right.

Curious, Kayo moved through the dark rooms toward the music.

The odd tune continued as Kayo approached.

She stopped walking when she saw the source of the music. A chill slid down the back of her neck and tingled through her arms to her fingertips. Kayo swallowed hard and backed away.

Rosie still waited outside the locked bathroom.

"Come with me," Kayo whispered.

"What is it?" Rosie asked. "What's wrong?"

"Shh." Kayo put her finger to her lips and led Rosie through the dark museum.

Kayo could tell when Rosie heard the music, too. She suddenly stopped walking and looked around. Kayo steered her around the corner and past more displays, barely visible in the faint light.

It was the same tune as before, repeated over and over.

The girls moved toward the sound until they stood together, staring into a glass display case. The odd music came from inside the case.

"Look," Rosie whispered.

Kayo whispered back. "It's the musical cat."

# Chapter

**W**atch the cat's back legs," Kayo said.

Rosie saw the legs of the mohair cat move rhythmically in and out as if hands were pressing and releasing them.

The odd music tinkled into the dark museum.

"How does that work?" Rosie whispered. "There aren't any wires. It isn't plugged in."

Kayo peered into the display case, her nose only an inch from the thick glass. "Maybe it's battery operated," she said.

"I don't think they had battery-operated toys in 1900," Rosie replied. "Besides, it says on the card that the cat plays music when the bellows inside it are squeezed."

"Someone's playing it," Kayo said.

"Someone invisible."

The music stopped.

*Thump.*

Both girls jumped at the sudden noise.

*Thump. Thump.*

The girls looked at each other, their eyes wide with alarm. They looked at the display case again. No one was there, yet they could clearly hear the thumping noise, as if a person were inside the case, pounding against the glass.

*Thump. Thump. Thump.*

"Who's there?" Rosie said.

The pounding stopped.

"Girls?" The voice came from downstairs. "Are you coming?"

Rosie and Kayo ran back to the rest room. Rosie tried the door again. This time it opened. Her umbrella stood in the corner beside the sink, where she had left it.

She grabbed the umbrella and they hurried down the stairs. The woman stood by the door, waiting for them.

"Sorry it took so long," Rosie said. "The rest room was occupied, so we had to wait."

"We heard music upstairs," Kayo said.

The woman opened her mouth as if to say something and then closed it again.

"It came from a toy cat," Kayo continued, "but we couldn't see who was playing it."

The woman hesitated for a moment, as if deciding how to reply. "We pipe in music on a sound system," she said at last. "That must be what you heard."

Before Kayo could disagree, the woman opened the door and held it, indicating that Rosie and Kayo should leave. "Come back soon," she said. She smiled pleasantly, but the girls could tell she wanted them to go.

Rosie put up her umbrella, and the two girls stepped out into the downpour. The woman closed the door behind them.

"That was *not* piped-in music," Kayo said.

"She knew what it really was, but she didn't want to tell us."

Rosie and Kayo started toward the bus stop.

"What do you think that pounding noise was?" Kayo asked.

"It was hands, banging on the glass."

"Hands we couldn't see," Kayo said.

"It was a ghost," Rosie said.

The girls stopped walking, and looked at each other.

"A ghost was playing the musical cat," Rosie said, "and when it realized we were there, watching and listening, it quit playing with the cat and started banging on the glass. It probably wanted to frighten us away."

Kayo shivered. "I didn't know you believed in ghosts," she said.

"I never thought about them much until now, but how else can you explain what happened?"

"I can't," Kayo said. "Someone we could not see was pushing that cat's sides in and out. And it certainly sounded as if fists were banging on the glass."

"I think a ghost locked the bathroom door, too," Rosie said. "The door was locked and then unlocked from the inside, but nobody came out, and there was no one in there when I went in to get my umbrella. It had to be a ghost."

"Why would a ghost lock us out of the bathroom?"

"I don't know."

"I thought ghosts always haunted old buildings," Kayo said, "such as old churches next to graveyards or old houses where they used to live."

"The museum isn't very old," Rosie said.

"But the dolls are."

As they waited at the bus stop, Rosie felt uneasy. It was a vague discomfort, a sense that something was not right, although she didn't know exactly what.

It's the rainy weather, she told herself. The low clouds and fog brought early darkness, and a damp chill seeped beneath her sweatshirt. Rosie shivered.

The uneasy feeling grew stronger.

Rosie had felt this way in the airport once, when she was waiting for her uncle's plane to land. That time Rosie had realized someone was watching her. When she had looked around, she saw one of the teachers from her school. Rosie waved, the teacher waved back, and the uneasy feeling disappeared.

Now, as Rosie waited for the bus, she had that same feeling. *Someone is watching us*, she thought, but every time she turned around the sidewalk was empty.

"Why do you keep looking behind us?" Kayo asked.

"That business in the doll museum has me spooked, I guess."

"It doesn't make sense," Kayo said. "We heard fists pounding on the glass, as if a person were inside the display case, trying to get out. But if it was a ghost, it could just go in and out through the glass, couldn't it?"

"I don't know."

"I thought ghosts could go anywhere they want. In movies they float right through walls and windows and even locked doors."

"Not everything in movies is true," Rosie said. She glanced around again. The feeling was stronger now. Although she saw no one behind her, she was sure someone was watching her.

"Here comes our bus," Kayo said.

Rosie glanced around one more time. She gasped and pointed. "Look back there," she said. "By that tree."

Kayo turned and looked. "What? I don't see anything."

"A man. I saw a man in strange clothes. He's watching us." Rosie had barely glimpsed the man, but she had seen enough to know he was wearing some kind of costume.

"I don't see anyone," Kayo said.

"He must have ducked behind the tree."

The bus rumbled to a stop and the door creaked open. Kayo got on. As Kayo dropped her money in, Rosie paused with one foot on the step, looking back at the tree.

"There!" she cried. "I saw him again! There *is* a man watching us."

# Chapter

**K**ayo bent to peer out the side window.

"Move to the back of the bus, please," the driver said.

Rosie stepped into the bus. Her hand shook as she released her coins.

Kayo slid into a seat by a window and looked toward the big tree. A faint blue light shone around the tree trunk.

Rosie sat behind Kayo, also by a window. She cupped her hands on the sides of her head, to see better, and stared at the empty sidewalk.

"I don't see the man," Kayo said, "but I see a funny light, as if somebody has a flashlight with a blue bulb in it."

"I don't see him now, either. He must be in back of the tree. That's where the light is coming from."

As the bus pulled away from the curb, Kayo moved back to sit beside Rosie.

"Are you sure the man was watching us?" Kayo asked.

"Positive."

"Maybe he lost something and was looking for it with a flashlight."

"No," Rosie said. "He was definitely watching us. I only got a glimpse, but he wore some kind of old-fashioned military costume, with a helmet."

"Weird," Kayo said.

"There was something very strange about that man."

"It's a good thing the bus was on time."

The girls rode along in silence for a few blocks, watching a young mother try to keep a toddler on the seat.

"I'm glad you're spending the night at my house," Kayo said. "Mom has a meeting tonight, and after what happened in the museum, and then that man watching us, I would not be thrilled to stay home alone."

The girls got off the bus at the corner nearest Kayo's apartment.

As soon as Rosie's feet touched the ground, she was engulfed by the same, strange feeling of uneasiness.

"Kayo," she whispered. "I think he followed us."

Kayo frowned. "How could he?" she said. "Wasn't he walking? You said he was behind a tree."

Rosie looked nervously in all directions, her anxiety growing.

"If he was on foot," Kayo said, "he couldn't possibly keep up with the bus. We only stopped a few times."

Rosie knew Kayo was right, yet she couldn't shake the feeling that she was being watched.

"All that craziness in the museum made you jumpy," Kayo said. She unlocked the door and put her foot carefully inside to keep Homer and Diamond from running out. When she had made sure the cats weren't lurking behind the door, trying to escape, she went in, and then held the door open for Rosie.

Rosie did not go in. She stood just outside the door, as if her shoes were glued to the steps.

"Are you coming?" Kayo said.

"I saw him again," Rosie said, her voice trembling. "He was right over there." She pointed toward the street.

Kayo stepped outside and shut the door. She surveyed the empty street. "I don't see anyone," she said.

"I don't see him now, either." Rosie frowned.

"But where would he go? There isn't any tree to hide behind this time."

"I know," Rosie said. "He just sort of—disappeared."

"Are you sure it was the same man?"

Rosie nodded. "Unless there are two people running around in an old uniform and a helmet, it was the same man I saw back at the bus stop."

Kayo looked both ways. She saw a young couple, their arms around each other, strolling down the sidewalk on the opposite side of the street. She saw the woman who lived in the apartment directly above Kayo, riding her bicycle home from the grocery store with a bag of groceries in the basket.

"There," Rosie whispered. "He's back."

Kayo looked where Rosie was pointing. "Oh!" she said. "I see him."

The man stood stiffly on the sidewalk, watching them. A faint blue light surrounded him.

He was tall, with a square jaw and large hands. He appeared to be in his mid-twenties, and he wore a dirty military uniform that looked as if it had been on him for weeks. The gray pants were tucked into knee-high leather boots, and he wore a helmet with a pointed ornament on top.

His blue-gray jacket had red piping and metal buttons on the front and sleeves. Shoulder straps were connected to a wide leather belt, from which hung four leather bullet containers.

"He isn't real," Kayo said, but before the words

were completely out of her mouth, the man vanished. One moment he was there and the next he was not, just like that.

Both girls remained still, staring at the spot where the man had stood. They waited, but he did not reappear.

Finally Kayo opened the door again, and this time Rosie followed her inside.

Kayo closed the door, locked it, and leaned her back against it. "Who do you think it was?" she asked.

"Who?" said Rosie. "Or what?"

"A ghost? Is that what you think?"

"He—it—disappeared into thin air," Rosie said. "What else can do that, besides a ghost?"

"I could see him," Kayo said, "but I could see behind him, at the same time."

Homer, Kayo's gray and white striped cat, came to greet them. Kayo leaned down to pet him as he rubbed against her ankles.

The doorbell rang. The girls glanced at each other in alarm.

Kayo looked through the peephole. "It's Sammy Hulenback," she said.

Rosie groaned. "Isn't he ever going to quit hanging around?"

Kayo opened the door.

"Are you having a meeting of your secret club?" Sammy asked.

"Yes," Kayo said. "And since it's secret, I can't invite you to come in." She started to shut the door.

"Wait!" Sammy cried, putting his foot inside the door to keep Kayo from closing it. "I have something to show you."

"Lucky us," Kayo said.

"What is it?" Rosie asked.

"It's an application to join your club." Sammy handed Kayo a piece of paper. "I want to track down thieves and catch vandals and chase after murderers, the way you do."

"That is not the purpose of our club," Rosie said.

"We'll consider your application and let you know," Kayo said. She closed the door.

"I've considered," Rosie said. "I vote no."

"I wouldn't let him in Care Club if he was a scout for the Yankees," Kayo said, "but we can't vote until we're having a meeting." She put Sammy's application on the small table beside the front door.

A low growl rumbled deep in Homer's throat. His fur stood straight out, making his tail seem three times its normal size.

"What's the matter with Homer?" Rosie said.

Kayo's orange cat, Diamond, stalked into the room. Her fur, too, stood on end, and her big amber eyes seemed focused on the same place where Homer was looking.

Homer hissed and swiped his paw across the air in front of him.

Kayo bent and tried to pick Homer up, but the cat backed away from her. "Nice Homer," Kayo said. "What are you growling at?"

"Kayo." Rosie's voice was little more than a squeak.

Kayo looked up.

The man in the uniform looked back at her. A faint blue light surrounded him. He stood in Kayo's front hallway, inside the door she had just locked.

"Who are you?" Kayo said. "What do you want?"

"*Komme,*" the man replied.

"I beg your pardon?"

"*Komme schnell.*"

And then, before either girl could figure out what the man meant, he was gone again. A faint musty odor remained behind, the kind of smell that comes from a long-sealed box that's been stored in a damp basement.

Homer and Diamond sniffed the place where the man had stood, and then, their fur slowly returning to normal, they rubbed on Kayo's ankles, demanding their dinner.

"I can't believe what just happened," Kayo said.

"Neither can I. But it makes me nervous."

"It must be the ghost from the doll museum."

"Why would he follow us?"

"I don't know. But we never had a man appearing and disappearing before, not until we heard the musical cat and the pounding. It must be connected."

"The question is, what should we do about it?" Rosie said.

"There isn't much we can do about it, is there? If he came in here once, he can come in again, any time he wants to."

# Chapter

"Did you understand what he said?" Rosie asked.

"No." Kayo shook cat food into two bowls. "It sounded like some other language."

"Maybe it wasn't a ghost. Maybe he's from another planet. Maybe a spaceship landed near the doll museum and we were the first Earth people he saw, so he followed us and he's trying to communicate."

Kayo put a bowl in front of each cat.

There was a knock at the door. Both girls jumped.

Kayo looked out the peephole.

"Is it him?" Rosie whispered.

"It's Sammy."

Kayo opened the door.

"Am I in the club?" Sammy asked.

"We can't consider your application," Kayo said, "until we have an official meeting." She started to close the door.

"Wait a second," Rosie said. "Sammy, did you see anyone outside this building just now?"

"Yes," Sammy said.

"You did?" said Kayo.

"Was it a man in a military uniform?" said Rosie.

Sammy looked surprised. "No, it was your neighbor—the one who always rides her bike to the store."

"Oh," Kayo said.

Sammy leaned toward the girls, water dripping from his yellow rain slicker. "Who did you think I saw?" he asked. "Who was here wearing a military uniform? Is your secret club helping the army this time?"

"No," Rosie said.

"What's going on then? Why did you want to know if I saw a man in a uniform?"

"Forget it," Rosie said. "I made a mistake. It's nothing."

"We thought we saw someone we knew, but we were wrong," Kayo said.

"I don't believe you," Sammy said. "You're doing something exciting again, aren't you? And dangerous."

"I hope not," Kayo muttered as she closed the door.

After Mrs. Benton left for her meeting, Rosie said, "Let's have our Care Club meeting tonight. It will give us something to think about besides the ghost."

Kayo called the meeting to order and asked, "Is there any new business?"

"I met a woman in the pet store yesterday," Rosie said. "She helps find homes for greyhound dogs."

"Only greyhounds?" Kayo said. "Why not other dogs?"

"Greyhounds are bred for dog racing," Rosie said. "Lots of them aren't fast enough, and even those that are can only race for a few years. Some of the dog breeders don't bother to find homes for the dogs that can't race."

"What do they do with them?" Kayo asked.

"You don't want to know. The woman had a newspaper article that made me sick to my stomach."

Kayo gulped. "Oh," she said.

"Some breeders are unscrupulous," Rosie said, smiling because she had used a former vocabulary word. "The woman I met belongs to a Greyhound Rescue group. They go to Florida and Arizona and Idaho and other states that have dog racing, and they take unwanted greyhounds and find good homes for them. Maybe Care Club can help."

"I can't adopt a greyhound. They're big and this apartment isn't."

"We don't have to adopt them ourselves," Rosie said. "We can do a report at school about the Greyhound Rescue efforts, or we can volunteer to help pass out their information, or we could raise money and donate it to them."

"Great idea," Kayo said. "I vote to help Greyhound Rescue."

"So do I. The phone number is at my house; we can call tomorrow and get started."

"There's one other piece of new business," Kayo said. "Sammy's Care Club application."

Rosie groaned, but Kayo went into the hallway, got the piece of paper, and brought it back to her bedroom. She unfolded it and began to read.

*"Here is why you should let me join your Secret Club:*
*"1. I am smart and can help you figure out clues.*
*"2. I have a good bike so I can get over here fast whenever you need me to help chase criminals.*
*"3. I can keep a secret. I would not tell anyone about our Secret Club activities."*

"It's signed, *Sammy Hulenback, Secret Agent Number Three.*"

"The trouble with this application," Rosie said, "is that Care Club is supposed to help animals, not solve crimes. Sammy wants to join because he thinks it will be exciting and dangerous, but I do not intend to get involved with any more criminals."

"Neither do I."

"Of course," Rosie added, "he also wants to join because he likes you."

"I move that Care Club reject this application," Kayo said.

"I second the motion," said Rosie.

"All in favor say aye."

"Aye," said Rosie.

"Aye," said Kayo. "The motion carries."

"The next time we see Sammy," Rosie said, "let's tell him that you have a boyfriend. If he thinks you like some other boy, maybe he'll quit hanging around."

"He'd want to know who it is," Kayo said.

"Tell him the boy lives out-of-town. He's a rock singer. Or a movie star. How about a boy from Texas whose family owns a bunch of oil wells?"

"The meeting," said Kayo, "is adjourned."

"Put in the minutes that we adjourned circa

eight o'clock," Rosie said. She took out her notebook and made a check mark on the page that said:

*Circa: around or approximately. Usually
used with dates.*
*Example: It was built circa 1889.*

Rosie awoke in the night, aware that Homer
lay across her feet. Kayo slumbered quietly in the
other twin bed.

Rosie moved out from under the cat, and
Homer quickly curled beside her again, purring
softly. Smiling, Rosie reached down and stroked
the thick fur.

She dozed then, half-asleep, half-awake. In this
drifting dreamlike state, she smelled the same
odd musty odor and realized the man was there.
Even with her eyes closed she knew he stood
erect in his rumpled uniform and his helmet, just
inside the door. Sleepily she wondered who he
was and why he was in Kayo's bedroom.

The smell intensified. Homer growled. A
matching growl erupted from Diamond, who lay
on the other bed next to Kayo.

The cats' warnings roused Rosie from her
dreamy condition. She opened her eyes. The
room was dark except for a glow of pale blue
light around the man.

Rosie reached for her glasses and put them on.

**31**

She could see him clearly now—his uniform, his face, his eyes. She sat partway up, leaning on her elbows.

He gestured to her to follow him.

Rosie shook her head no.

As she gazed at the man, she knew he was not from this world. Although she could see the man, she also saw Kayo's closed bedroom door, which was directly behind him. She could look at the man and look right through him, at the same time.

She saw the buttons on his jacket, and the ornament on top of his helmet. She saw his pants, tucked into the tops of his high leather boots. At the same time she saw the doorknob and the poster of Willie Mays that Kayo had tacked to the back of her bedroom door. For an instant the drab gray-blue military uniform and the San Francisco Giants' uniform, with its black and orange lettering, blurred together.

Then the man took another step toward her and the blue glow intensified, blocking out the poster and everything else in the room.

Both cats leaped to their feet, with their fur extended and their backs humped up. Diamond hissed. Homer continued to growl.

Rosie reached across to the other bed and shook Kayo. "Wake up," she whispered.

"Umm," Kayo mumbled.

Rosie shook harder, her own fear flowing from her hand into Kayo's shoulder. "Wake up!"

Kayo opened her eyes. "What?" she said.

"He's here," Rosie said. She heard the sharp intake of breath as Kayo saw the man, too.

Kayo sat up in bed, clutching the blanket tightly under her chin.

Curiosity mixed with horror as the girls watched the ghost.

Homer jumped to the floor and crept toward the ghost, his ears back and his body low.

The ghost held both hands out and beckoned to the girls to follow him.

"*Komme,*" he said.

"Go away," Kayo whispered. "Leave us alone."

The ghost's eyes shone with intensity, and he waved his hands toward them again. "*Komme so schnell wie möglich!*" he said.

Kayo reached for the bedside lamp and switched it on.

The instant the light came on, the ghost disappeared. Only a faint musty smell remained.

# Chapter 5

*H*omer and Diamond sniffed the place where the ghost had stood.

Kayo got out of bed and walked to the closed door, avoiding the spot that the cats were examining.

She opened the door and looked into the dark hallway. "He's gone," she said and shut the door. "For now," she added.

Rosie took her notebook and pencil from the table on her side of the bed and began to write.

"This is not the time for vocabulary words," Kayo said.

"I'm trying to write what he said, so we can remember it." Rosie continued to write. "And I'm writing a description of his clothes. Maybe we can go to the library tomorrow and figure out where he's from and what he's trying to tell us."

"Why would a ghost want to talk to us?" Kayo said. She moved nervously around the room as she spoke, taking shirts and jeans from the back of a chair and hanging them on hangers. "This whole thing gives me the creeps."

"He wants us to go somewhere with him," Rosie said.

"No way. I wouldn't go two feet with that—that—"

"Spook," Rosie said.

"Whatever he is, I wouldn't follow him if he offered me tickets to the World Series," Kayo declared. "Never! Never, never, never!"

"Shh," Rosie said. "You'll wake up your mom."

Kayo pulled a pair of sneakers from under a chair and put them in the closet. She wadded up a dirty sock, stretched her arms over her head, and pitched the sock into a hamper.

"Maybe he wants us to go back to the doll museum," Rosie said.

"What?" Kayo stopped cleaning the room and looked at Rosie.

"The doll museum is where all of this started," Rosie said. "He has to be connected somehow to the music and the thumping on the glass. I think he was in the museum, only we couldn't see him then, and now he's followed us home."

"I don't like it," Kayo said. "I don't want a ghost in my bedroom."

"Let's look up ghosts in your encyclopedia," Rosie said. "Maybe there's a way to get rid of him."

"Good idea." Kayo removed the G volume from the bookshelf and turned the pages until she came to the heading GHOST. She read aloud, "The spirit of a dead person, seen by the living."

Then she skimmed the rest of the material silently until she came to, "Although belief in ghosts is known in all parts of the world, their existence has never been proven."

Kayo handed the encyclopedia to Rosie. While Rosie read, Kayo went to her closet and got out her camera. "If he comes back," she said, "I'm going to take his picture."

"That would be proof," Rosie said. She looked at the words she had written. "Maybe he was speaking Italian. The words sounded Italian, don't you think?"

"I wouldn't know," Kayo said.

"Why would the ghost of a soldier be hanging around the doll museum?"

"Why is the ghost of a soldier hanging around us?"

"He wants to tell us something, or show us something." Rosie squeezed her eyes shut tight, the way she always did when she was trying to think. "Maybe the ghost saw the burglar," she said. "Maybe that's what he's trying to tell us." She opened her eyes. "The ghost saw the thief, and he knows there's some evidence at the museum that nobody has noticed and he wants to show it to us."

"Why us?" Kayo said. "We aren't F.B.I. agents. We aren't police detectives. We aren't even Girl Scouts. If a ghost knows who broke into the doll museum, he should let somebody from the museum know, not us."

"Perhaps they can't see him," Rosie said slowly, thinking it through as she spoke. "Maybe kids are more likely to see a ghost than adults are. I read one time about a three-year-old boy who talked about his friend, José. His mother thought it was cute that little Benjamin had an imaginary playmate and wondered where he had heard the name José, since the family knew no one by that name.

"One day Benjamin saw one of those Missing Child photos on a milk carton, and he pointed to the picture and said, 'There's José.' When his mother read the information, the missing boy's name was José."

"What did she do?" Kayo asked.

"Benjamin kept talking about his friend, and the games they played, so the mother called the

Missing Child hot line and asked if José was still missing."

"Was he? Was Benjamin really playing with José?"

"No. They said José's body had been found, three weeks earlier. He had drowned in the river."

"So the little kid was playing with a ghost," Kayo said.

"That's what the mother thinks. She never saw or heard José, but Benjamin played with him for a couple of months."

The girls were quiet for a moment, thinking of the little boy and his imaginary friend.

"My point," said Rosie, "is that kids are more open to unusual ideas, and so we saw the ghost, rather than an adult."

"Maybe some of the museum people see him and won't admit it," Kayo said. "The woman at the desk said the music we heard was their regular piped-in music, but I suspect she knew it wasn't."

"Exactly," Rosie said. "Maybe the ghost saw us admiring the dolls, and realized how much we like them, and thought we might be able—and willing—to help. So he tried appearing to us and now he knows we can see him."

"Every time he comes he stays longer," Kayo said.

"Or we see him longer every time. He might be here all the time but it takes practice for us to see him. You didn't see him at all at first, and I only had brief glimpses. But now that we've learned how, we see him more easily."

"I would just as soon quit practicing," Kayo said.

"We need to go back to the doll museum," Rosie said. "Tomorrow. We'll stay until it closes and then make up some excuse to go back upstairs. If the ghost is there, we'll find out what he wants."

"How?" Kayo said. "We won't be able to understand him any better tomorrow than we did tonight, so it won't do much good to follow him."

"At the museum he won't have to talk; he can show us what it is he wants us to see."

"It's worth a try," Kayo said. "I'll try just about anything if it will keep that spook out of my house."

Kayo got back in bed and turned out the light. The cats settled themselves again, but both girls lay staring into the dark.

"What are you thinking?" Rosie whispered.

"I wonder if we'll see him again tonight," Kayo said.

They did, just before dawn. The cats sensed his presence first, and their growling woke the girls.

This time the ghost didn't say anything. He didn't get a chance. As soon as Kayo woke up, she grabbed the camera from her bedside table, aimed it at him, and clicked the shutter.

The flash went off.

The ghost vanished.

# Chapter

The next afternoon Rosie and Kayo returned to the doll museum.

"I want to do this," Kayo said as they walked to the bus stop, "but I'm scared."

"So am I. I've never seen a ghost before. I don't know anyone who's ever seen a ghost. I like to read ghost stories, but I always thought they were made up."

"In the books I've read," Kayo said, "the ghost always wears a long, flowing white gown. I never heard of a ghost in a military uniform."

"He doesn't act as if he wants to hurt us," Rosie said. "He only wants us to follow him."

"Still, it's scary the way he suddenly appears out of nowhere, and I can't help wondering what will happen if he gets angry."

"If he appears at the museum, we will follow him," Rosie said. "Since that's what he wants, there would be no reason for him to get angry."

"What if something goes wrong? What if we get in major-league trouble and no one hears us call for help?"

"We won't leave the doll museum. What could go wrong there?"

"If we don't find out what the ghost wants," Kayo said, "he may keep appearing in my room at night. That idea is more scary than following him."

While they waited for the bus, Sammy rode up on his bicycle.

"Where are you going?" Sammy asked.

"To the doll museum," Kayo said.

Sammy wrinkled his nose, as if something smelled bad. "You don't still like dolls, do you?"

"As a matter of fact, we do," Rosie said.

"Dolls are for babies," Sammy said.

"Strike one," said Kayo.

"I thought you wanted to be a professional baseball player," Sammy said.

"I do," Kayo replied.

"Baseball players don't have anything to do with dolls," Sammy said.

"Strike two," Kayo said. "The doll museum even has a Jackie Robinson doll."

"Who?"

"You don't know who Jackie Robinson was?"

Kayo said. "I don't believe it." She removed her Chicago Cubs cap, pushed her long blond hair away from her face, and put the cap back on. "Jackie Robinson," she said, "was the first black player to play on a major-league team. He put up with insults and racial slurs, but he was Rookie of the Year and the National League's Most Valuable Player. He was the first black person to be inducted into the Baseball Hall of Fame."

Kayo planted both hands on her hips and glared at Sammy. "Until Jackie Robinson came along," she said, "only white men could play in the major leagues. He was a hero! How can you not know who Jackie Robinson was?"

"He knows now," Rosie said.

"I wouldn't go to a stupid doll museum if you paid me," said Sammy.

"Strike three," said Kayo.

"Nobody asked you to come," said Rosie.

Sammy said, "Tell me the truth. Where are you *really* going?"

"We told you," Kayo said. "We're going to the doll museum."

Sammy folded his arms across his chest and gave them a suspicious look. "It has something to do with the army, doesn't it? You guys are too smart to go look at a bunch of sissy dolls in a dusty old museum. You're going somewhere to meet the man in the military uniform."

"He's on to us, Kayo," Rosie said. "We may as well tell him the truth."

"Go ahead," Kayo said.

Rosie leaned toward Sammy and whispered, "We're going to the hospital. Some genetic scientists are doing secret experiments on human intelligence, and they asked us to participate. They want to know why we are so smart."

"We're going to have an operation," Kayo said.

Sammy gulped. "Both of you?"

"Yes," Kayo said. "On our big toes."

"Huh?"

"The theory," said Rosie, "is that the most highly intelligent people do not get their reasoning power from their brains, as everyone thinks. It comes from their big toes."

Sammy looked down at his feet.

A large green bus wheezed to a stop.

"Here's our bus," Kayo said.

"When will you get home?" Sammy asked.

"Circa midnight." Rosie made a check mark in her notebook.

The girls climbed on the bus and dropped their money in the coin receptacle.

"Typical Sammy," said Rosie as they found seats toward the back. "He's never been to the doll museum, but he thinks he knows all about it."

"If he knew how beautiful and valuable the

old dolls are, or what a gorgeous big building the museum is, he'd change his mind."

"What mind?" Rosie said. "That boy needs a new brain."

Kayo grinned. "Or a new big toe," she said.

They arrived at the doll museum at four. A different volunteer docent greeted them.

Upstairs, many people viewed the displays, admiring the beautiful dolls. Rosie and Kayo moved quickly from exhibit to exhibit.

"I'm too nervous to enjoy this," Kayo said. "I feel the way I did before I pitched in the league championship game." She raised both hands over her head, stretched, and threw an imaginary baseball.

"Maybe that's a good omen. That's when you pitched your perfect game." Rosie looked at her watch. "Four-thirty," she said. "I wonder if the ghost knows we're here."

By four forty-five, Rosie and Kayo were the only people remaining on the second floor. They waited by the musical cat.

"We're here," Rosie whispered. "You can come any time."

"The sooner, the better," Kayo added.

"Maybe he's here," Rosie said, "but we can't see him because the lights are too bright."

"He had better come as soon as the museum

**45**

closes. We'll have only a couple of minutes after five to find out what he wants. Then we'll have to leave."

"What if he doesn't come?" Rosie said.

"Then we'll know he didn't have anything to do with the doll museum, after all. We guessed wrong."

At one minute to five Rosie went downstairs. As she approached the desk, a group of women came chattering out of the museum store, headed toward the exit.

"My friend is in the bathroom," Rosie told the woman at the desk. "I'm going to wait for her; we'll be down soon."

The woman nodded agreement as she waved goodbye to the group of women and, at the same time, answered her telephone.

As Rosie rushed back up the stairs, the second-floor lights went out. She waited a minute at the top of the stairs, letting her eyes get used to the dark, before she walked through the exhibit rooms to where Kayo waited.

"Anything?" Rosie whispered.

"No."

The girls stood still, watching for the ghost in the uniform.

While they waited upstairs, the woman at the desk downstairs hung up the telephone, snatched her purse from a shelf, and let herself out of the circular reception area.

She rushed into a small office. "Would you lock up for me, please?" she said. "My neighbor called; her mother had a heart attack and she needs me to watch her baby while she goes to the hospital."

The woman dashed out the door and down the steps to her car. She was nearly home before she realized she had forgotten to say there were two girls still upstairs. No harm done, she decided. The girls would have come down long before anyone locked the doors. They would be on their way home by now.

But Rosie and Kayo were not on their way home. At five-fifteen, as the locks clicked into place downstairs and the burglar alarm was activated, the girls stood in the dark on the second floor of the doll museum, staring in disbelief into the display case which held the musical cat.

The ghost in the uniform did not appear.

A different ghost did.

# *Chapter*

*I*t began with the music.

The brief tune played over and over, just as it had the day before. This time Rosie and Kayo recognized the sound of the musical cat and were not surprised to see its sides moving in and out as an unseen being pushed on it.

When the music stopped they waited, expecting to see the ghost who had followed them home. Instead, they saw the ghost of a small girl, not more than five or six years old.

She wore an ankle-length cotton dress, with a long white apron over it. A blue kerchief, folded in a triangular shape, was tied at the back of her neck, beneath her brown hair. Her face and hands were pale, and her whole body, including her clothing, was transparent.

"It's another ghost," Kayo whispered.

Rosie nodded. The ghost of a small girl was not as scary as the ghost of a large man in uniform. The child would have been appealing, except for one thing: Her face was contorted with grief. Sobs racked her small body and tears streaked her sorrowful face as she knelt inside the display case, pounding her fists against the glass.

*Thump. Thump. Thump.*

It was the same sound as before except this time Rosie and Kayo could see who was pounding. The ghost girl wept and banged frantically at the glass.

"Is she trapped in there?" Kayo asked as chills rippled down her arms.

Rosie did not answer. She had never seen anyone look as unhappy as the ghost girl looked.

The little girl did not appear to see them. Although her face was only a few inches from the inside of the glass, and Rosie and Kayo were only a foot from the outside, the ghost girl seemed to look right through them, without noticing that they were there.

*Thump. Thump. Thump.*

Rosie raised her own fist, hesitated a second, and then beat on the outside of the case. The thick glass vibrated.

The ghost, clearly startled, stopped pounding and blinked at them. She stared for an instant, the tears still rolling down her pale cheeks. Her hands reached through the glass toward Rosie and Kayo, as if she were begging for help. *"Petit chat,"* she said.

And then she vanished.

Rosie and Kayo pressed their faces to the glass but saw no more sign of the unhappy child.

A deep voice directly behind them said, "I think you do not speak French. Or German."

Rosie jumped. Kayo gasped. Both girls spun around to see who was there.

A blue glow lit the room, making all the dolls look as if they wore pale blue clothing and had blue skin. The same musty smell that had been in Kayo's bedroom filled the air.

The ghost in the uniform said, "You came. That is good." He spoke haltingly, with an accent; the girls had to listen hard to understand him. "And you know this language?"

"Yes," Kayo said. "We speak English."

"Good. I have not spoken for many years. It was difficult to know which Earth language to use."

"Who are you?" Rosie asked.

"I am Werner von Moltz." He saluted.

"Nice to meet you," Kayo said. "I think."

He pointed into the display case. "I did not mean to do it," he said.

"Do what?" Kayo said.

"I saw a sudden movement and thought the French were attacking me. I fired before I knew it was a child. In a war one does not wait for the enemy to fire first."

Rosie's voice was barely a whisper. "You killed her?"

He winced at the question. "I did."

"When?" Kayo asked.

"The war had just begun. We thought it would be over quickly and Germany would be victorious."

"Which war?" Rosie said.

"We called it The Great War, but I learned there is nothing great about war except the suffering. So many dead. So many wounded. And for what? What was gained? What was learned?"

"I don't know," Kayo said.

"The Great War," said Rosie, "was World War I."

"*Ach!*" Werner von Moltz slapped his palm to his forehead. "So many wars they must be numbered, to keep them straight."

Rosie glanced over her shoulder, wondering if the other ghost had returned, but she had not.

"After The Great War," Werner von Moltz said, "our noble leaders returned to their high offices and thought of new reasons to fight. They learned nothing, and I died knowing I had killed an innocent child."

"It was an accident," Kayo said. "You didn't mean to shoot her."

"Thank you," he said. He bowed slightly. "Thank you for believing that."

Werner von Moltz stepped close to the display case and looked in. "For all these years," he said, "I have tried to bring peace to Chantal's spirit, to make up for robbing her of her life. But I cannot make her happy. The only thing that will erase her sorrow is the return of her toy." He pointed into the display case.

"The musical cat?" Rosie said.

"Yes. She weeps for her kitty. She cried for it as she died, and she will grieve through all eternity if I do not find a way to help her."

"How terrible," Kayo said.

"I left my own body a few hours after Chantal left hers," Werner continued.

Rosie and Kayo glanced at each other, horrified, and then looked at the ghost again.

"I saw the child's sorrow and vowed to help her. When the fighting moved on, we went together, Chantal and I, to her home, but her kitty was not there. Perhaps it was hidden in a soldier's knapsack, a gift for some other child at war's end. I had no way to know who had it, or where.

"I searched for decades, roaming through all continents, to find this toy. I found it and brought Chantal here, but it is not within my power to dry her tears. I am unable to remove the kitty from its place."

"You came in my house through the locked door," Kayo said.

"Chantal and I can go anywhere because we are not of the Earth anymore. But her toy cat is physical, and I have no way to move it past the locked glass."

"If she can go in there she can play with the cat any time she wants," Rosie said. "Why is she still so unhappy?"

"She longs to be on French soil, just as I wish to return to Germany. Chantal needs to be near her home and near the graves of her parents. She wants her kitty there with her, in France."

"She was speaking French, wasn't she?" Rosie said.

"Yes. Chantal's language is French. Like her heart."

"Were you speaking German last night?" Rosie said.

"Yes. I asked you to come, as quickly as possible." He smiled at them. "And here you are."

"Why did you follow us?" Kayo said.

"I have followed many others since I found Chantal's toy. Only you acknowledged my presence. The rest do not see me or pretend not to see me. Or they are too frightened to listen."

"We can't help you," Rosie said. "We don't have a key to unlock the display case."

"*Ach!* I feared as much."

"We could talk to the people who work here," Kayo said. "If we tell them what you just said, maybe they would agree to open the display case."

"The musical cat is probably worth a lot of money," Rosie said. "The museum people may not want it to leave."

"Chantal will need her kitty only a short time," Werner von Moltz said. "If she can take it home to France, and play with it there, her tears will be gone, forever. And her unhappy spirit will be at peace. Forever. When that happens Chantal will no longer appear as a ghost. She will no longer care about Earthly toys."

"But the cat will be somewhere in France," Kayo said.

"I will try to return it," Werner said. An expression of great longing came over his face. "If Chantal's spirit finds peace," he said, "that will allow me to find peace, also."

"So you wouldn't appear as a ghost anymore, either?" Rosie said.

"That is correct. But I will try, before that happens, to return the musical cat."

Rosie turned to Kayo. "I think we should help him," she said.

"So do I," Kayo replied.

"You will speak to them?" Werner asked. "You will try to help me?"

"Yes," Kayo said. "We will try to help you."

"We'll do all we can," Rosie said.

"I thank you." Werner von Moltz saluted again, clicking his heels together sharply. The blue glow grew brighter and then he was gone, leaving Kayo and Rosie blinking into the darkness. Only a trace of musty odor remained.

"No one is going to believe this," Kayo said.

"We promised we'd try."

"I want to try," Kayo said. "That little girl was shot accidentally because she happened to live where a war was being fought. It seems only fair for her ghost to have her toy cat, if that is what she needs to be happy for all eternity."

"Last night," Rosie said, "I was afraid of the ghost, but now that we know what he wants, I'm not scared anymore."

"The woman at the desk is probably wondering what's taking us so long. Let's go tell her what happened and ask if she has keys. Maybe she would open the case right now."

They started toward the stairway.

"It's awfully dark in here," Rosie said. As soon as she said it, she realized why. While they were talking to the ghost, the lights from the first floor and stairs, which earlier had spilled onto the second floor, had been turned off.

Kayo said, "I hope she didn't forget we are here."

They walked carefully down the dark stairs until they reached the landing. From there they could see the main floor, with the circular reception counter. The lights were out throughout the entire museum. The only light filtered through the front windows, from the museum's outdoor lighting. Even the skylight looked shadowy.

"Everyone's gone," Kayo said. "It's already dark out."

Rosie pushed the button that illuminated the dial on her wristwatch. "It's after five-thirty," she said. "We missed our bus."

"I didn't know it was that late. We talked to the ghost a long time."

"My parents don't let me ride the bus after dark unless they're with me," Rosie said. "We'll have to call home."

"I'll call Mom," Kayo said. "She should be home from work by now."

"If she isn't we can call my dad. And we had better look for a night number for the museum. We can probably unlock the door and get out, but we wouldn't be able to lock it again. We can't go off and leave the doll museum unlocked. And what if we set off the burglar alarm?"

## The Ghost Followed Us Home

They started down the second half of the stairs, moving slowly in the dark so they wouldn't fall. They were nearly to the bottom when they heard a creaking noise, ahead and to their right.

Both girls froze.

Another ghost?

# Chapter

8

*T*he girls crouched close to the side of the staircase.

Rosie's mind raced. It can't be the janitor, she thought. An employee would turn on the lights. And the two ghosts had moved silently. Except for his conversation Werner von Moltz made no sound.

Someone else was in the museum.

The creaking grew louder. It sounded like a wheel, as if a rusty wagon was being pulled toward them.

Kayo nudged Rosie with her elbow as two people entered the main room from the direction of the museum store. Both wore black clothing, including gloves. They had black ski masks over their heads, with cutouts for their eyes, noses, and mouths.

One of them pulled a low four-wheeled cart with a flat surface. Kayo had seen similar carts at a discount grocery store, except this one was piled with dolls.

The two people in black pulled the cart toward the bottom of the second stairway, the one visitors used to exit the second-floor displays.

"I hope these keys fit the second-floor displays," one of them said. It was a woman's voice. "We made the keys in a terrible hurry."

"We got in, didn't we? The key turned off the alarm. You got in the museum store and got the dolls you wanted." The second voice belonged to a man. "Why would the upstairs displays be any different?"

The man walked away from the cart. He stood between the museum door and the circular counter, looking outside. The woman started up the exit stairs.

"Make it fast," he said.

She paused. "I would be a lot faster," she said, "if you had thought to measure the elevator to be sure the cart would fit."

"The exercise will be good for you," he said.

"If climbing up and down stairs is so great, why don't you come and help?"

"I'll keep watch while you open the cases and get out the dolls you want. Then I'll come and help you carry them. The first rule of successful burglary is 'Always post a lookout.' "

The woman climbed the other stairs and went out of Rosie and Kayo's view.

Moving together as if they were doing a choreographed dance, Rosie and Kayo slowly stood and backed up the stairs, keeping their eyes on the man.

They did not realize when they reached the landing. Rosie backed into the child-size oak piano that stood on the landing, and the piano slid across the floor, making a scraping sound.

The man turned.

Rosie and Kayo stood still on the dark landing, hardly daring to breathe. They could see him because he was next to the glass door, where the outside lights shined in.

"Was that you, Darlene?" he called.

"Yes," a voice replied from the second floor. "Come and help me carry these dolls."

The man loped up the stairs, returning shortly with his arms full of dolls. He dumped them on the cart.

"Be careful with those," the woman snapped as she, too, came down with an armload of dolls. "Break off one little pinkie and the price plummets."

"Only a crazy person would pay one hundred thousand dollars for a bunch of dolls," the man said.

"Mrs. Tuttle is not crazy. She's a shrewd businesswoman who will triple her money on these dolls." As she spoke the woman carefully laid the dolls she carried on the cart and then straightened the ones the man had dumped.

"Triple her money? You mean she's going to make more than we do on this deal?"

"We're making plenty."

"We should make the most. We're taking all the risks. My ears are still ringing from that burglar alarm shrieking the night we came in here to copy the keys."

"It was loud, all right."

"Tuttle's at home eating dinner right now while we take a chance on prison terms."

"Mrs. Tuttle has the contacts. She'll sell these to collectors in other countries, who have no idea they are stolen. What would we do with them? Do you have any pals who will pay big bucks for a Shirley Temple doll?"

The woman stomped back up the stairs. The man returned to his lookout post.

Rosie edged carefully past the small piano, and the girls crossed the landing. They started up the second half of the stairs.

Part way up, when they could no longer see the man, Rosie put her hand on Kayo's arm, indicating she should stop. She whispered in Kayo's ear, "I have an idea."

61

Kayo waited, growing more nervous by the second.

"I'll go back down," Rosie whispered, "to where we were when they first came. You wait on the landing. When he goes upstairs to help her carry the next load, you run to the second floor, make a big racket, and then lock yourself in the bathroom."

Kayo shook her head, no, but Rosie continued to whisper. "They'll go up to see what the noise is, and I'll dash to the telephone and call the police. The thieves will get caught in the act."

"What if they see you?" Kayo said.

"If they see me I'll run up the stairs and you can let me in the bathroom with you."

"Maybe we should both hide in the bathroom until they leave, and then call the police," Kayo said.

"We can't give descriptions of them or of their car," Rosie said. "They would get away. They would get all the dolls."

Kayo thought about Rosie's plan. "You should be the one to distract them and hide in the bathroom," she said, "and I'll make the call. I can run a lot faster than you. If they chase me I can probably get away; they might catch you."

Rosie knew Kayo was right. Kayo ran two miles every day as part of her training to be a professional baseball player. Rosie ran only when she was required to do so in P.E., and then she always finished last in the sixth grade.

Kayo sat and bumped down the stairs on her bottom. She scooted across the landing and then slid silently down the rest of the steps, pausing at each step to be sure the thief had not turned around.

The man stood as before, with his back to both stairways, looking out the front door.

Rosie crouched on the dark landing, careful not to touch the little piano. She also watched the man.

When Kayo's feet reached the main floor, she stayed seated on the second step up. Her hands pressed on the step and she leaned slightly forward, ready to spring up and run when it was time.

"Come and get them!" the woman called.

The man looked out the door in both directions, and then started toward the exit stairs.

As soon as he moved, Rosie ran. When she reached the second floor she let out a bloodcurdling scream, the kind she had heard in an old monster movie. Her voice echoed through the empty museum.

The man swore and began climbing up the stairs two at a time.

When he reached the landing Kayo shot to her feet and ran toward the circular reception area.

She had seen the telephone earlier, behind the counter.

She fumbled for the doorknob to open the waist-high door that led inside the area.

The door was locked. Kayo reached over and tried it from the inside, but the door did not open. It must need a key, Kayo thought. She put her hands on the marble counter and jumped, swinging her legs up.

Rosie screamed again.

The man stopped part way up the steps and looked behind him. As soon as he turned, he saw Kayo. Instead of continuing up, he ran back down.

Intent on climbing over the counter, Kayo took her eyes off the man and did not realize he had changed directions. She swung her feet inside the counter area and slid to the floor.

When she looked up the man in black was only a few feet away, rushing straight toward her.

Kayo knew instantly that she could not get away. He was too close. If she had been outside the circular reception area, she could have run, as planned, and joined Rosie in the bathroom.

But there was not time now to climb back over the counter and run. He would catch her easily.

Instead of running she searched for the telephone. Her fingers felt frantically along the ledge beneath the counter, where she had seen the woman pick up the telephone earlier.

The man put his hands on the counter and vaulted over the door. Kayo moved away from him as she continued to hunt for the telephone.

There! She found it. She raised the receiver as his feet hit the floor inside the reception area.

Kayo put her face close to the telephone, trying to read the numbers. She punched number nine.

The man lunged. Before Kayo could hit number one, his fist swung out, knocking the telephone from her hand.

# Chapter

The telephone receiver clattered over the ledge and dangled toward the floor.

Kayo edged sideways away from the man, her back pressed against the rib-high counter.

Upstairs, the screaming stopped.

"Dutch!" the woman's shrill voice cried. "Come up! There's somebody in here."

The man did not answer her. He stepped closer to Kayo. "What are you doing in here?" he said. He spoke as if he owned the museum and Kayo had no right to be trespassing.

"I have permission to be here," she said. "I'm doing research on ghosts."

"Sure you are," the man said, "and I'm the President of the United States."

The woman upstairs yelled again. "Dutch! Do you hear me? Someone is up here. He's locked himself in the bathroom."

"How did you get in?" the man asked Kayo. "Did you see me unlock the side door and turn off the burglar alarm? Or did you and your buddy come in during regular hours and hide somewhere until everyone left?"

"There's no one with me," Kayo said. "I came alone."

A nasal-sounding voice spoke from the floor near Kayo's feet. Kayo jumped.

The man's head jerked as he looked down.

The voice said, "If you'd like to make a call, please hang up and try again. If you need help, hang up and then dial your operator."

I would love to dial the operator, Kayo thought. I would trade my Johnny Bench rookie card for a chance to dial the operator.

"If you'd like to make a call," the voice repeated, "please hang up and try again. If you need help, hang up and then dial your operator."

"Be quiet," the man said, kicking at the telephone.

"There's no one in the bathroom," Kayo said. "That screaming you heard was one of the ghosts. They like to lock the bathroom doors as a joke. They do it all the time."

"There are no ghosts."

*Beep beep beep beep beep.* The telephone emitted a series of sharp sounds designed to attract attention. The man reached down, grabbed the receiver, and replaced it in its cradle.

Taking advantage of his momentary distraction, Kayo leaped up on the counter. She slid across it and dropped to the other side. When her feet hit the marble floor, she ran for the front door. It was much closer than the stairs. If she could make it out of the museum, she was sure she could run faster than the man. She would get to a telephone and call for help.

She knew Rosie would be safe in the bathroom. The thieves had keys to the museum and the display cases, but they would not have a way to unlock the bathroom door when it was locked from the inside.

The man jumped over the counter and started after Kayo.

Kayo stretched out her arm as she neared the door. She was almost there.

As Kayo's hand closed around the door handle, the man caught her. His hands clamped down on her shoulders and spun her around to face him.

The woman ran down the stairway. "Can't you hear me?" she said. "There's a person upstairs. Maybe more than one." She stopped running when she saw Kayo. "Who's that?" she asked. "How did she get in?"

Kayo stood with her back to the door, facing the thieves. Light from the museum's outdoor lights shone dimly in on their black clothing. Their eyes glittered angrily through the openings in the ski masks.

"She says she's here doing research on ghosts," the man said.

The woman stiffened. "Ghosts?" she said. "There are ghosts in here?"

"Yes," Kayo said, sensing the woman's anxiety. "Lots of ghosts. The museum is haunted."

"My grandmother claimed she once saw the ghost of her father," the woman said. "Grandmother was only ten at the time, but she talked about it for the rest of her life."

"Are we going to stand around and swap stories about our dear old grannies," the man said, "or are we going to get those dolls?"

"There's a person upstairs in the women's bathroom," the woman said. "I heard terrible screaming, and when I went to investigate, I heard the bathroom door close and lock. Someone is in there."

"It's one of the ghosts," Kayo said. "The screaming was a ghost, too."

Maybe I can scare them off, Kayo thought.

Maybe I can make her so nervous she leaves, and he would go with her.

"The ghosts scream when they're angry," Kayo continued. "They don't like it that you're taking the dolls away."

As Kayo spoke the woman kept rubbing her hands together and looking over her shoulders.

The man said, "Don't give us any more ghost foolishness. We know better." He turned to the woman. "She probably has a friend with her," he said "and the other kid screamed."

"I thought there was a person upstairs," the woman said, "but I didn't actually see anyone. I heard the screams and then I heard the door click shut, and when I tried to open it, it was locked from the inside. Maybe it is a ghost, Dutch. Maybe this place *is* haunted."

"And maybe I'm going to win an Olympic medal in figure skating."

I wish the ghost would appear, Kayo thought. If the ghost of the German soldier materialized right now, this woman would faint for sure.

"If you take the dolls," Kayo said, "the ghosts will follow you."

"I don't like this, Dutch," the woman whispered. "Let's take what we have and get out of here."

"And let her call the cops before we get it

loaded in the van?" the man said. "No way. We are not leaving without everything we came for."

"My friend and I were here yesterday," Kayo said. "A ghost followed us home."

"That's enough about ghosts," the man said. He took Kayo's arm and dragged her past the cart that was now half covered with dolls. He climbed the exit stairs, pulling Kayo with him.

The woman trailed after them. "What are you going to do with her?" she said.

"I'll think of something."

"We don't have a lookout now," the woman said.

"I know that," he snapped. "It's more important to keep this kid under control."

When they reached the second floor, Kayo saw that the thieves had a flashlight, the kind Rosie's parents bought for their motorhome. The flashlight sat on the floor, throwing light across the displays of dolls and toys.

Several of the glass display cases stood open, their contents gone.

"Get the rest of the good ones," the man said to the woman.

She put a key into the lock on the display case containing dolls of Little Red Riding-Hood and the Wolf, and Goldilocks and the Three Bears. She opened the case.

Kayo looked toward the display case that held

the musical cat. It remained locked. She wondered what would happen if the woman opened that case.

Would the crying ghost of the little girl appear to claim her toy? Would Werner von Moltz come?

If I can get the ghosts to come, Kayo thought, they might scare the thieves away.

# Chapter

# 10

You're leaving behind the most valuable toy in the whole collection," Kayo said.

"What?" the man said. "Which one?"

Kayo pointed. "The musical cat."

The woman walked quickly to the display case and looked at the cat. "Not true," she said. "It's a nice little toy and it's in good condition, but it won't bring nearly as much as the dolls we're taking."

"It will if you know its history," Kayo said. "That cat belonged to King George of England when he was a little boy."

Kayo had no idea who had ruled Great Britain at the time the musical cat was made, but she thought there had been a King George at one time.

"This kid should be writing fiction," the man

said. "First ghosts and now the King of England. Gimme a break."

"If the toy had a royal background," the woman said, "you can be sure the museum would advertise that fact." She turned away from the cat's display case.

I went too far, Kayo thought. I'll have to be careful what I tell them or they may not believe anything I say.

The woman lifted Goldilocks out of the case.

"My mother is coming to pick me up soon," Kayo said. "If I'm not waiting for her by the front door, she will call the police."

Maybe Mom *will* come, Kayo thought. Rosie and I are supposed to be on the bus that gets home at 5:45. When we aren't on it Mom will worry that something is wrong. She'll try to find us.

"I'm going to start loading the van," the woman said. "It's too risky to stay here."

"The ghost that followed us was a German soldier," Kayo said. "He was killed in World War I."

The woman dropped Goldilocks. She turned to look at Kayo. "My great-grandfather died in World War I," the woman said. "When my grandmother saw his ghost, he was wearing his uniform."

"This ghost wore a uniform, too," Kayo said, "and a helmet. There was a blue light all around him, and even after he disappeared, we smelled a damp musty smell where he stood."

The woman gazed at Kayo, her eyes wide. "She's telling the truth, Dutch," she said. "I know she is. She couldn't make up a story like that."

"The ghost followed my friend and me home from the museum," Kayo said. "Last night he appeared in my bedroom in the middle of the night."

"Just like Grandma," the woman said.

"That does it!" the man said. "I don't care if the ghost of Christopher Columbus follows us home. We have a job to do here, and the longer we stand around talking, the greater the chance we'll get caught. So let's quit yakking and get on with it."

"What about the girl?" the woman asked. She picked up the doll she had dropped. Kayo was glad Goldilocks had landed on the carpet.

"We'll lock her in one of these empty cases," the man said. "She won't be able to call the cops from in there."

"There's still somebody in the bathroom, too."

"Let her stay there; she hasn't seen or heard anything. From the way she was screaming she's probably so scared she'll stay in there all night. By then we'll have our money from Tuttle and be on our way to Spokane."

"It's a ghost in the bathroom," Kayo said.

The woman hesitated for a moment, looking at Kayo, before she carried another armful of dolls down the stairs.

The man pulled Kayo to an empty display case next to the one that held the cat. The glass door stood open.

Kayo looked at the enclosure. All of the display cases were higher than the museum floor; most had large drawers below them which pulled out to display other exhibits. Kayo guessed that the case was four feet wide, four feet deep, and about five feet high. Kayo would fit inside the case, but there wouldn't be any room to spare. She would be able to sit down only if she drew her knees up to her chest.

He pulled out the drawer, to make a step. Two china baby dolls in white dresses lay in the drawer, their innocent eyes looking up at Kayo and the thief through a covering of thick glass.

"Climb in," he said.

There won't be enough air, Kayo thought. He might as well lock me in a glass coffin.

"In," the man repeated, shoving Kayo toward the drawer. His dark gloves felt warm on her shoulders. She caught a whiff of aftershave lotion blended with sweat, and her stomach turned over.

The man put his hands on Kayo's waist, lifted

her, and set her feet on top of the drawer. Then he shoved her into the display case. He pushed with such force that she hit her head on the back wall, stunning her long enough for him to close both the drawer and the glass door.

The woman rushed back up the stairs. "The phone rang while I was downstairs," she said, "and an answering device came on. The caller was a woman who said her daughter and a friend visited the museum this afternoon and failed to arrive home when they were supposed to. The woman said since there was no answer she assumed the girls had left. Unless someone from the museum calls right back, she is going to call the police and report them missing."

Yes! Kayo thought. Call the police, Mom. Now!

While the man held the door shut, he spoke over his shoulder to the woman. "Go downstairs and play that message back. Get the phone number and call the kid's mother. Make up a name; tell her you're from the museum. Say that the girls missed their bus and an employee is driving them home."

Listening to the man's instructions, Kayo clenched her fists in frustration. His plan would work. Even if Mom had already called the police, she would call them back and tell them they didn't have to look for two girls, after all, because

**77**

someone from the museum was bringing them safely home. Mom would wait another hour before she would suspect that something was wrong, that no one from the doll museum was bringing the girls home. By then Kayo might be out of air.

"Give me the keys," the man said as he held out his hand. "And be sure to erase the message after you listen to it."

The woman nodded and tossed the ring of keys to the man before she hurried downstairs.

He made a one-handed grab for the keys and missed. They rattled to the floor. When he bent to pick them up, he moved away from the glass door for an instant.

Kayo shoved hard from the inside. The door opened far enough for her to squeeze one foot out.

The man tried to stuff Kayo's foot back inside the case. She leaned her shoulder into the door and pushed. The door jerked open, striking the man's collarbone.

He stumbled backward, accidentally stepping on the keys. His ankle twisted and he flailed his arms, trying to catch his balance.

Before he could slam the door shut again, Kayo jumped out of the display case.

The man grabbed her arm.

Kayo wrenched free, spun away, and sprinted

through the dark museum toward the rest room. If she could make it there, Rosie would let her in and they would both be safe.

Heavy footsteps pounded behind her.

He was close. Too close.

And he was getting closer.

# Chapter

# 11

Rosie paced nervously around the bathroom. She looked at her watch. Six-fifteen.

Why didn't Kayo come?

It's been too long, she thought. If Kayo made it to the telephone and called for help, the police would be here by now. As soon as they arrived Kayo would come to get me.

But Kayo had not come, nor had the police.

Something went wrong, Rosie decided. Kayo never made the call. The thieves must have caught her. If so, where was she now? Were the thieves still in the museum? Had they tied Kayo up and left? Had they taken Kayo with them?

Rosie turned off the bathroom light. She couldn't wait any longer, not when Kayo might need help.

## The Ghost Followed Us Home

Rosie unlocked the bathroom door and cracked it open. Putting an ear to the opening, she listened. She heard voices somewhere in the museum, but she could not make out who it was or what they were saying.

Rosie opened the door and slipped out, easing the door shut so it wouldn't make any noise.

The museum was still dark. Rosie's heart beat faster. If the police had come they would have turned the lights on. The voices must be the man and woman in ski masks.

It sounded as if they were on the second floor. Rosie moved slowly through the dark museum toward the voices. Although her eyes adjusted to the darkness, she held her hands out in front of her as she walked, fearful that she would bump into something and make a noise again. Each time she came to the end of a corridor, she peeked around the corner before she continued into the next display area.

She was getting close to the voices when her hands hit glass. Rosie stopped. It was the door of a display case, standing open. The case was empty. She came to other empty display cases where the thieves had removed the dolls.

Anger surged through Rosie. Those thieves were not only stealing from the museum owner, they were robbing all of the people who liked to come and enjoy the collection. It wasn't right.

"Rosie!" Kayo's cry jolted Rosie, setting every nerve on edge. "Unlock the door!"

She's running from the thieves, Rosie realized. She's headed this way, toward the rest room, and I'm not there.

"You won't make it!" the man shouted, and Rosie knew instantly that his voice was too close. She could not get back to the rest room before he saw her.

Instead of running she climbed into an empty display case and pulled the door shut. She smiled and held her arms out, waist high, spreading her fingers. She stood absolutely still, barely breathing.

There are some life-size dolls, she thought. I might get away with this.

Kayo ran past the stuffed horse pulling a wagon load of dolls. She ran past the doll hospital.

When she rounded the corner the man was only a few feet behind her. Kayo was fast but so was the man, and with his long legs he gained on her with every step.

Rosie saw them coming. Run, Kayo! she thought. Run fast! The bathroom door is unlocked.

Just as Kayo passed the case where Rosie was, the man leaped forward and tackled her. His hands closed around her ankles.

Rosie watched, horrified, as Kayo fell.

Rosie wanted to jump out of the case and attack the man, but she knew it was better to stand where she was, with her smile frozen on her face and her unmoving hands in the air. If he didn't realize she was there, she might be able to sneak downstairs and get to the telephone. It was smarter to call for help than to fight with the thief.

The man stood up, pulling Kayo to her feet. Holding her by both shoulders, he pushed her in front of him, out of Rosie's sight. As soon as they were gone, Rosie climbed out of the case and tiptoed back toward the stairway.

The man pushed Kayo to where the keys lay on the floor. Still holding on to Kayo, he picked up the keys. Then he pulled out the drawer, lifted Kayo onto it, and shoved her inside the empty case.

He leaned his body against the door while he tried to insert a key in the keyhole. It didn't fit. He tried a different key. It wouldn't work, either.

On the third try the key slid smoothly into the keyhole. Kayo heard the *click* as the door locked.

The woman returned. "I talked to the mother," she said. "I told her I was driving the girls home, and she believed me."

Rosie passed the rest room, wishing she could go back inside, lock the door, and wait until help arrived, even if nobody came until morning.

If she were alone with the thieves, that is what she would do. But she couldn't think only of her own safety; she had to think of Kayo, as well. The man had seemed angry when he caught Kayo. Rosie had no idea where he had taken Kayo or what he planned to do. For all she knew the thieves were armed.

Tempting as it was to wait alone in the safe rest room, she could not do it.

Instead she made her way down the stairs, moving slowly and carefully. At the landing she sat down, the way Kayo had, and bumped down the rest of the steps.

The downstairs room was empty. She heard voices from upstairs again. Maybe she could call for help now, before they came down.

Rosie ran to the circular counter and felt for the doorknob. The door was locked.

She heard voices at the top of the exit stairs. The thieves were coming down.

Rosie ran to the far side of the counter and squatted down.

"I still say we should leave now," the woman said.

"One more cart load," the man said. "Then, if you're still jittery, we'll go and come back for the rest another night."

"No," the woman said. "I'm never coming

back. And if any ghosts follow us, I'm dumping the dolls."

The thieves reached the landing and continued down. Where is Kayo? Rosie wondered. What have they done with Kayo?

"I can't believe you let that kid scare you," the man said. "There are no such things as ghosts. She was making up stories, trying to frighten us, just like she lied when she said her mother was coming to pick her up. None of it was true." He began pulling the cart full of dolls away from the stairs.

"Maybe so," the woman said. "But the idea of seeing a ghost makes my hair stand on end."

Rosie hesitated for only a moment. If she hid and waited to call the police after the thieves had left, they would probably get away with all the dolls. She wanted to make them leave now, before they took the dolls out of the museum.

"Goooooo," Rosie said. She spoke softly with a waver in her voice, making the word sound like a moan. It was the way she had imagined a ghost would sound until she actually heard the ghost of Werner von Moltz speak.

The thieves stopped.

"What was that?" the woman said. "Who's there?"

Rosie moaned again, slightly louder. She cupped her hands around her mouth and tried to make it sound as if her voice came from the empty office. "Gooooo awaaayyy."

"It's the ghost," the woman said. "Dutch! The ghost is here."

"Don't be an idiot," the man said. "It's probably the second kid, trying to scare us."

"Goooo nowwwwww," moaned Rosie.

"You can do what you like with the dolls," the woman said. "I'm not staying where there are ghosts." She hurried down the hallway toward the elevator and the employee workroom.

Swearing, the man approached the counter, making no effort to be quiet. As he came around the counter one way, Rosie moved quickly the other way, bent at the waist.

The man suddenly reversed directions and sprinted around the counter.

Rosie could not respond fast enough.

"I knew it!" he cried as he spotted Rosie. "Darlene! Come back. There's no ghost; it's the other kid, just like I said."

The woman returned.

Rosie stood and faced the thieves. She could not see their faces through the ski masks, but she knew she would never forget their voices.

"Some ghost," the man said. He grabbed Rosie's arm. "Come on. Let's go visit your pal."

Rosie did not struggle. She knew she was not fast enough or strong enough to get away.

"I've been thinking about the toy that belonged to King George," the man said to the woman as they climbed the stairs. "Maybe the kid knows something the museum isn't advertising. Her parents probably know the owner or she would not be in here at night. Maybe that really is the most valuable piece in the museum, but they don't want the public to know."

"Maybe they're afraid of theft," the woman said.

The man laughed.

"I'll go get it," the woman said.

He handed her a ring of keys.

Rosie tried to think which toy had belonged to King George, but she could not remember.

When they reached the second floor the woman kept going. The man stopped in front of the first empty display case, a freestanding square one. He gave Rosie a push.

"In you go," he said.

A chill of horror prickled Rosie's scalp.

He is going to lock me in there, she realized, and I won't have enough air.

*Thump. Thump. Thump.*

The noise came from around the corner, in the next corridor where the musical cat was. It's the ghost girl, Rosie thought. She's there, pounding on the glass.

Rosie expected the woman to come running

back. She had seemed genuinely afraid of ghosts, and she must hear the noise.

"Get in," the man said.

*Thump. Thump. Thump.*

"Do you hear that?" Rosie said. "That's one of the ghosts. She wants us to open the case she's in."

"And I'm head coach of the San Diego Chargers," the man said.

*Thump. Thump. Thump.*

"It is a ghost," Rosie said. "I'll prove it to you. Come on." She walked around the corner toward the thumping noise.

Chuckling, the man followed.

Rosie started toward the musical cat and then stopped when she realized the thumping came from a display case on the other side of the cat. She looked toward the noise.

"Oh, no!" she gasped. It wasn't the ghost girl pounding on the glass. It was Kayo.

*Thump! Thump!* Kayo beat her fists on the inside of the door, looking angry and scared and helpless.

"Let her out of there!" Rosie demanded.

"Anything else you want to show me?" the man said.

# Chapter

# 12

The man reached for Rosie's arm.

Rosie twisted away from him and ran. Fear put speed in her feet; she sprinted around the corner and toward the stairs.

He caught her before she could start down. He pulled her to the corridor where the woman was and pushed her to an empty case near the one Kayo was in.

Rosie remembered the doll that had been in that case. It was a French doll with a beautiful long dress. Rosie had always liked the doll's ringlets and the wreath on her hair. They took it, she thought, and they're going to get away with it.

"Get in," he said. "Now."

"No."

He raised his hand as if to strike her.

Rosie swallowed her anger and climbed into the case. Tears stung her eyes as she wondered what would happen now. She knew Mrs. Benton would call Rosie's parents when the girls did not arrive.

Mom and Dad would look for her and Kayo. Mrs. Benton would look for them. Before long, the police would look for them. Probably whole search parties would look for them.

But would anyone look in the doll museum? Rosie worried that everyone would assume something happened to the girls on their way home. No one would think to look for them here.

We'll be found tomorrow morning, Rosie thought, when the museum opens. But will we still be alive?

Kayo watched as the woman put a key into the lock on the display case that contained the musical cat. Yes, she thought. Open that one.

Kayo waited holding her breath. She was certain that Chantal, the ghost girl, would appear as soon as the door opened.

Kayo hoped both ghosts came to get the cat. She wanted the ghosts to appear right in that awful woman's face and scare her out of her wits.

The woman turned the key.

The door swung open.

"Chantal!" Kayo cried. "The case is open. Come and get your cat!"

Nothing happened.

There was no sign of the weeping child.

Kayo's shoulders sagged. What a joke, she thought. I lay awake half of last night fearing a ghost would come, and now I'm disappointed because a ghost didn't come.

The woman reached in and picked up the mohair cat.

Me and my big mouth, Kayo thought. They did not plan to steal the musical cat until I made up that stupid story about King George. Now the thieves think the cat is worth a ton of money. Thanks to me our favorite toy is going to be sold to some collector overseas. We'll never see it again, and neither will any of the people who visit the doll museum in the future.

Why didn't I tell them it was the big doll in the same case with the cat, the one sitting in a chair, that was valuable? Or I could have said the oil lamp in that case belonged to King George. All I wanted was for them to unlock that door. Why did I mention the cat at all?

She watched as the woman examined the cat, turning it over in her hands.

Maybe the ghosts are waiting until the cat is outside, Kayo thought. Maybe the German soldier and the crying ghost girl will follow the thieves and take the cat later, when there are no more doors to get through.

She hoped so. If the musical cat could not stay here in the museum, Kayo wanted it to go to France, to make little Chantal happy and to ease Werner von Moltz's guilt. She wanted both ghosts to find peace.

The woman carried the cat past Kayo's case. Kayo pushed on the glass again even though she knew it was hopeless. The woman did not look at her.

The air was already stuffy inside the case. Kayo pressed her warm forehead against the smooth, cold glass.

If she wasn't found quickly, she feared she would be a ghost soon herself. And Rosie, too.

The man stood in front of Rosie's door, holding it closed.

The woman tucked the cat under her arm. She handed the keys to the man so he could lock the case that Rosie was in.

He inserted the key in the keyhole, but before he turned it, the woman screamed.

Her shrill cry bounced off the glass display cases.

The man spun around to see what was wrong.

The woman fainted, crumpling to the floor at his feet.

The musical cat did not fall with her. It remained suspended in the air as if supported by invisible hands.

"What?" The man backed away from the cat, leaving the keys dangling from the door of the display case.

The sides of the cat began to move in and out. The strange music filled the air.

The man knelt and shook the woman. "Wake up!" he said. "We're leaving."

The woman remained motionless.

So did Rosie. She was afraid if she moved or made a sound, the man would realize he had never locked the door. Standing as still as one of the dolls, she watched the man gather the woman in his arms and carry her toward the stairway.

The musical cat continued its song.

As soon as the thieves turned the corner, Rosie pushed on the door of her case. The door swung open, and Rosie climbed out.

She pulled the keys from the lock and ran to the display case where Kayo was.

She tried keys until she found the right one. When the door opened, Kayo jumped to the floor.

Neither girl spoke. Holding hands, they walked to the top of the exit stairway and looked down. The man was halfway down the steps, still carrying the woman.

The music stopped.

The thieves reached the bottom of the stairs.

When they got to the cart full of dolls, the man lowered the woman's feet until they touched the floor. Supporting her under her arms, he shook her again. "Wake up," he said. "You have to walk while I pull the cart."

The woman blinked and swayed. "I saw a ghost," she said. "Did you see her, Dutch? Did you see the ghost?"

"Calm down," the man said.

"Where is she?" the woman said. "Where is the ghost now?"

"There isn't any ghost."

"You didn't see the little girl? She had on an old-fashioned dress and an apron, and she took that mohair cat out of my hands and started playing music with it. She was right there in front of us. You must have seen her."

"Well, I didn't," he said. He grabbed the cart handle and pulled it toward the hallway.

The woman staggered after him.

The cart squeaked louder now that it was loaded with dolls. The woman continued to talk about the ghost while the man insisted she had imagined it.

Kayo and Rosie crept down the stairs and hurried to the front door.

Rosie turned the handle. As she pushed the door open, Kayo tapped her on the shoulder. Rosie looked back.

Chantal's ghost floated toward the door, carrying the musical cat.

Rosie and Kayo glanced at each other, nodded agreement, and pushed the door open wide. Standing together they held it open and waited for the ghost.

Chantal cradled the cat close to her chest as if it were a baby. She paused at the threshold and smiled at Rosie and Kayo. Her face shone with happiness.

"*Merci,*" Chantal said.

"You're welcome," Rosie whispered.

The girls felt a gentle, cool breeze when the ghost passed them. A faint scent of fresh hay lingered after her.

Rosie and Kayo watched as Chantal Dubail and her musical cat drifted across the museum steps, floated high above the parking lot, and disappeared into the night sky.

Rosie started to close the door, but Kayo stopped her. She pointed to the left. A large van was parked close to the building, far in the corner.

"There must be a back door," Kayo whispered. "Let's go in and call the police. They might get here while the thieves are loading their van."

The girls went inside. The cart's squeak came from far down the hallway.

While Rosie carefully closed the front door,

Kayo climbed over the counter. She found the telephone and dialed 911.

"We need help," Kayo whispered. "At the doll museum."

Rosie looked over the counter. Kayo motioned for her to come. Rosie climbed over the counter and sat on the floor next to Kayo.

"The emergency operator said the police would be here in a couple of minutes," Kayo whispered. "It's probably safer to wait here than to go outside."

The squeaking stopped.

Rosie and Kayo listened.

"The door to the workroom is locked," the man said.

"It can't be," the woman said. "We left it open in case we needed to get out fast."

"Somebody locked it, and I can't open it without the key."

"It was those girls," the woman said. "Those girls must have locked the door."

Kayo and Rosie smiled at each other in the dim light. They had a good idea who had locked the door. It was the same person who had locked the bathroom door yesterday so that Rosie and Kayo would have to stay in the museum when everyone else was gone. Werner von Moltz.

"Give me the keys," the man said.

"I don't have the keys," the woman said. "You have them."

"No, I don't."

"I gave them to you so you could lock up the second girl."

"I left them in the lock," he said. "I'll go get them."

"I'll come with you. I'm not staying here alone. The ghost might come back."

The voices came closer. The thieves were walking fast.

We should have run when we had the chance, Rosie thought. By now we would be a block away instead of huddled here, hoping the thieves don't look over the counter.

"There was no ghost, I tell you. Look around. Do you see any ghost? Do you hear any music? No. Of course not. Because you imagined the whole thing. You let those kids and their wild stories get to you."

"What if she follows us?" the woman said. "If that ghost appears in my bedroom tonight, I'll have a heart attack."

The voices were entering the reception area.

"Maybe we can get out this door," the woman said.

"The van is next to the back door. And we have to load the dolls. I'll run up and get the keys."

"We could move the van and take the dolls out this way."

"Sure we could. And every car that drives past would see us. Why not just put out a sign: Burglary in Progress?"

"I am never setting foot in this place again," the woman said.

Rosie and Kayo heard heavy footsteps clomp across the floor and go up the stairs.

"They're gone!" the man yelled from above. The footsteps pounded back down.

"The kids are gone, and so are the keys." His voice shook with fury. "They got away and took our keys with them."

"They're probably hiding in the bathroom," the woman said.

"I'm going to disconnect the telephone," he said. "We need time to load the van. I don't want them to sneak in here and call for help."

Putting both hands on the countertop, he vaulted over.

When he landed, he looked down.

"Look who's here," he said. "A pair of ghosts."

# Chapter

**13**

*T*he girls stood up, facing the man.

"Give me the keys," he said.

"We don't have them," Rosie said.

"The ghost took them," Kayo said.

"You two have spoiled a perfect job," the man said, "and now you're going to wish you hadn't."

"We called the police," Kayo said. "They are on the way."

"More lies," the man muttered. His hands, in the black gloves, reached toward Rosie.

"Help!" Kayo shouted. "Werner! We need help!"

As Kayo called his name she wondered whether the ghost was still there. Now that Chantal had left with her toy, there was no reason for Werner von Moltz to stay at the museum. By now he might already be in France with Chantal. Or back in Germany. Or even at peace so he didn't appear as a ghost any longer.

The gloved hands closed on Rosie's arms.

"Werner!" Rosie cried. "Help!"

A blue glow lit the room behind the girls. Rosie and Kayo could smell the musty odor.

The man's hands stopped.

"Dutch!" The woman's voice vibrated with fear. "Look!"

The blue light grew brighter.

The man dropped his hands and took a step backward, away from the girls.

The woman screamed.

The man turned and climbed over the counter. He and the woman ran together toward the front door.

Werner von Moltz, in his uniform and helmet, appeared in front of them. He held one hand up.

"Halt!" he commanded.

The woman slumped to the floor.

The man tried to walk around the ghost.

"Halt!" Werner von Moltz repeated.

The man stopped. "Who—who are you?" he said.

Sirens screamed in the street.

The thief turned toward the hallway, but Werner von Moltz again blocked his way.

The thief made a fist and swung at the ghost.

His fist went straight through the ghost and out the other side. Werner von Moltz did not flinch.

The thief pulled his hand back and looked at it as if he had never seen fingers before.

"They are not yours," the ghost said.

The thief stared at the ghost, his mouth open. "What?" he said. "What do you want?"

"The dolls are not yours. They are loyal childhood friends and they must stay here, where those who loved them can visit and remember."

Red lights whirled in the dark outside as two police cars pulled into the museum parking lot. The sirens stopped.

The spinning red lights shone through the glass door from outside, blending with the blue glow inside.

It's like a crazy laser video, Kayo thought.

Bright flashlights came on in the parking lot, pointed at the door.

The ghost vanished.

The woman moaned and sat up. "It's all over, Dutch," she said.

"No!" he cried. "We can still get away. Run!" He turned and dashed down the dark hallway toward the locked door.

The woman got to her feet.

Rosie and Kayo heard the man kicking at the door, trying to force it open.

As the girls climbed over the counter, they heard the sound of wood splintering.

The woman started groggily toward the hallway, but Kayo grabbed the back of her ski mask and held tight.

"Dutch!" the woman yelled. "Help! The ghost caught me!"

Two police officers ran up the museum steps. Rosie opened the door.

Officer Ken Bremner and Officer Julia Harig rushed into the museum.

Rosie pointed down the hallway. "That way," she said. "He's trying to get out the back door."

Officer Bremner ran down the hallway.

"This is his partner," Kayo said, letting go of the woman's ski mask. "They tried to steal the dolls."

"They locked us in the empty display cases," Rosie said.

The woman in the ski mask leaned against the reception counter.

"Are you Kayo Benton and Rosie Saunders?" Officer Harig asked. When the girls said yes, she said, "Call your parents. They reported you missing about half an hour ago. They are plenty worried about you."

Kayo reached over and lifted the telephone on to the counter. She called her mother, and Rosie called her parents.

Another police car arrived and two more officers came in. A woman ran up the steps behind them and started to follow them in the door.

"Sorry. No admittance," an officer said.

"I'm Lauren Verrilli," the woman said. "I'm a docent at the museum." Rosie and Kayo recognized her as the woman who had been at the reception counter the day before.

"Let her in," Officer Harig said.

Lauren entered. "I live across the street," she said, "and I saw the police cars. What happened? Did someone break in?"

"Can you turn the lights on?" Officer Harig said.

Lauren went into the small office, and seconds later the museum lights blazed on.

Rosie and Kayo listened as Officer Harig read the woman in the ski mask her rights.

"There are ghosts here," the woman said. "I saw them. One was a little girl and one was a soldier. They played music on the toy cat."

"Better order some mental tests on her," one of the officers said.

Officer Bremner returned with the other thief.

"There's a cart full of dolls at the end of the hall," Officer Bremner said. "Looks as if they planned to go through the workroom and out the fire-escape door to their van."

Lauren ran to get the cart.

"Tell them, Dutch," the woman said. "Tell them we really saw ghosts."

"I didn't see any ghost," the man said.

Rosie reached in her jeans pocket. "Here's a set of museum keys," she said.

Officer Bremner looked hard at Rosie and Kayo as he took the keys. "Aren't you the same girls who caught the vandals at the school?" he asked.

"Yes," Kayo said.

"And you found the poisonous plant in that old woman's yard."

"Mrs. Tallie," Rosie said.

"That's the one," he said.

"Maybe we ought to sign them up for the police force," Officer Harig said. "They solve half the crimes in Oakwood before we do."

Lauren Verrilli put the dolls and toys away while Rosie and Kayo told the police what had happened. Neither girl mentioned the ghosts. It seemed better, somehow, just to tell about the thieves and leave Chantal Dubail and Werner von Moltz out of the story.

Part way through, Mr. and Mrs. Saunders drove in to the parking lot. Mrs. Benton was with them. Rosie and Kayo started over and told everything again.

They had just finished answering questions from the police when Lauren came downstairs.

"There's only one item missing from the upper

level exhibits," she said. "It's a musical cat, made in France. It wasn't on the cart and it isn't in any of the display cases."

"The ghost took it," the woman said. "I've been trying to tell you that."

"Let's get her to the hospital," Officer Harig said.

"Dutch!" the woman said. "Tell them what happened. You saw the second ghost, too. I know you did."

"I don't believe in ghosts," the man said.

Officer Bremner clamped handcuffs on the man's wrists and led him to the patrol car. Officer Harig followed with the woman.

"They must have hidden the cat," another officer said. "We didn't find anything in their van except some reference books with the current prices of antique dolls."

"I wonder why they took that one item?" Lauren said. "It isn't nearly as valuable as many of the others."

Kayo and Rosie smiled at each other and said nothing.

# Chapter

# 14

"It was you, wasn't it?" Sammy Hulenback demanded the next day, when Rosie and Kayo got to school. "You caught the thieves at the doll museum."

"What can he be talking about?" Rosie said.

"I have no idea," Kayo replied.

"I heard all about it on the radio this morning," Sammy said. "You caught the thieves and called the police."

"Were our names mentioned?" Kayo asked. She knew they were not, because Rosie's parents always insisted that the girls' names not be used in any news report.

"No," Sammy admitted, "but as soon as the reporter said the doll museum, I knew right away it was you. You didn't have operations on your big toes yesterday. You went after the thieves."

"Maybe we did and maybe we didn't," Kayo said.

"Your club goofed this time," Sammy said.

"The thieves are in jail, aren't they?" Rosie said.

"Ha!" Sammy cried. "It was you! I knew it."

The girls walked toward their sixth-grade classroom. Sammy followed.

"You goofed," he said, "because one toy is still missing. It said on the radio that the thieves hid a musical cat somewhere and the police can't find it."

"Don't believe everything you hear on the radio," Kayo said.

"Do you know where the cat is?" Sammy asked.

The girls did not answer.

"You probably kept it yourselves," Sammy asked.

"Strike one," Kayo said.

"You did! You're so crazy about animals, you stole the toy cat yourself and you're letting the thieves take the blame."

"Strike two," Kayo said.

"The radio said the cat was really old," Sammy said.

"It was made circa 1900," Rosie said. She took

out her vocabulary notebook and made a check mark.

"If you were going to steal a toy cat," Sammy said, "why wouldn't you take a new one?"

"Strike three," Kayo said. "You are out of this conversation."

The girls sat in adjoining desks in the front row. Sammy, who always sat in the last row, stood beside them for a moment. "I heard the dolls that were nearly stolen are worth six hundred thousand dollars," he said.

"That's right," Kayo said.

"Do you want to go to the doll museum with me after school today?" Sammy asked.

"We can't," Kayo said. "We're picking up information about Greyhound Rescue, for a school report."

"We probably aren't going back to the museum for a long time," Rosie said.

"I'm going today after school," Sammy said. "I'll look around for that musical cat. If I find it, will you let me in your club?"

"You won't find it," Kayo said.

"How do you know? The thieves might have tossed it into the bushes."

"The cat is not in the bushes," Rosie said.

"Where is it then?" He squinted at Rosie as if he could see inside her head and read the answer to his question. "You know where it is, don't you?"

Rosie motioned for Sammy to lean down so she could whisper in his ear. "The cat is in France."

"You're lying," Sammy said. "How would it get to France? You lied about your big toes and you lied about going to the circus at midnight, and now you're lying about the cat." He stomped back to his own seat.

"Circus?" Kayo said. "What circus?"

Rosie was laughing so hard she could hardly answer. "When he asked what time we would get home yesterday, I told him *circa* midnight. He thought . . ." Both girls gave in to a fit of giggles.

When they finally quit laughing, Rosie said, "Do you realize we had an adventure that was not an official Care Club project?"

"It may not have been official," Kayo said, "but we did help an animal get returned to its home." She smiled at Rosie. "A toy animal."

"Chantal looked so happy last night," Rosie said. "Maybe we should add a line to the Care Club charter, vowing to help all ghosts."

"I do not plan to meet another ghost," Kayo said.

"I'm glad we met the ones we did, though. I wonder if Werner von Moltz will bring the cat back after Chantal doesn't need it anymore."

"He'll try."

"It's odd, isn't it?" Rosie said. "That first night, when he appeared in your house, we were terrified. Now we think of him as a friend. I kind of hope we'll see him again."

"We were scared of the unknown," Kayo said. "Once we understood the ghosts and their problems, there was no reason to be afraid."

"The only thing I'm afraid of now," Rosie said, "is that Sammy will keep bugging us to let him join Care Club."

OAKWOOD DAILY HERALD        Sunday Edition

MUSEUM'S TOY CAT FOUND IN FRANCE

A musical cat which was stolen from the Oakwood Doll Museum is being returned to the museum, but its return is as much a mystery as its theft.

A clerk at the American embassy in Paris found the mohair cat this morning on the desk of the American ambassador to France.

Neither the clerk nor the ambassador could explain how the toy got into the embassy during the night. Nothing in the building, where night security guards were on duty, had been disturbed or removed.

The musical cat, which was made in France circa 1900, was stolen from the doll museum last Wednesday night. No one at the museum knew how the toy got to France.

"We thought the thieves hid it around here," said Lauren Verrilli, the museum docent who cataloged the items that had been removed from their cases during the break-in.

According to Police Officer Julia Harig, two people were arrested for attempted burglary and for assault on the girls who discovered them in the museum. The alleged burglars remain in the county jail.

The American ambassador to France called Oakwood police because an anonymous note with the cat asked that it be sent to the Oakwood Doll Museum.

The note was written in German.


On Monday morning Kayo said, "I used up my film yesterday, and Mom said she would drop it at Fine Fotos on her way to work. My pictures will be ready this afternoon."

"Let's go get them after school."

When the girls picked up the prints, they flipped quickly through photos of Homer and Di-

111

amond, Mrs. Benton's birthday cake, and Kayo's baseball team.

They both wanted to see the one picture that was taken late at night in Kayo's bedroom.

When they found it they held it between them and stared.

The picture had a faint blue tinge as if the developer had made a mistake.

It showed Rosie's bedroom door, with the Willie Mays poster.

It showed part of Homer, with his back humped high and his tail huge.

And, barely visible, it showed a German soldier in a World War I uniform.

# Author's Notes

All of the dolls and toys described in *The Ghost Followed Us Home*, including the musical cat, are currently on display at the Rosalie Whyel Museum of Doll Art in Bellevue, Washington, recipient of the Jumeau Trophy for The Best Private Doll Museum World Wide.

I am grateful to Rosalie Whyel for her help and cooperation. She answered questions, offered assistance, allowed me to describe her beautiful facility, shared photographs, and even took the musical cat out of its case so I could touch it and listen to its song.

The cat's World War I history came from my imagination. Chantal Dubail and Werner von Moltz are fictional characters, and so are their ghosts.

*     *     *

# FRIGHTMARES

There are several nonprofit organizations whose sole purpose is to find homes for ex-racing greyhounds. For more information, contact the Greyhound Adoption Network, 1–800–G–HOUNDS. You will be referred to the adoption group nearest you.

# About the Author

**Peg Kehret's** popular novels for young people are regularly nominated for state awards. She has received the Young Hoosier Award, the Golden Sower Award, the Iowa Children's Choice Award, the Celebrate Literacy Award, the Sequoyah Award, the Land of Enchantment Award, the Maud Hart Lovelace Award, and the Pacific Northwest Young Reader's Choice Award. She lives with her husband, Carl, and their animal friends in Washington State, where she is a volunteer at the Humane Society and SPCA. Her two grown children and four grandchildren live in Washington, too.

Peg's Minstrel titles include *Nightmare Mountain; Sisters, Long Ago; Cages; Terror at the Zoo; Horror at the Haunted House;* and the *Frightmares*™ series.

Don't miss any of the adventure!

# FRIGHTMARES™

Whenever pets—and their owners—get into trouble, Rosie Saunders
and Kayo Benton always seem to be in the middle of the action.
Ever since they started the Care Club ("We Care About Animals"),
they've discovered a world of mysteries and surprises. . .and danger!

## #1: CAT BURGLAR ON THE PROWL

## #2: BONE BREATH AND THE VANDALS

## #3: DON'T GO NEAR MRS. TALLIE

## #4: DESERT DANGER

## #5: THE GHOST FOLLOWED US HOME

# By Peg Kehret

 A MINSTREL® BOOK

Published by Pocket Books

1049-05

# Bruce Coville's <u>Alien Adventures</u>

What happens when a tiny spaceship crashes through Rod Allbright's window and drops a crew of superpowerful aliens into the middle of his school project? Rod is drafted by Captain Grakker to help the aliens catch a dangerous interstellar criminal—in a chase that takes them all over the galaxy!

## ALIENS ATE MY HOMEWORK

## I LEFT MY SNEAKERS IN DIMENSION X

## THE SEARCH FOR SNOUT

## by BRUCE COVILLE

 A MINSTREL® BOOK

Published by Pocket Books          1043-03

# The Single Girl's Manifest~~x~~a

iving in a stupendously superior
ingle state of mind

## Jerusha Stewart

SOURCEBOOKS CASABLANCA™
AN IMPRINT OF SOURCEBOOKS, INC.®
NAPERVILLE, ILLINOIS

Published by Sourcebooks, Inc.
P.O. Box 4410, Naperville, Illinois 60567-4410
(630) 961-3900
FAX: (630) 961-2168
www.sourcebooks.com

Library of Congress Cataloging-in-Publication Data

Stewart, Jerusha.
  The single girl's manifesta : living in a stupendously superior single
state of mind / Jerusha Stewart.
      p. cm.
   ISBN 1-4022-0503-1 (alk. paper)
   1. Single women. I. Title.

HQ800.2.S76 2005
646.7'0086'52--dc22

2005019861

Printed and bound in Canada
TR 10 9 8 7 6 5 4 3

In recognition of the mother and father,
sisters and brother who love the
original last single girl in the world.

*Author's Note*

**Some of the names have been changed to protect the innocent and harbor the guilty.**

# Acknowledgments

The Book. Who knew two simple, one-syllable words could come to carry such weight in my life? In the beginning there was Rhoda London, the angel on my shoulder who was the first to say, "You *have* to write a book, you know." Next, my author friend Judith Briles piped in, unsolicited, with, "You really *should* write a book."

Then along came publishing veteran Marie Brown, who said, "You know, you really *can* write a book." And then my dear friend Kathryn Leary hugged me close and said, "You *are* going to write a book."

Which led to me having a conversation with my crazy friend Melissa Penn who countered, "You *can't* write a book about *being single!*"

"But it's what I *really* know!" I insisted. And I'm stubborn—tell me I can't do something and it only makes me want to do it even more. Lucky for me my wonderful fairy godmother of an agent Nancy Bell-Ellis, and Deb Werksman, my straight-shooting editor at Sourcebooks, agreed with me, and they showed me how to write *that* book. When I'd come in for my monthly hair appointment, my stylist Ella Thomas prodded, "What about the book, girl?" And, always, my mentor Steven McIntosh just kept saying, "Jerusha, finish the book!"

Which brings me to subjects of the book, thank you single friends and strangers who honestly opened your hearts for the book.

And through it all sisterfriend Deirdre McGruder read, edited, cried, screamed, laughed, and drank cheap wine with me until one day she announced: "It's A Book!"

Mahalo Nui Loa, I couldn't have done it without every one of you!

# The Table of
# Self-Serving Contents

**Step One.** Be Revolutionary
*Value Your Single-Mindedness*

## Step Two. Indulge in Random Acts of Selfishness
### Sustain the Single State of Being

## Step Three. Claim Your Space
### Establish a Singular Sense of Place

# Step Four. Embrace the "L" Word
Be the Love of Your Life

# STEP ONE
## Be Revolutionary

Value Your Single-Mindedness

# Chapter One

# Bypassing the Altar
# Can Be Life Altering

"You're born alone and you die alone. They don't make caskets for two." Decades later, I still remember my father's wisdom on the singularity of life.

It was common sense advice, coming from him. Why waste so much energy on finding a mate, becoming a couple, and getting married when you're going to die all by yourself? Yet, as I get older, I contemplate what it means to live life on this planet as an unattached person.

My father's sage advice was of little comfort as I grew up and faced being a single woman in a married world. As kids we're all afraid of the dark, jumping off the high dive, and the boogey man under the bed. As we age, we conquer old fears and replace them with new ones. The granddaddy of them all is the fear of growing old alone.

I've seen that "look" in the eyes of my women friends as they glance at me knowingly. "I'm not going to be like Jerusha, single at forty-five." Or they look away in sadness and think, "Poor Jerusha, over forty and alone."

I want to scream at them: "DON'T BE AFRAID!" What's the worst thing that can happen if you're not married at thirty or thirty-five or—God forbid—ever? What evils lurk behind the curtains of single life? The single stories you are about to read unmask the fear of the unknown unmarried existence. Face the fear of being single and you will be free to choose to marry or not with confidence.

At this moment, there are over one hundred and five million single adults residing on America's shores. We could form the Single State of America! Heck, there are enough of us here to create another country—worldwide, possibly enough to colonize another planet. Think about that for a minute.

These days, the question for singles seems not to be *when* we'll get married, but *if* we'll get married. The definition of "relationship" has expanded exponentially to range from the traditional boy-meets-girl-dates-girl-marries-girl route to the growing popularity of the "tribe" of committed friends. It's becoming more acceptable to consider education goals, career focus, and individual growth as important—if not more so—than love, marriage, and children.

It's no accident that so many singles are happily avoiding the altar. I would wager that only a small minority actually woke up one morning and declared, "I will never marry!" These mingling millions have consciously or unconsciously opted for another choice. Their everyday decisions have played a major part in how they live. For most women, it's been a gradual coupling of financial advancements and rising self-satisfaction with their single lives, which has resulted in their declaring their marital independence. Singles did not make a *single* choice. They seized a series of opportunities, which led them towards the sensational solo life.

However, marriage is still the ultimate goal for so many women and men. In my case, I don't know if "happily ever after" means eternal singleness, but I never believed the doctrine that I must marry to be happy.

I recently took a fresh look at my single status after I attended a play at Stanford University, my alma mater. Minutes before the curtain rose, one of my former classmates unexpectedly slid into the seat next to me.

"Jerusha!" she shrieked, startling people around us. "It's Karen!" I returned the squeal of joy as I was engulfed in her huge hug. Karen still had her dancer's body, but she was now crowned by a cloud of white—not brown—hair styled in an Afro.

"It's so good to see you after all these years," she exclaimed. "I'm here to see my husband perform—he's one of the musicians."

"Wow!" I shouted. "I didn't know you were married!"

"Yes! We've been together for five years now. Remember Jesse from the dorm? He's in the band as well. You remember him. He just got married in March to Renee. And this is my friend Ally," Karen said, turning to the laughing, copper-haired, copper-skinned woman beside her.

"Hi, Ally, I'm the last single girl in the world," I said by way of introduction. After hearing the marriage update, that's how I felt. Was I without the must-haves of the grown-up woman's wardrobe: little black dress accessorized by the tall, dark, and handsome husband?

Now, I am certainly not "the last single girl in the world," but I often wonder if I will be. With the epidemic of televised "love" connections and the proliferation of dating websites, the whole world seems to be in mating overdrive. Would the real, truly single people please stand up?

In my quest for compatriots, I interviewed more than two hundred single men and women of various ages, races, and sexual orientation to discover how they arrived at this place in their lives. Did they choose to visit Singlehood and stayed past the altar's closing time? Or did they take a detour and just never return to the marriage speedway, complete with kid laps and divorce pit stops?

This book poses the question, "What does it mean to be single in a married culture?" And it's a book about all the stuff that can and does happen when you're living in the world on your own. These pages are filled with real accounts of a lifestyle that's often mistakenly rated second-best. The people you'll meet here are not defined by their singleness, they are living proof that you can live a blameless and shameless life as a single adult. You'll learn the how, why, when, where, and wow of living *la dolce vita* solo.

There's a saying: "You only live once, but if you do it right, once is enough." The courage and diversity of these single lives could redefine what is right for each of us.

So there's no need to apologize; it's perfectly acceptable for you to celebrate your own brilliance, polish your shining star, and totally toot your own horn. It's your responsibility to celebrate your birthday and impersonate Santa Claus and the Easter Bunny to ensure you get exactly what you want, and it's your duty to take yourself out to dinner occasionally just because. It's your right and responsibility to be really into beautiful, funny, sexy, incredible, and wonderful you!

## The Last Word

**Being single is a choice—a choice you are free to make along with millions of other women just like you.**

### A Singles Declaration of Independence

I am an unmarried revolutionary.

I promise to value my single-mindedness.

I will indulge in random acts of selfishness.

I claim my space as a single person.

I embrace the "L" word. I love my life.

# **Chapter Two**

## The Other Happy Ending,
### a.k.a. the Stupendously Superior Single State of Mind

Welcome to your world. If you're single, it's all about you. And if you're not, you can pretend as you flip through these pages.

If you're single you do not possess anyone nor are you possessed by another. You may not be engaged, but that's never stopped you from engaging in maximum fun. Let's face it: if you're single, it's because you *choose* to be, not because you're *doomed* to be. There aren't enough words to describe being single because it's an individual place for each of us. Our lives as soloists are as unique as our names, the freckles on our noses, or our hearts' desires.

Why does this choice make sense for anyone or me? I want to live longer. Studies show single women are healthier than their married counterparts. I want to work less. It's no fun leaving the office to come home to clean up after a spouse and kids. Single women have fourteen extra housework-free hours per week. All work and no play make Jill a dull girl.

I always get the last laugh, the first and only long hot shower, and the last piece of dessert. We're truly the queens of our castle exercising control over all we survey—the remote *and* the checkbook. Generally, the more control people exercise over their lives, the happier they are.

Welcome to my world.

## My Not-So-Humble Beginnings

I read once in Forbes magazine that "Jennifer" was the most popular name for the second wives of wealthy executives who traded up for younger models. The majority of their first wives had names like Mary and Susan. Is this the case of a rose by any other name not smelling as sweet? I mean, how important is a name in the mate selection process? Does labeling a child with an unusual name place them in the singles market forever? If so, with a name like Jerusha, I've found my niche.

I was the one daughter out of five children whose name was chosen to satisfy a bet. My parents were expecting a boy for their firstborn child. Every old wife's tale was consulted; my mom craved "boy" foods and dreamed "boy" dreams. Relying on those unmistakable signs, my parents bet my grandmother that if I were a girl, she could name me.

Singular Sensation #1

*Imagine an unmarried future.* Cut pictures out of magazines that look like where you'll live and what you'll be doing with your time. It's the fear of the unknown that makes life scary. Paste the pictures on a board and create a beautiful mosaic of the life of your dreams.

**10**

I was born while my mother slept under a cloud of anesthetic. Imagine her surprise when the doctors introduced her and my equally disappointed father to their brand new baby girl. The first sound I heard was my mother screaming, "It's not mine! It's not mine! I ordered a boy!" Whereupon the nurses took me away and then my smiling grandmother brought me back and said, "Look, isn't Jerusha beautiful?"

And so I entered the world with a very distinctive name and a very distinctive beginning.

"Jerusha" (Jeh RUE shah) is a Hebrew word that means inheritance or treasure. Jerusha. I am wedded to my name. I love how musical it sounds with its combination of strong consonants and short vowels. My name labels my wide face with its high forehead and Native American nose, my particular set of long, dark brown arms and heavy, muscular legs. When I was growing up there were no dreams of a shining knight on a white horse to come to my rescue. My name was Jerusha; I could take up that damn lance myself and set off to conquer the world.

But growing up, I was never the cute one. If cuteness is a requisite quality for attracting boys, I've failed miserably. At birth, I was not in the line where they were handing out cute button noses or cute little figures—and even worse, everyone seemed to notice it. My earliest memory of my deficiency is as a chubby child playing in the neighborhood sandbox. I was one of those rough-looking black kids with dark, ashy brown skin that always looked dusty, no matter how much Vaseline my mother rubbed on my elbows and knees.

I actually remember a little boy blurting out to my younger sister, "You're cute," and then running away. She *was* cute. Everyone said so. She had skin the color of *café au lait*. She had beautiful brown eyes with long dark lashes that curled wickedly at the ends. Even her lisp was cute.

I sat there next to my cute sister, seething as I watched the boy dart back to the safety of his friends. "That's right, run," I thought as I gripped fistfuls of sand, gearing up to toss them at his head. But the impulse passed as quickly as it came, and I let the sand trickle through my fingers. I looked at my sister, watching me with those wide brown eyes, and lowered my head. I've never felt *less* cute in my life than at that moment.

As I grew older, things got worse. I was big for my age and was often mistaken as the parent of my four younger siblings. But I was still only about nine years old when I overheard the conversation that would set the tone for the rest of my life.

I was out in the back yard playing with my dolls while the grown-ups had dinner. A few people drifted out onto the lanai of our Hawaii home. I had wandered over to the side of the house when I heard the first voice say, "You know, it's a shame. Jeri's not that pretty at all."

I stopped in my tracks and quickly glanced around. They couldn't see me. It wasn't until later that I realized I had been holding my breath. Then a second voice responded, "No, not pretty—

## Singular Sensation #2

*Indulge your inner child.* Treat yourself to a "security" bracelet to twist between your fingers when you're nervous or a fuzzy teddy bear or warm blanket to curl up with after a bad day. You'll instantly feel better!

but she's smart. She'll do alright." I was crushed, but I was also mad as hell. That was the moment I realized that life wasn't fair and that "cute" counted for more than I could ever imagine.

"But she's smart…" I heard that voice saying, over and over again in my head. Yes, I was smart. I vowed to study hard. I would get better grades than anyone else in my class. If I couldn't attract the boys, I'd beat them, I told myself. *That* would get their attention—maybe even more than being cute ever could.

> ## Singular Sensation #3
> *Fa la la la luscious!* Take voice lessons. It will improve your speaking voice and give you renewed self-confidence every time you open your mouth.

**Thirty-five years later: Marina**

Marina stretches across the foot of my bed, her head hanging off the edge.

"What are you doing?" she asks with the impatience of the nine-year-old she is. We were supposed to go play miniature golf fifteen minutes ago.

"Just five more minutes. I'm making a couple of notes for the book," I reply, distracted. I'm multi-tasking like a fiend, making the bed, packing a suitcase, and, indeed, scribbling notes for the book.

"Oh, that singles thing again," she says with a loud, dramatic sigh, rolling her big brown eyes. She twists her body so suddenly that she almost falls off the half-made bed.

"When I'm all grown up, I'm going to be single," she announces, batting her eyes at Jolene, my good friend and her adoring mom. Marina's voice is so authoritative you'd think she just proclaimed, "When I grow up, I'm going to be president."

But I don't think this will be a case of like mother, like daughter. Jolene struggled with a teenage pregnancy and never got to fully appreciate single life. As Marina quizzes me about the people in my book, I'm fascinated as she tries to figure out how life fits together: childhood, singlehood, and adulthood.

**Now, Back to My Own Happy Ending**

Once I reached adulthood, I realized that drive to be *seen and heard* is one of the most compelling aspects of being single. In a world where couples are the norm, sometimes so much of your energy is spent trying to get someone's attention. Ah, but by the time I was twenty-five, I had no trouble garnering attention. I had just passed the prestigious California Bar Exam, and was ready to take my place in the world. But when I proudly informed my mother I had decided not to practice law, she blurted, "Now *no one* will marry you!"

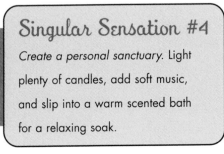

**Singular Sensation #4**

*Create a personal sanctuary.* Light plenty of candles, add soft music, and slip into a warm scented bath for a relaxing soak.

I was hurt by her comment, but at the time, marriage was the farthest thing from my mind. I could have a fling anytime I wanted with a variety of eligible (and not-so-eligible) men, so I was fully satisfied with my love life. I didn't have the time, energy, or desire for full-time romantic engagement. Yet as the years crept by, my independence sometimes felt more like a curse than a calling.

Here's one vivid memory: It's Friday night and I'm thirty. I'm sprawled across my futon couch, reading a back issue of

*Cosmopolitan*, the guide for the single girl, and munching on chocolate-covered macadamia nuts. I'm restless. *I should be dancing!* I think. I should be flirting with strangers in a crowded bar. I should be anywhere but home alone.

I'm the girl who received a dozen long-stemmed red roses, each one with a poem attached, each one individually hand-delivered by a different stranger. But the designer of this delicious delivery was a friend who was engaged to be married in a couple of months.

I'm the girl who found a romantic poem to die for and a single yellow rose left on her doorstep from a most appreciative lover from the night before, a Kennedy-esque blond with the bluest eyes ever. We dated for a while, and then he lost his heart to a Eurasian ballerina.

I'm the girl being tested for AIDS/HIV. The first time, I was staying with my best friend in Denver; she's a doctor. She asked me about being tested. I was having a rather passionate on again/off again throw-caution-to-the-winds sexual relationship at the time. Neither of us practiced safe sex on a regular basis with our other partners. I was definitely living dangerously.

> ## Singular Sensation #5
>
> *First up.* What could you be first at? First in your family to take flying lessons? First among your friends to learn Photoshop? First at work to make quota? Go ahead, be number one!

It's Friday night and I'm thirty. Another night older and alone.

I've had to face some hard facts about my life—such as that our lives are what *we* make of them. My high school sweetheart and I had pledged to marry each other at thirty unless we met someone better. He did; I didn't. Oh, I did do a short stint as married person in my mid-thirties, but we divorced after four years. He wanted a house and a picket fence. I wanted to run away with the circus—literally.

## Steal This Life: Courtney's "Conversation Points"

**Skip the husband habit and add a personal signature to your everyday solo routine.**

"I think this is something people could do well to remember: if you have something unusual, something that draws a little extra attention, that's a starting point for a conversation," advises Courtney as she removes her tinted designer sunglasses. In the last town where she resided, her infamous "Court" specials became her trademark at the local coffee shop, where she was greeted by name. Some people are defined by their life partner, others such as Courtney are distinguished by their brand of unabashed uniqueness.

Elevate your game. Develop a signature style—wear mismatched earrings or socks. Cultivate a skill. Take fencing classes or create your own house cocktail. Try taking an ordinary object and making it into something that showcases your amazing single girl singularity. Why not collect dinner plates from different patterns and amuse yourself at dinner with an ever-changing palette? Invite friends over for a meal and the eclectic dinnerware mix will make your dining room table a healthy topic of conversation.

I'm trying to remember when I first realized I enjoyed being single. Could it be the first time a smile crept across my face as one of my married friends complained about her husband's tight grip on the purse strings? Or was it after a day of racing through the city for back-to-back job interviews, I came home exhausted, collapsed on the sofa, and relaxed for a couple of hours, browsing through a favorite home-design magazine while watching the sun set in a sherbet-colored haze? I remember thinking how nice it was not to have to answer another question, not even a "How was your day, dear?" And I just listened to the sound of my own heart-beat, uninterrupted by the sound of another's voice or footsteps.

I never thought I'd come to treasure the soft velvety sound of silence. Some hours it's almost as seductive as a lover's whisper. The absence of sound envelops me in a cozy wrap of my own thoughts as I digest the day's happenings.

And yet, I have always loved people—the crazy blur of many voices speaking at once, quick gestures, rapid body movements. A thriving and activity-filled day is still my preferred way to spend my time. So what's different?

Sometimes I just want to sate my desire for simplicity and simpatico with self. I treasure silence and its companion, slowness. The slow sound of a jazz composition winding its way from my living room speakers into my bathroom lit by candlelight. Soup simmering on a stove for hours. Carefully putting my things away after a fast-paced day. The slow movement of my fingers on the keyboard as I ponder a thought or search silently for just the right set of words. I appreciate the texture and rhythm of my daily rou-tine. A place for everything and…sigh…just me in my own place.

## Steal This Life: Hit Singles!

**So many men, so little time is one of the proverbial myths of singledom. Got time on your hands? Do what single folks do!**

- Become the first black woman secretary of state of the most powerful nation on earth. (Condoleeza Rice, Secretary of State, the United States of America)
- Build billion-dollar empires. (Martha Stewart)
- Earn the respect of every nation in the world. (The Pope, the Dai Lai Lama)
- Start a gazillion-million dollar media empire. (Oprah Winfrey)
- Become a jack-of-all-trades and master them all. (Artist, scientist, inventor, mathematician, and philosopher Leonardo Da Vinci)
- Enable millions to search the wild World Wide Web with ease. (Sergey Brin and Larry Page, the founders of Google)
- Become the first black woman to fly off into space. (Astronaut and physician Dr. Mae Jemison)
- Become one of the greatest artists the world has ever known. (Painter and sculptor Michelangelo)
- Write best-selling series of children's books that appeal to the adventurous child in all of us—and raise kids as a single mom in the process. (*Harry Potter* author J. K. Rowling, who later tied the knot)
- During your more than thirty-year reign, make your nation a dominant world power. (Catherine the Great, Empress of Russia)

- Live to be over one hundred and tell about it. (Authors of *Having Our Say,* a lively oral history by sisters Sadie and Bessie Delaney, who lived to be 101 and 103 respectively)
- Inspire the world with your care for others. (Mother Teresa)
- Become one of the greatest composers the world has ever known. (Ludwig van Beethoven)
- Define eccentric, exuberant, extraordinary living. *(Auntie Mame)*
- Become known as the world's greatest lover. (Casanova)
- Be the single girl with the ultra best toys. (Barbie, Mattel's bestselling bachelorette doll)

**There's No Sin in Single!**

It's just fine if you want to...

- Get all dressed up just to go out with your girlfriends.
- Own a                              .
- Have your own personal space—even if it's a big three-bedroom house—and not share it with anyone.
- Tell the "not the guy" guy that little lie—"I just got back together with my ex-boyfriend."
- Ask for help to fix your computer, the toilet, and your car—all in the same week.
- Use caller ID to screen calls from your family.
- Give the hot guy at the deli the once over.
- Skip the housework and hire a maid to clean up after just you.
- Believe you are the center of your universe.

## Singular Sensation #6

*Call out of the blue.* When you're thinking of someone, pick up the phone and call them. Chances are they were thinking of you too!

## Note to Self

Celebrate National Friendship Week (mid-August) by recognizing your special friends who are near and far. None of us hears often enough how special we are. Spread the word.

## You Gotta Have Friends

Friends are so important when you're single (they even had their own long-running hit TV show named after them). Friendships fill that emotional void between our oneness and our bonds of romantic love and familial blood. Friends are the people who accept the invitation to share your life and stay through your first bra, that down and dirty breakup where you lost ten pounds, and the shock of your first gray hairs. But they're also there to celebrate your stellar climb up the corporate ladder and wallow in laziness with pizza and bad movies. You don't necessarily have to live with your friends, and luckily for most of us who are single, we don't have to live with*out* them.

The average person has one to two best friends, four to six close friends, and ten to twenty casual friends, said author and sociologist Jan Yager to the "friends as family" co-hosts on a recent *Today Show* segment. As singles we're busy making friends, keeping friends, enjoying friends, taking advantage of friends with benefits, or looking for the best friend we'll spend the rest of our life with. Researcher Heidi Reeder commented on the same *Today* segment that the majority of people, whether married or single, enjoyed spending time with friends more than anything else, including being with their spouses. She pointed out that our families used to be our main area of support but in today's highly mobile society we now look to our friends to get us to the airport or take care of us when we're sick. And yes, girls and guys can be friends. Reeder's research found that in only 14 percent of friendships with the opposite sex did one person have romantic feelings for the other. So we may want to marry our best friend but not our *real* best friend, okay? But 50 percent of us think our friend is attractive and that someone else would like them. So see, we may not be that into you, but the girl across the room…

So are you and your pals more like Lucy and Ethel, Thelma and Louise, or Will and Grace when it comes to having each other's back? It doesn't matter as long as you have time for friendship through the many courtships and work shifts in your life. We strengthen these unconditional bonds of love by feeding them the mundane details of each other's lives. How many times have you heard or said, "We have to get together more!" These singles say it and mean it.

### Southern, Twenty-three

Southern lives in Virginia Beach, Virginia, and a lot of her girlfriends are married. So she really treasures the time she sets aside to hang out with her female friends. "I really have to try hard to pin 'em down," she says with a little laugh when I ask her about having so many friends who are hitched at such a young age. But Southern has a determined

> ## Singular Sensation #7
>
> *Date my friend.* The next time you and your friends hit the club scene, act as each other's matchmaker. Each woman commits to introducing at least one guy to her friend. This will take the pressure off you and the guys as well. Take chances. Increase the dating pool by fixing each other up with men you'd normally ignore.

look on her face when she says, "That's been the best thing really, for them and me to keep on spending time together."

Southern herself was briefly married for a year and remembers not having enough "space" to nurture those relationships. Now she says she knows that just talking is important, even when your friends are just in casual relationships. "Just to have that connection with other girls makes you feel sane."

One of the lucky ones, Southern has kept in touch with a pal she's had since she was three years old—proving, as she says, "That I've been a girlfriends' kind of a person since I was young." They've kept in touch on and off over the years. When Southern returned to Virginia Beach, they established a standing "Thursday night date." The two get together for a couple hours at a restaurant or each other's homes just to catch up on their lives. Southern says, "It's nothing special." But I can tell by the smile on her face that it's the special nothingness that makes it oh so right.

I have a couple of friends I've stayed in touch with since high school and we're all scattered across the country. So I can relate when Southern says, "It's just someone who knows you so well that it doesn't matter where you're living. If you're across the country, you can pick up the phone and call someone who knows you."

## Singular Sensation #8

*Start your own club.* Interest your friends in a book, movie, or restaurant of the month adventure. Bond with your buddies over literature, pop culture, and fine food.

## Singular Sensation #9

*Stride right.* Grab your homies for a regular evening stroll. Make a date to burn calories, play catch up, and increase your cardio fitness.

**Monica, Thirty-two**

"I actually have dinner with my married friends once a month. We've been doing it for almost three years. It's just a way to stay in touch. It was one of my friends' idea who is married that we all get together because we were all kind of going separate ways, with getting married and having families.

## Steal This Life: Make a Friendship Bracelet

**Remember when you and your girlhood friends would sneak away to your secret space under the stairs, or the clearing in the woods, or the clubhouse where no boys were allowed? You'd spend hours sharing stories and swearing oaths to always be true friends to one another. Well, who says you can't do that now that you're all grown up?**

Invite your dearest friends to create or reunite the circle and celebrate your bonds of unconditional love for one another. Come together and build your own special friendship bracelet. You can ask each member to bring a charm bracelet to the gathering and then take turns each year gifting one another with a single talisman to celebrate the personal milestones, special gifts, and unwavering support that you've given one another over the years.

Whether you decide to add a charm per year to your collection or a gift from each member every year, it's an occasion that will reinforce the singular status of friendship in your lives.

*the other happy ending*

"They asked me initially—they just felt like we weren't seeing each other as much. It can be as few as eight and as many as twenty, on the first Thursday of the month. We rotate houses. Whoever hosts is responsible for the main course and people bring appetizers, desserts, side dishes, beer, wine, whatever… and yes, they've come to my place."

### Darryl, Thirty-nine

"Every Saturday morning we walk. We use the walk to catch up with each other on what's going on in our lives. There are six to eight of us. We don't work together anymore, but we all met at Oracle in 1988. I worked there until 1995, so we haven't worked together since then. So here it is 2005 and last year in 2004, we started the tradition of meeting every Saturday morning and walking along the beach.

"The time is key. It's 9 a.m. Sometimes we complain about the fact that's it's so early, but it doesn't interfere with the rest of your day. It's a two-mile walk. We walk a mile, go to the café and have some coffee and a muffin, and then we walk back to our cars.

"I started it because it was something I was doing anyway. Then I wanted to keep in touch with my friends, so I invited them along. And they started showing up. Some are married; some are single. And now

> ## Quickie Fact
>
> Married or single women rate spending time with friends and relatives as the most enjoyable part of their day—even higher than hanging out with spouses or significant others or their children, according to the Day Reconstruction Method (DRM) study in 2003 by researchers from several American universities.

we have the spouses coming. The spouses started asking, 'What do you guys do every Saturday morning? Are you really exercising or is it…?'"

## Cheryl, Forty-Nine

Cheryl, a personal financial counselor, advises individuals to boost their social lives and their bank accounts by starting a home-based, part-time business. She and a girlfriend host spa parties at least once a month. "Women love getting together. We were networking, making connections, talking about business," she says. "And it was nice to be talking about business instead of talking about how come we're not in a relationship.

"Life is too short to be sitting around complaining about the fact that you don't have a man!"

## Julius, Forty

"It's a New Year's Eve tradition—we get together the same group of people every year. We talk about how our lives are doing, how we're aging. The same person has hosted it for the last fifteen years. He's the anchor. He's single and he's the link between all of us.

"Lots of food and booze. He typically does the basics and we all bring something. There's a core group of six to eight people,

> ## Singular Sensation #10
>
> *Ultra-fabulous homeschooling.* Host a private party with a guest chef from your local favorite restaurant. Or have the salsa teacher from the local dance studio add zest to your next themed gathering. You'll have great fun learning the tricks of their trade.

> ## Singular Sensation #11
>
> *Post your feelings.* Keep your address book updated, and a stack of postcards and stamps handy. (Ikea and restaurant/bar hotspots have great postcards for free.) Send quick "hellos" to faraway friends when the mood hits you.

## The Single Best Attitude

Don't take people for granted—that's the easiest way to make certain that they'll disappear. A single person is not automatically sentenced to a life of aloneness. The choice to have people who care about you in your life is always up to you. If you make others a priority in your life, they'll return the favor. Like any relationship, friendships require care and feeding to stay alive. You've got to work at them, but they're worth it. How else would you find out about that great new steak place in town, the opening at the company you're dying to work for, or the amazing stylist who knows how to work with baby-fine hair? Stay in touch with your friends. They'll help you stay in touch with the world.

then there's more. Some people bring friends; it varies.

"Lots of laughing. We call each other on stuff. We tell embarrassing stories. It feels like your surrogate family. We're really supporting each other. Talking about the issues in our lives, the serious issues, funny issues, semi-serious issues, but humor is threaded all the way through."

**Make New Friends When You Lose the Old; the Single Wear Silver and the Married Ones Gold.** Single status doesn't have a guaranteed place in your status quo or that of your friends. As life moves along, your friend-filled college days are replaced by a shrinking group of gal pals. All your close friends are answering the call of wedding bells and becoming obsessed with matrimonial plans. And your repeat bridesmaid appearances are draining your bank account. Are you drowning in tossed bridal bouquets? Don't despair; you can win new girlfriends to join your single escapades.

How's this for multi-tasking? Attend singles events where you'll meet women your own age who are single and with at least one thing in common with you: the desire to meet men! Adopt a spirit of cooperation rather than competition. The men will find your self-confidence irresistibly attractive and your newfound gal pals will appreciate finding a kindred spirit. You can joke about your bad dates, surf the online personals together, or expand your shopping horizons on out-of-town boutique browsing adventures!

I met some great friends by checking out the male offerings at an 8minuteDating event. Those types of parties lend themselves to making new friends because you spend a decent amount of time talking with the guys you meet and can compare notes with the other women during the breaks. Also, 8minuteDating lets you choose dates for multiple reasons—friendship, business, and a first date. So the next time you visit a meet market, make sure you engage your fellow female shoppers!

## The Last Word

**Being single is a choice. You made it. Don't subscribe to the myth of "the unchosen." No one else can make "the choice" for you.**

1. Being single is not the same as being dead to the world. Use your free-from-spouse time wisely. You can conquer the world, or at least that small part of it that interests you the most.

2. Singles have friends who double life's pleasures. Nurture those relationships.

3. Now move on and enjoy your dolce vita solo!

# Chapter Three

## Cultivate the Single Sense

*"What would you do if you knew you could not fail?"*
—*The engraved paperweight on my desk*

At forty-five, I am truly a *single* person...*and I love it!* I'm spoiled rotten. I've come to realize that being single was a deliberate choice. Or better stated, it was a collection of small, medium, and super-size decisions made every day of my life. I am a laugh-loud, live-large black woman with an ever-changing sense of personal style. I dress however I want, go wherever I want, talk to whomever I want, do whatever I want. I am fearless. I am a woman to be reckoned with, and I don't apologize for that. If Dr. Phil, TV's number one shrink, is right and men really are intimidated by smart, funny, sexy, and confident women, then I'm probably their worst nightmare.

I enjoy flaunting the power of being one. This single sense that one is enough. My single-mindedness tells me I have everything I need—in fact, I had it all the time.

How does it feel to be a successful single person? We possess the common traits of fun, fearlessness, and heightened self-confidence, which support our solo decision-making and marriage-defying actions. We're more likely to engage in "future think": Who am I going to have dinner with next week? Who can I call for drinks tonight? Who's free to join me for a last-minute trip to the islands?

Singled out, we're happy to opt out of marriage in the pursuit of our own individual brand of uber *joie de vivre*. We tend to connect with the world at large: being best friends with people, parties, and places rather than relying on a partner or family for support. Forget the boring, home alone single stereotype; we're fully engaged in developing our own social community. You'll find us at the gym, the flicks, the restaurants, and clicking online, trading spontaneity and freedom for the contentment of coupling.

Singleness is a place where all our options are still open. We haven't committed to another; in fact, we're more interested in making and keeping commitments to ourselves. Our heightened sense of self alerts us to the many opportunities for choice, as in, "I choose not to marry. I choose to be a single mother." Or, "Yeah—I'd rather live together than get married." Discarding the conventional wisdom that says marriage is the ultimate goal,

> **Singular Sensation #12**
>
> *Words to live by.* Visit the local paint-your-own-pottery studio. Paint your favorite affirmations on tiles to hang throughout your home.

more and more we're exercising our freedom to stretch beyond the societal bonds of sex and relationship.

Outside those boundaries you're free to ignore those who judge you, and you can engage in a constant process of redefining and reinventing yourself. See, routines make people feel safe. In a committed relationship, there's an expectation of who you are and who you should be, and you could find yourself becoming that role rather than becoming *yourself*. If you keep redefining yourself, it can threaten the foundation of a relationship built on an unspoken agreement of "this is who I am and this is who you are." When you're single, however, your agreement is a personal one, and the only person you have to answer to is yourself.

This is not to say that the single sense is only for singles; everyone can benefit from strengthening this aspect of themselves. Each of us will more than likely spend a good percentage of our lives alone, whether we never marry or because of divorce or the death of a spouse. By developing our single sense we can meet the challenges of everyday life with a renewed confidence. For those in a relationship, leveraging their single sense allows them to extend the ties that bind without breaking the knot.

## Quickie Fact

A higher percentage of married couples (32.7 percent) than singles (21.2 percent) volunteer to better the quality of life in their communities. Okay lonely girl, want to feel better about yourself? Help someone else feel good. Get involved with something larger than your life!

### In Love with Living Single

You can learn to love your single life. You can get used to calling the shots, getting what you want, and doing whatever you please. Just ask Leslie, a single mom with seventeen-year-old twin daughters and a younger daughter aged thirteen. I liked Leslie immediately. She exudes energy. Her naturally buoyant personality carries her through the ups and downs of being unattached.

"Hallelujah, praise the Lord, hot damn, I'm single!" she yells, falling into a chair at a café on the Stanford University campus, where she is the high-profile director of the alumni association. Leslie views being single through a refreshing prism of sharp and sometimes off-color observations on life since her divorce a dozen years ago.

She's forty-seven and has the perfect potential Mr. Right but adamantly refuses to marry or live with him. She has the guts to maintain her singleness within her coupled existence. It's not mandatory for your personal independence to end when a relationship begins.

"I'm *single*! I just like the way the word 'single' sounds. You know, like when you fill out forms and check that box," Leslie says, making an invisible check mark in the air. She doesn't have to tell me that she's a very social person, but it would come as a surprise to most people how much she treasures being alone. "I love being with people," the brunette in perpetual motion assures me, "but I really need my alone time to recharge my batteries."

Time alone is definitely an undervalued perk of singlehood. How many times have you been thankful to come home from

> ## Singular Sensation #13
>
> *Move your body.* Dance! Salsa. Tango. Hip-hop. Swing. Take a class or enjoy an evening on the dance floor and tap into the rhythm of your life.

## Steal This Life: Stress Less

**Single life demands quite a bit of mental, physical, and spiritual flexibility. Start the day with a stretch and you'll feel happier. End the day with a stretch and you'll sleep better. Stretching your muscles can be a metaphor for the rest of the day, encouraging yourself to move past obstacles to reach your highest potential.**

It feels great to get the kinks out before you go to sleep. Curl up into a tight ball, pulling your knees tight into your chest. While lying on your back, release by pushing your legs out straight in front of you and flexing your toes. This move will stretch the back muscles that have tightened during the day and will leave your body deliciously liquid and languid as you sleep.

work and not have speak to another person? Answer that question truthfully and I'll bet more than once you've been happy just to relax in front of the television alone.

"I'd much rather come home to an empty house. Relax, feel at home, just putz around," Leslie says, rearranging her slim body in the chair. "And then the doors open and my lover or my children are introduced into the environment." Anchoring herself first allows her to better enjoy the company of others.

Leslie and her ex-husband share custody of the girls, so she gets to celebrate the joy of reconnecting with them every other week. "Tonight they're coming home and I can't wait to see them," she says, her brown eyes sparkling. "It's hard being a single parent, but also great because you have every other weekend to yourself," she says, admitting her guilty pleasure. "What other situation allows you to have kids *and* have time to yourself?"

I have to think about that one. The girl's got a point. I think my married-with-children friends would surely enjoy regularly scheduled timeouts from their bundles of joy. Leslie's lucky because she has that elusive great rela-tionship with her ex. "Sure, it's hard deciding where the eigh-teenth birthday party is going to be and missing out when your daughter gets her first period because she's at the ex's house, but everyone has to give to get in this situation."

And, like Leslie, I'm sure there are times when you'd rather go it alone. She prefers arriving at certain social events without her boyfriend in tow so she can visit with everyone she wants to. She and her lover have even developed their own personal party rating system. "'One' means I really need you there. There are people I want you to meet. 'Two' means I could go either way and 'three' means please don't come," she says putting up her hands to ward off the designated date.

I love the way Leslie honors her right to be single. She could retreat to the security of coupledom, but she claims her singleness

> **Singular Sensation #14**
>
> *Explore your senses.* Take a "trust" walk with a friend. Take turns blind-folding one another and allowing the other person to lead.

> **Singular Sensation #15**
>
> *Adopt a cause.* Find an organization, person, or idea you think the world can't live without. Lend them a hand.

on a regular basis to stay at the top of her game. You too could develop her appreciation for aloneness.

## Recipe for Romance

What book on being single would be complete without at least one recipe for embracing your romantic self? In the Far East, they say if you want to attract love, you must be love. In the West, we regard love as something totally outside ourselves that materializes when we find our other half. It's evident in the language we use: "I'm looking for love." "I want to find true love." I wonder, does *love* know it's lost?

This ritual can be performed on Valentine's Day, or whenever you want to remind yourself that love can be found within.

### Note to Self

Make your home an adoring castle. Place a vase of fresh flowers or a scented candle by the front door. Put your stereo on a timer. Place framed pictures of friends and family in prominent places. Tonight you'll come home to a welcoming space where you'll be greeted by an inviting scent and serenaded by your favorite tunes.

### Romance Thyself Ritual

Still searching for that perfect valentine? Misplaced your Love Potion No. 9? Wish that Mars and Venus had never been discovered? Stop and look in the mirror. You're going to celebrate your one true love: yourself!

Love is empowering. Empowerment begins with knowing who you are and accepting yourself as you are. Shakespeare preached those immortal words of self-love and self-esteem: "To thine own self be true."

The first step in attracting love is to be loved. So take time to fall in love again...with yourself. To begin, follow in the footsteps of some of the greatest lovers of all time and write a love letter to your beloved. Address this message of amour to *vous*. This will not be an "I'm so great because..." kind of letter. Express the spirit of your truest self and create an intimate portrait.

*What You'll Need*

- A favorite pen
- Inspiring stationary or handmade papers
- Scent or fragrance—fresh flowers, candles, incense, essential oils
- Adornments of desire: ribbons, old movie tickets, dried flowers, fairy dust
- A comfortable place to write

*What You'll Do*

Borrow tactics from some of the best teachers. Create your own personal rendition of "How do I love thee, let me count the ways..." Take your time. A love letter cannot seem rushed, but must be written with great attention to detail. Write by hand. There's nothing as sensual as the human touch. Plus, you can decipher your own handwriting.

Breathe in the aromas of roses, magnolia blossoms, irises, or the seductive scent of patchouli oil. Cleopatra seduced Antony in a bedchamber knee deep in rose petals. Let the subtle

## Quickie Fact

As we age, singles still sing freedom's song. More than 50 percent of free agents in their forties, fifties, and sixties rank independence as their favorite thing about being single. *AARP, Lifestyles, Dating & Romance, September 2003* language of scent color your prose. Choose your words carefully, lovingly, reflecting upon what you find most enchanting about your appearance, habits, talents, and beliefs. Can't find the right words? Add lines of poetry, movie dialogue, or scenes from a favorite novel.

What wows you about you? Unwrap your own unique gifts as you write—express your fantasies, hopes and dreams for the future, private aspirations, gentle yearnings of your heart. With the stroke of the pen uncover your deepest strengths, define your character at its best, and promise yourself fidelity always. Be as explicit as possible. You'll want to read and reread this tribute to yourself and be inspired to be the person you were meant to be. Use this opportunity for self-discovery. Talk to yourself through your letter writing. Be spellbound.

Enclose meaningful mementos: a ticket from an outdoor concert under the stars, a beautiful photo of yourself, shells gathered on a stroll across an exotic beach. Feeling adventurous? Write your missive while naked by

## The Single Best Attitude

You know the old saying, "Absence makes the heart grow fonder"? You love your friends and family, but then it's time for them to go home. Being single allows you to be on intimate terms with your private time and personal space. One of the most underappreciated luxuries of solitary living is the control you have over the ebb and flow of being with other people. You can shut the door and keep the chaos of others out. You are not obligated to be with another. And yet you are always free to invite people in to share your life.

## Singular Sensation #16

*Silence please.* Be still. Be quiet. Listen to the sounds of silence. What do you hear?

the light of a full or waxing moon. Remember: you are your most ardent suitor.

Then send it. There's nothing so exciting, especially in these days of electronic communication, as receiving a hand-addressed envelope. It doesn't matter that it's from you; distance will make that self-made prose all the sweeter. Your words of love have traveled out into the universe and found their way back to you—just as you affirm the true love of another will.

On this day, in your quest for love, choose to look within.

## Steal This Life: Kill Yourself with Kindness

**Leslie offers this bit of advice to other singles: "Be kind to yourself. Life is hard and when you're single you have to say sometimes it's okay that I didn't make a great decision today, or wow, I could have done better at this. Sometimes it's okay to just be."**

"Treat yourself like you would a friend," she adds. "We need to comfort ourselves along the way."

Leslie suggests we give ourselves more TLC—tender loving care. "If you're going to be single, I think you really sometimes have to be a little more gentle on yourself than a lot of people are."

**Be a Thriving Single!**

Now, do *you* have what it takes to be single? Take this self-test. Check all that apply to the way you currently live.

_____ can sleep in

_____ can sleep all day and not feel guilty

_____ have a take-charge-of-self personality

_____ have the ability to go deep within

_____ carry a credit card in your own name

_____ can fly to Bali on a week's notice

_____ have time to read the great American novel

_____ dislike crowds

_____ crave alone, recharge-your-batteries time

_____ have a personal checking account

_____ have time to learn to make soufflés

_____ are a self starter

_____ can feed yourself

_____ can dress yourself

_____ can talk to your girlfriend at 3 a.m.

_____ have left the house at midnight to answer a booty call

_____ have ten things you need to accomplish before you die

_____ possess the ability to amuse yourself

_____ are made of character-building blocks

_____ are an expert in self-care

_____ have left dirty dishes in the sink...for days

_____ will use the eject button on bad dates

_____ own a first-aid kit

_____ have an emergency number besides your parents

_____ show a well-kept persona

*cultivate the single sense*

_____ care for a pet

_____ know where to borrow a pet

_____ stick to your exercise routine

_____ have bought yourself flowers for no reason at all

_____ try out a new vibrator…bi-monthly, quarterly, annually

_____ actually could survive on a desert island a la
Robinson Crusoe

_____ think Mae West got it right when she said, "It's not
the men in my life. It's the life in my men."

_____ believe your happiness is a primary concern

_____ believe you are the center of the universe

_____ have coupling and uncoupling skills

_____ claim to be the master/mistress of the First Date

_____ have a Second Date Rule

### *How to Score*

• If you checked all, congratulations! You're an Uber Single.

• If you checked half, you're well equipped to live outside the state
of matrimony.

• If you checked six or less, well…send me an invitation to your
wedding.

## *Singles Must-Haves for Success*

1. The Outfit. You know, the clothing combination that
brings out the color in your eyes, enhances your curves, and
shows off your assets—the one that makes you feel too
good too resist!

2. A Shoulder to Cry On. Everyone gets lonely. Remember

the old joke that says a woman needs three men to fulfill her? One to pay her bills, one to rock her world in bed, and one to talk to about the other two.

3. Karaoke Song. If you can't sing, be sure to choose a tune that doesn't require perfect pitch.
4. A Clean Joke.
5. A Dirty Joke.
6. Savings. You gotta have backup.
7. Scented Candles. A great way to refresh and relax you and your home, and hey, everyone looks better by candlelight.
8. Feel-Good Movie. Something to pop in on a rainy day, the day the cat dies, the day you lose your job, or have a fight with your best friend.
9. Talent. You should be adding something to the party—why else would friends and strangers have you over? Bring good wine, know how to juggle, add witty conversation.
10. Personality. Self-explanatory. It can be cultivated.
11. A Great Smile. It's free and provides instant attraction!
12. A Signature Cocktail. It sparks conversation...and wouldn't you rather look confident ordering a cool drink than clueless fumbling with a drink menu?

## Singular Focus: Work and the Single Girl

"Work is love made visible," Buddha, the born-again single, is reported to have said. What if your work was your heart's desire? I met two twenty-something women who are lucky enough to have found their bliss—and a supportive environment of single acceptance. Over coffee and ice cream in a neighborhood café in

Chicago, we discussed the pressure to marry and their free-to-be-single work lives.

"Right now the only commitment I'm concerned about is the commitment to myself—and doing what I want to do, which is [concentrating on] my career and my friends. Being in a relationship is a choice and right now the biggest relationship commitment I'm making is to myself and no one else," Leah states. After college graduation she accepted a position with the Adolescent Child Network and UCSF's Center for AIDS prevention studies. She's fully committed to her career in public health and feels lucky to be able to work in her chosen field.

## Note to Self

Once a week declare a workday lunch a "no man's land." Use the extra time to discuss career goals, work issues, or the best places to get half-price designer shoes. You'll learn tons, laugh lots, and find you have a lot more important things to talk about than why he didn't call.

Both twenty-two, Brooke and Leah have embraced the belief that being in a committed relationship is a choice, not a requirement of a grownup life. And they are weighing that choice against other goals they have for their lives. Were you thinking this way at their age? It seems you came to a similar conclusion. You decided to pursue a life path that was more personally rewarding for you and in which you contributed to society's general well-being. Don't beat yourself up for succeeding at being single. You made your bed and now you're entitled to relax in it. "So many women our age seek out relationships to fulfill something that's not within themselves," Brooke says, her elbows resting on the wooden table as she adjusts her baseball cap and straight blonde ponytail. Brooke's found her dream job

## Steal This Drink: Marvelous Mojito

**McKinley is the quintessential bicoastal bartender. He's perfected a cocktail that gets him invited to the best parties in the urban singles meccas of Manhattan and San Francisco. Why don't you play bartender at a home happy hour with friends, or adopt this recipe as your signature drink? Stir up some serious mojo, baby!**

*McKinley's Blood Orange Mojito*

2 oz. light rum

1/2 blood orange

Juice of 1/2 lime

1 tablespoon sugar or simple syrup

Club soda

Mint leaves

Use a tall, narrow glass. Take the blood orange sections, ten mint leaves, sugar, and lime juice; muddle in the glass. Add ice to fill the glass. Pour in the rum; stir well. Top off with a healthy splash of club soda and garnish with more mint leaves.

Feeling a little weak in the knees?

working in television. She's freelancing in the production department of the *Oprah Winfrey Show* and hopes for a permanent job with the show when she graduates. Brooke has appeared on the show twice and describes Oprah as "my mentor from afar."

Brooke describes the environment at Harpo Studios as full of single, independent, driven women and says that's why she loves it so much. She compares it to her days working in Top 40 radio, where there was always gossip about everyone's sex life. Brooke remembers asking her boss-to-be during the initial job interview at the studio if she had a boyfriend. The women replied that she didn't and Brooke had the audacity to ask, "Why not?" The producer candidly answered her question saying, "I just don't have time for that. Honestly, Brooke, I'm so involved at work and that's fine with me. Yes, I date but it's not really central to my life right now." For Brooke, who had just ended a long-term relationship with her media boyfriend, this was a breath of fresh air and a new role model for a personal lifestyle.

**Singular Sensation #17**

*Take a television timeout. What will you do with all that extra time? Explore new forms of entertainment.*

You, too, are an independent single woman excelling at living life on your own terms. Don't shy away from opportunities to present another way of being to young people around you. They'll receive plenty of marriage messages, but some may be looking for validation that there is life outside those bonds. Take the time to discuss the freedom and fulfillment of solo living with those around you. You may face a few fears of your own and nurture members of the next generation of single adults. It's more than okay to say, "I'm good at being single and I love it. Here's why."

At the studio of one of the most powerful single women in America, Brooke is inspired by the focus on the corporate mission to empower people and the thought-provoking conversations about the world at large that happen around the water cooler rather than the endless chatter on the status of romantic relationships or lack thereof.

"Well, look at who is in charge: someone who doesn't believe in marriage," Brooke exclaims, referring to "Ms. O." "She does not believe you have to have a certificate to dedicate your life to someone and have the government say you're married."

### The Single Best Attitude

You've heard the old adage "seeing is believing." If you see yourself having an awesome solo life, then you'll believe in the power of self. If you can see it, you can be it. If others see you having the time of your life, they'll believe it can happen for them.

Leah, a round-faced brunette, seconds Brooke's relief at having found a cadre of colleagues where dating is not always the topic du jour. She grew up in the cornfields of Illinois, where becoming a twenty-something twosome is near mandatory. I can't believe that her parents are already expecting grandchildren rather than a college degree. But Leah just laughs it off. "It's not enough that we have careers, we're going places, we have great girlfriends, great apartments, a fun social life. People will still be like, 'oh, who you dating?'"

### Singular Sensation #18

*Your first time.* When was the last time you did something for the first time? Learn something new. Knitting, cooking, rockclimbing, or motorbiking will all get your juices flowing.

## Sensational Presents for a Singular Presence

The art of giving and receiving is a constant thread running throughout fifty-two-year-old Kathryn's life, whether she's showering others or herself with love. I've known her for more than a decade, and on several occasions I've seen how much people enjoy being in her space. It's obvious that not only is Kathryn engaged with life around her, she's also intently focused on herself and her own comforts. Since she doesn't short-change herself, her guests know they won't be short-changed, either.

When you treat yourself well, others will follow your lead. Your actions say that you care about yourself and won't accept anything less from those around you.

One of Kathryn's best practices is her habit of giving herself presents on every and any occasion. "You get a new job, you get a present; you complete a project, you get a present; the election

## Steal This Party Line!

**Brooke and Leah introduced me to the Midwest party circuit. They host "Stop and Go" or "Traffic Light" parties with their friends. An invitation to their house party comes with a request to dress the part.** If you're available, wear green to signify "go ahead and chat me up." If you're unsure of your availability, as in "I'm dating someone but my profile is still active on Match.com," you wear yellow. Those taken can attend the festivities, but they wear red for "Warning! I belong to someone, who by the way might be at the party and is watching my every move. Please don't ruin my night!"

To keep things moving they serve red, green, and yellow cocktails and finger foods. Caution! Dangerous curves ahead!

doesn't turn out the way you want and you get an election comfort present. You give yourself gifts all the time," I tease her gently.

Rewarding one's self for doing well is a great idea. There's nothing wrong with a well-meaning bribe every now and then to get you going on a new project or to raise your spirits. Small indulgences are a wonderful way to remind yourself of your own greatness and they won't break the bank. Kathryn certainly isn't waiting around for someone to recognize she's special. And neither should you.

"I don't know when that ritual began, but it was one I created myself," Kathryn says in her precise, yet melodious, voice. "In a marriage, traditionally the husband buys the wife the flowers. Well then, it occurred to me if I want flowers I'd better buy some, because right now I don't have someone buying me flowers," she says with unabashed practicality.

Kathryn certainly honors the spirit of ritual—the importance of having a way to say, "I matter." This is so important. You may not always feel as if you have someone in your life who celebrates the very fact of your existence. Whether you're married or single, you should hold yourself dear. In your own heart of hearts,

> **Singular Sensation #19**
>
> *Great party trick.* Take a palm reading or handwriting analysis class. Delight your friends with your new-found talent.

> **Quickie Fact**
>
> A study of twenty-four thousand people published in the *Journal of Personality & Social Psychology* concluded that after the initial honeymoon phase, most people were no more satisfied with life after marriage than they were before. *Grace Woman Sept/Oct 2003*

## Note to Self

The next time you clean the house, walk the dog, or finish your taxes on time, buy yourself a little something to mark the occasion. It can be a dime store accessory or a Tiffany bauble. The important thing is not the cost. It's that each time you handle the object, you'll remember the occasion it commemorates.

## Singular Sensation #20

*Recipes for success.* Write your favorite creativity tips on index cards. Use them as idea starters when you're feeling stuck on the job.

you must know that "I matter." Reinforce that thought on a daily basis with flowers, candy, a private moment of relaxation—whatever touches you deep inside.

"I just realized that life is so amazing. You work so hard and you accomplish something and there's a joy in the accomplishment," Kathryn says, her long, manicured fingers raised in confirmation. "It's nice to cement it with something special that every time you look at that thing it reminds you that yeah—you did this," she says holding one of her newest treasures: a small tortoiseshell bag handle she'll fashion into a necklace. What a great idea: you celebrating you!

## Singular Sensations

**#21** *Change your color palette.* Skip basic black and reach for warm browns or cool blues to refresh your wardrobe. Choose to wear a new green or a haute pink.

**#22** *Treat yourself.* Since you know what you really, really like, establish a habit of rewarding yourself with a small treat on a regular basis. It could be reading five pages of that new novel at lunch, buying a flower for your desk at work, or a single chocolate truffle. Don't always live in denial; make yourself happy.

**#23** *Present place.* Gift yourself with a private place to store presents. Turn a shelf in your closet into a gifting space. Collect ribbons, wrapping paper, and unusual containers for decorating hostess gifts and party favors. Practice the art of giving.

**#24** *Stop the clock.* Pick a time of day that's all yours to do with as you please. Don't answer the phone. Don't clean the house. Reserve a special activity, like finishing a favorite novel or drinks with friends, for your personal time of day.

**#25** *Cover naked cash.* Cash is always in fashion but dress it up before you give it away. Put a music store gift card inside an

### The Single Best Attitude

What better cause for celebration is there than you? Why not praise yourself for scaling new heights at home or at work? No need to wait for others to recognize how special you are. You should value your own opinion of self as much if not more than anyone else's. After you achieve a miniature milestone acknowledge your feat with cartoon heroine Dora the Explorer's chant, "I did it! I did it! I did it!" Give yourself a little pat on the back in private and you'll smile throughout your day. Honor yourself. Nurture yourself. Value yourself. Believe in yourself. Those are the greatest gifts you'll ever receive.

old album or music CD cover. Pair a clothing store gift certificate with a coupon to clean out a friend's closet. Always accessorize your cents.

## The Last Word

**Being single is a choice. And with that choice comes a singular perception of the world and your place in it. Be aware and act accordingly.**

1. Everyone should nurture their sense of singleness; it will keep them a free person.
2. Being single and having relationships are not mutually exclusive states of being.
3. Share the wealth. Mentor other singles.
4. Reward yourself. You deserve the best!

# Chapter Four

## Technically You're Single
### If That's How You File Your Taxes, Right?

When I first set out to write a book about singles, I thought they'd all be like me. You know, single, unmarried, not in a relationship, not sporting a band of gold or any other outward signs of attachment. I thought figuring out who's single would be the easy part. Boy, was I wrong!

Like the time my married friends pointed out a tall, dark, and handsome stranger at a holiday event and literally pushed me towards him, saying, "Girl, he's been checking you out all night. See how he keeps coming around and smiling at you. Go over there and introduce yourself." Well, seeing as I'm not the shy type and the first rule of singleness is meet and conquer, I went for it. "Hi, my name is Jerusha. Are you single?" I asked giving him my best "I-want-to-get-to-know-you-much-better-real-quick" smile. He answered quickly and with the smoothest "I'm-definitely-interested-in-gettin'-me-some-of-that" smile. "Yes! And thank you for asking." After the event, we got to know each other better over dinner and drinks.

Three weeks later we met at a business meeting. On this occasion he was visibly uncomfortable during my presentation. Mr. Single informed my partner and I that he hadn't had a chance to review our proposal in depth as he'd been busy over the holidays buying a home with his fiancée. Fiancée! Like that's what Santa put in his stocking!

## Steal This Spy: Who Can You Trust?

**Not always the opposite sex. When in doubt about a potential date's facts and figures, let your fingers do the walking across your keyboard—Google him!** Yes, that whole privacy thing can be demolished on the Web. I know a woman who met a guy at a singles gathering. He asked for her number—yippee! She put his name into an online search engine only to have newspaper accounts with his photo pop up relating to him having been questioned for the gruesome murder of his wife's lover a year earlier in another state. So if you haven't been personally introduced or you get that funny feeling in the back of your neck, go ahead, Ms. Sherlock Holmes, rely on a very public private eye.

### Single By Any Other Name

Technically, we're all single because human beings come packaged individually. Possibly that's where the confusion comes in, because "single" isn't simply defined by most of us as "unmarried." The next time you ask someone if they're single, keep the following interpretations in mind. Oh, and remember: single does not equal available.

> **Singular Sensation #26**
>
> *Getting to know you.* People tell you who they are when you meet them. Listen. Don't make them into something they're not.

"Single is a state of mind. A situation in which you're comfortable with yourself. You can or cannot be a loner. You've made a choice to be single in certain phases of your life." —*Steve S., 41*

"Looking." —*Arielle, 25*

"To not bitch and moan about it." —*Sally, 43*

"You have your options. Options are everything sometimes. Selection. You're not stuck with one person. You could have three individuals you're seeing because they give you three different things." —*Pam, 34*

"Single to me just means not married. In other words, if you're in a relationship with someone, technically, you're single. You're available because it's less hassle to get out of the relationship; you don't have to get a divorce." —*Price, 45*

"Waking up alone." —*Melissa, 35*

"I suppose technically not being married. Single doesn't necessarily mean available. Although if you read Craigslist, there are married people who are available." —*Russell, 42*

"Having a job, paying your bills, and going on Match.com because everybody else does." —*Nadia, 32*

"There is no *significant* other. No one else but your self. All you take care of is you. That's single." —*TuJuania, 25*

"A perk of being single is I can afford my outrageous life and the outrageous designer clothes. I thought about that today 'cause I was actually shopping at Neiman Marcus and I bought myself some really expensive stuff. I won't be able to do this if I have kids. I'm going to be shopping at Target. Maybe I'm just not there. Maybe myself buying a new frickin' Gucci purse is more important than kids right now." —*Jen, 31*

"If there's somebody you'd introduce as your girlfriend, then you're not single. Whether it's [to your] parents or friends or whomever...then you're off the market." —*Greg D., 34*

"Society pretty much defines it that if I have my own house, and I have my own car, and make my own way, and do my own work, and even if I'm having sex with someone as my only partner, I'd still be single." —*Anna, 56*

"Does single mean you're not married? Or does single mean you're not dating? I don't know. The lines are so blurred. I'm dating somebody but he doesn't like to have a girlfriend. So I guess I'm single." —*Jennifer, 31*

"Blissful state of control where you get to choose how you want to live and who you want to live it with." —*Aaron, 32*

"History in the making. Because women are no longer subjected to the status or whatever else everybody wants them to be." —*Pamela, 34*

"Trying to figure out who's next." —*Jeri, 22*

"Definition of single: unattached. Single is non-monogamous. That's bad, isn't it? Function of my age, not a function of my morality." —*Mike, 48*

"Being single is just being free. At the end of the day you don't have to explain yourself to anybody except for you." —*Sofia, 27*

"If you're in a relationship but you're still not married. Then you like each other enough to be in the relationship, but not enough to be married, so you're single. For women there's every incentive to be aligned with one person. For men, non-alignment ain't a problem." —*Greg C., 38*

"Being single. I'm not beholden to anyone and no one's beholden to me. Amen!" —*Lucille, 80*

> ## Singular Sensation #27
>
> *Singular presence.* Don't be afraid of being singled out. Raise your profile at work with an excellent performance. Being the center of attention can have powerful results.

## Singular Lifestyle Trends

Chances are if you're single—or acting like you are—the life you're living today is what others will be living tomorrow. Singles connect with the world differently than their married counterparts. From food to fun, it matters if we're talking onesies or twosies.

### Singling

It's official—singles are the new couple. "Singling" is the latest form of mingling in today's world. According to the U.S. Census' latest population figures, close to 48 percent of individuals in the United States line up everywhere without a partner. Marriage is no longer the required rite of passage in grownup life. You're three times more likely today to list your marital status as single than you were thirty years ago. More people than ever are living past the century mark, and living longer solo. Being single alone, single with friends, single at work, single on vacation, single buying a house, and seriously single as in "not looking to get married" is evolving into the new norm.

For instance, according to Nielsen/ NetRatings, singles spend twice as much time surfing the Web as those who are married and their main reason for surfing the tech wave is to hook up. Singles are three times more likely to visit dating sites and social networking sites as they are to go shopping online.

And from food to relationships, everything is being singled out. Consumer analysts have finally figured out that it's easier to digest stimuli in small bites. So everything is offered in single servings, from fruit snacks to music downloads of hit singles to customized television programming by way of TiVo to single-meal size packaging at the grocery store. The happiness of the one trumps the needs of the many. A strong sense of individuality tops the herd mentality. The tyranny of the "we" is succumbing to the presence of "I." The world is catching up with what you already know. Being single is sensational!

## Singular Sensation #28

*Gold rush.* Buy yourself an incredible of piece of j-e-w-e-l-r-y. Not costume, the real thing. Get some karats to match your sparkling personality. Make it special by having lunch first and then go shopping for the big bauble. Take your time to lust after several pieces before picking "the one."

## Sexual Healers

Our sex lives have been under a major attack with the rise of AIDS and herpes and the return of syphilis and gonorrhea. Singles have been in the trenches of the sexually transmitted disease warfare, but after a decade of dissin' intimate human contact, singles are responsible for the new sexual healing taking place in bedrooms across the planet. We're defending the right to human touch outside the bonds of marriage and leading the sexual healing movement.

Singles sex education advocates the power of sensuality. We're turning up the heat in ways people had never admitted before, from sexual outercourse (sexual contact with clothing as a barrier), anal sex, oral sex, deep kissing, and sexual self-gratification. Sexual peer counseling services are springing up on campuses across America and new adult education courses for post-graduate work are being offered through community education sources. Having sex is okay again…and the more ways the better.

Online and offline. With your partner and by your self. Opposite sex and same sex. Singles who live without partnership restrictions are exploiting the continuum of human contact like never before. Wanting to know more and do more. Knowing better and doing better has become the mantra of twenty-first-century sexuality. The increasing consumption of pornography by both sexes, the popularity of real people sex diaries and web cams

> **Singular Sensation #29**
>
> *Leave a legacy.* Recognize that the people who are close to you are family. Designate a cherished piece of your jewelry as a family heirloom and pass it on to a favored niece, nephew, or family friend. Preserve your link in the family chain.

on the Internet, and urban exotic erotic clubs means that sex is sexy again. Hallelujah!

### Totally Inner-Active

Only one is number one. Singles are proving that the most important relationship we have is the one with ourselves. We're just as likely to need our own space to recharge as we are to share our space with a significant other. The National Association of Home Builders reports that twice as many singles own their own homes today than a decade earlier and the building industry is scrambling to meet the demand of younger, more affluent single home-buyers.

And singles are going public with their necessary indulgences. Charlotte's and Carrie's shoe fetishes on *Sex & the City* opened the closet doors to women who could finally admit their secret passions for high heels, handbags, hair products, and anything in basic black. Diamonds remain a girl's best friend, especially when we can buy the one we want, when we want, to celebrate whatever we want. These no longer guilty pleasures are our way of saying we don't need anyone else to tell us we're worth it.

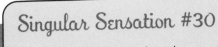

**Singular Sensation #30**

*Dates to remember.* Get the cake and candles. Keep a birthday book. Never forget to celebrate a loved one's special day ever again.

We are determined to satisfy our needs even if it means delaying marriage to do it. Worldwide, men and women are marrying later, sometimes living at home with their parents or shacking up with friends while they pursue their careers, educational opportunities, or childhood dreams, whatever they might be. The feeling is, it's my world and I can choose to invite you into it.

### The New Fairytale Family

Most people want a family to call their own. Singles are leading the way when it comes to retelling the story of "us" and "how we became family." Whether it's friends as family, single parenting through birth or adoption, or a multi-generational hybrid situation, singles rule when it comes to exploring what it means to be a family. Not willing to accept marriage as the standard incubator for creating a nest, singles are building social networks of their own and changing how society at large views this most basic of communities.

One **Liner**

"The irony of the single thing is... We're all self-contained. [Even] married people. They get up themselves. They wash themselves. They brush their teeth. They do all kinds of things that you'd do if you weren't living with someone. They go off to work. They have daydreams." —Anna G., 56

Marriage avoidance is leading to changes in legal, cultural, and marketplace assumptions. Contractual relationships, civil unions, and commitment ceremonies can announce the formation of a household, which may just easily end through nontraditional dissolution rituals. Singles who make alternative lifestyle choices like communal living and surrogate births are being forced to rethink their answers to standard questions like, "How do you know each other?" "Who gets the house when you all breakup?" and, "How did you lose the weight so fast after the baby?" They are forging new traditions like "orphan" holiday gatherings and annual non-blood family vacations. As singles, we're choosing selective, more meaningful activities with friends instead of large chaotic family gatherings.

> ## Singular Sensation #31
>
> *Bollywood Babe.* Start belly dancing. Exotic movements, sensual music, and sexy costumes—what more could you want in an exercise routine? I found tons of information on classes and costumes as well as inspiration for getting started at www.shira.net and www.bellydancingvideos.com.

Disputing the myth that we're home alone, singles are trading partners for significant other connections with organizations, causes, and avocations. And following in the footsteps of the United Way, Single Volunteers, Inc., focuses worldwide on singles having fun while doing good. And the number of singles heading post-9/11 services, Iraqi war outreach, and disaster relief efforts is impressive.

Just because we're unattached doesn't mean we're not connected. Our replacement sisterhoods, brotherhoods, tribes, and village people are all part of the modern expansive neighborhood.

### Fusion Flirting

"Fusion flirting" is the toe-in-the-water test as interracial dating enters the mainstream. Society has succeeded in fusing tastes, preferences, and cultures in the arenas of cooking, music, and fashion; now it's time for love. Affirmatively stating racial dating preferences has become politically correct in the border-crossing twenty-first century. Match.com even allows online profiles to decline a match by stating race as the reason. For those seeking cultural compatibility, singles groups now cater to racial and religious preferences offering black, Jewish, Asian, Indian, and Christian exclusive events. Maybe singles will start another revolution. The last one, the sexual revolution, was quite successful. The exotic has always been erotic; maybe now it's romantic as well.

## Steal This Life: Always Sexy Singles

**Being single is sexy. There's something very mysterious and alluring about those of us who have eluded capture.** Doris Day and Rock Hudson's cat and mouse play is just as risqué and funny today as it was in the frilly housewife '50s when few women worked outside the home. The well-dressed working girl in her chic suits still causes everyone to whisper, "Why isn't she married? She's so cute, sexy, fun to be with, and always looks damn hot and has fabulous shoes." Which leads to the next thought; "Damn! Why did I get married?" Which is, of course, why husbands across America discourage their wives from spending quality time alone with their single girlfriends.

Increase your powers of attraction. Leverage the power of red. There are a thousand shades of the passionate hue; find the one that best suits you. Irresistibly kissable red lips get him to focus right on target. Pair a silky red blouse with your favorite black suit or add fiery red pumps for the ultimate surprise finish to a night on the town look. Slip into satiny knickers and observe Red Panty Day during the month of October.

## Singular Fact or Fiction?

Where do you have the best chance of running into someone single? According to the most recent population numbers from the U.S. Census, that would be (in order) California, New York, Texas, Florida, and Illinois. You're least likely to find someone truly single in the states of Wyoming, Alaska, Vermont, and our nation's capital, Washington, D.C. Most singles clink drinks in metropolitan areas. And although there are slightly more available women than men nationwide, the opposite sex match-up varies by age.

Single? How much are you like other unattached members of the singular nation? Married? How well do you know your single friends?

**1.** "Parasite singles" are most likely to be found:

    a. Living at home in Tokyo, Japan

    b. In your neighborhood sports bar

    c. At a lecture on "How to Marry a Millionaire"

The answer is (a). "Parasite single" is the moniker used in the media to describe the increasing number of single Japanese women who live at home with their parents and forego marriage.

**2.** Look around. Are you and your friends delaying marriage until:

    a. Early 20s to mid 20s

    b. Mid 20s to late 20s

    c. Late 20s to early 30s

The answer is (b), according to the U.S. Census.

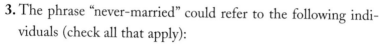

3. The phrase "never-married" could refer to the following individuals (check all that apply):

    a. ＿＿＿ Single
    b. ＿＿＿ Cohabitating
    c. ＿＿＿ Annulled
    d. ＿＿＿ Single mom
    e. ＿＿＿ Engaged
    f. ＿＿＿ Single dad
    g. ＿＿＿ Friends with benefits
    h. ＿＿＿ Single parents

You should have checked all of the above.

4. You're more likely to be married if you're:

    a. Hispanic
    b. Caucasian
    c. African American

The answer is (a). Hispanics have the highest percentage of married households, according to U.S. Census studies.

5. The "why wait for marriage?" trend is fueling:

    a. Diamond sales
    b. Home sales
    c. Leisure travel sales
    d. All of the above

The answer is (d).

**6.** Three times as many men over age forty as women in the same age group admitted to having multiple sexual partners at the same time.

      a. _____True

      b. _____False

False. Only twice as many men as women admitted to playing musical beds. (*AARP, Lifestyles, Dating & Romance, September 2003*)

**7.** West Coast singles are more likely to lock lips on a first date than singles elsewhere.

      a. _____True

      b. _____False

False. The sought after first-date kiss is more likely to happen under the stars on the plains of the Midwest. (*Yahoo! Personals nationwide survey, September 2004*)

**8.** Men pay to play. On average, guys spend which of the following amounts on dating each month?

      a. Between $75–$100

      b. More, more: $100–$150

      c. Still higher: $150–$200

      d. Big spenders: Over $200

The answer is (d). According to a survey of their members by the dating service It's Just Lunch, the average man spends $220 per month wooing the ladies.

**9.** Do we put our money where our hearts are? Online spending at dating sites tops spending on business information like stock quotes and investment advice or leisure entertainment such as videos and digital music.

      a. True_____

      b. False_____

True. In 2003, online dating sites captured $450 million in revenues, according to a May 2004 Online Publishers Association report.

**10.** You qualify for single taxpayer status with the IRS if:

      a. You divorce on the last day of the tax year for which you are completing a return and then remarry the following year.

      b. Are legally separated on the last day of the tax year for which you are completing a return.

      c. Widowed and your spouse died during the year for which you are filing taxes.

According to the tax code the answer is (b). So yes, he's only technically single if that's how he files his taxes.

## The Last Word

**Being single is a choice. Choose to define what it means for you.**

You are not alone. Along with many more single adults, you are changing the nature of 21st century relationships you have with others and your self.

# STEP TWO
## Indulge in Random Acts of Selfishness

Sustain the Single State
of Being

# Chapter Five

# But I'm Too _____ to Be Married!

Given the power of choice, most of us have our own reasons for remaining single. You reject the reasons society has bestowed on you for not being married. Yours are perfectly okay and true.

I found out that the unmarried people I interviewed were *not* too:

| | | |
|---|---|---|
| old | loud | chubby |
| fat | boring | popular |
| ugly | happy | pretty |
| stupid | interesting | depressed |
| unpleasant | "out there" | picky |
| young | arrogant | sexual |
| unattractive | sexy | busy |
| poor | opinionated | free |
| short | humble | rich |
| thin | unique | shy |

...to be married.

In fact, more than a few of them were quite charming. Several were knockouts. And for most, if not all of them, I found myself wondering why weren't they married.

In answer to the question "Why are you single?" I heard...
- Live in the wrong city
- Fell in love with the wrong person
- Bad timing
- Not looking for anyone
- Not interested in marriage
- Too busy
- Don't know why I'm still single
- Getting to know myself better
- Freedom is more important
- Travel too much
- Different calling
- Don't possess the "marriage gene"
- Marriage is not an option

What they didn't say...
- Haven't met the right person
- Never thought about it
- No one I know is happily married

But heck, maybe they aren't too anything to get married. They just don't want to get married.

**Singular Notion: Whose Eyes Are You Looking Through?**

"I'm not married. I've never been married. I have no girlfriend. I want a girlfriend. I'm Aquarius. I'm average in bed. I'm a good footballer. I like food and I can move things with my mind."
—*British pop star Robbie Williams, via AP Television News*

> ## Singular Sensation #32
> *Journal your singling.* Acknowledging making the choice to live solo means you're not a victim of circumstance. Shop for the perfect journal and record your thoughts about the solo life. Recognize yourself as the great decision maker.

"I've been stumbling into this so much! Everyone around me is getting married, having babies, buying houses. It's more than a different language, not like you're from another planet. But a belief in a religion I'm not a believer of—I'm a family atheist." —*Deirdre, 33*

"If he's not going to be great I'd rather stay single. I'm older, not picky, but if I've waited this long…" —*Nancy, 36*

"The sense of the individual is just so strong for me. I have a really strong sense of my individuality and I'm comfortable in my individuality." —*Kathryn, 52*

**Loves Blue Jeans, Lacks Marriage Gene**

For some of you, like Vanessa, a thirty-year-old journalist, being single is the straightforward choice of your heart. It's perfectly fine with you if a good man gets away.

As we begin to discuss her adventures, the proper reporter is quickly replaced by the straightforward homegirl. "I don't have, like, a maternal instinct. Never went through the whole thing of picking out china patterns in my head and wondering what my wedding's gonna be like."

Clad in tight jeans and a snug-fitting top that dives to showcase ample cleavage, Vanessa's *definitely* not dressed like she's saving anything for marriage. Instead, she craves the excitement of the first date, when everyone is on his or her best behavior.

"You're, like, shaving your legs every other day because you don't want no kind of stubble nowhere. In case they reach out a hand and try to touch your thigh," she explains. She then demonstrates by stroking her own leg and purring. I can't control my guffaw of laughter as she continues. "It's before you find out about their criminal record or how skuzzy they are. And you're just like ...GAWD..." She waves her hand, almost knocking over my empty wine glass. In the beginning, "they're so much cooler than fill-in-the-blank whoever you went out with the last time. I'm so glad I met this person because they're so not like fill-in-blank person you dated two times ago."

Vanessa's current beau, "Mercedes Boy," is still on the A-list, but maybe not for long. He's in the process of buying a high-rise city condo, and he's definitely got his jones on for marching to the altar and nesting. As Vanessa lies back on the sofa, studying the ceiling and twisting her locks between well-manicured fingers, she surmises that Mercedes Boy's biological clock is ringing because his older brother recently got engaged.

"Yesterday, he tried to take me to his grandma's house," Vanessa says, frowning. "He called me today saying, 'You want to

> ## Singular Sensation #33
>
> *What dreams may come.* When you were young, what was the life you dreamed of? Did it happen? Why or why not? Include these thoughts in your Singling Journal.

go to my soccer game on Sunday?' Like he's trying to lock...*it*...DOWN," she intones.

"I honestly don't think I want to get married. And, I think that's why I'm not married, truly. Because I mess over perfectly good people all the time," Vanessa says, without a trace of bragging in her voice. "This is not the first time I've met a stable, well-educated, employed black guy who worships me...and I'm like 'eh,'" she says with a shrug as she settles back into the couch.

Wow, I love her honesty. I don't want to do it; that's why I'm not doing it. Makes sense to me. Not wanting to get married is nothing to be ashamed of or explained away. Other things can and will fulfill your heart's desire. What's not okay is denying your feelings so you can be "normal" or be one of the girls. You're not in high school anymore. It wasn't okay then, either, but you didn't know any better. Now you're all grown up. And to paraphrase Maya Angelou's mother wit, "Now you know better, so, girl, go do better and better!"

Vanessa clearly relishes her role as serial temptress, and she doesn't care that it complicates her chances of finding a life partner. She'd rather not enter the marriage lottery. "I have control

### The Single Best Attitude

Stop explaining yourself. It's no one's business but your own why you've chosen not to marry. You are fully aware of the choice you've made and are willing to accept the consequences. You have a healthy understanding of the concept of cause and its effect on your personal happiness. You have permission to graciously deflect those "why aren't you married?" inquiries with a wave of the hand and a "I've been too busy to give it a second thought!" Just think: could it be that others are so fascinated by your single status because "the grass is always greener on the other side"?

*but i'm too _____ to be married!*

over my career. I have control over where I live. I have control over whether or not I'm doing something that makes me happy. I have control over whether or not I'm at peace with my relatives. I can control whether or not I'm getting sex. I want my happiness to be linked to...things I have control over. I don't have control over whether or not I'm gonna fall in love with somebody."

Vanessa is determined to exert control over her world and therefore takes responsibility for her own happiness. Not content to leave her destiny in the hands of fate, she's taken off the rose-colored

## Steal This Life: The Choice to Remain Single

**Why are you choosing to be single? List the reasons here. Feel free to rationalize, invent, and otherwise embellish your life.**

1. The reason you tell your parents:


2. The reason you tell the guys you date:


3. The reason you tell your friends:


4. The reason you tell your best friend:


5. THE REAL REASON:

glasses, preferring to meet life on her terms. I encourage you to stand by your choice and like Vanessa, be a brave warrior in the battle for your own heart.

## The Revenge of the M.R.S. Degree Dropouts

Do you have what it takes to be a single survivor? The things that disqualify you for marriage may make you a perfectly great single person. The big challenges of adulthood traditionally are securing employment and getting married—securing yourself. In fact, we use the same language for both: finding a job and finding a husband.

> ## Note to Self
> Embrace the power of the word "no." Stop saying "yes" or "maybe" when deep inside every fiber of your being is screaming "Nooo—not ever!" When a not-your-type man asks you out to dinner, don't say, "Well, maybe next week," and then get annoyed when he promptly asks you out again on Monday. Be clear about your feelings right up front so you don't encourage the "boomerang effect."

Ever notice how the whole process of mate selection closely resembles the hiring process? The main objective of either is to narrow down a wide pool of applicants to that perfect candidate. The goal of a first date and an initial interview are the same: to rate the elusive call back.

Rob, an attractive, well-to-do forty-eight-year-old architect from Lake Tahoe, confirms my suspicions. "When you go out on that first date it does look like a job interview. I've felt like that, like I'm being interviewed to be married," he says, shaking his head. "I've actually felt like the questions are so direct that I'm on an interview for a job." Well, Rob did manage to get two callbacks that lead to trips down the altar. But he didn't make it to retirement with either one.

but i'm too _____ to be married!

## One Liner

"One thing I do value is being me, and sometimes in a marriage you don't get enough of that. You don't find enough room to be you and be enough for the other person as well. And it's not really about being single; it's about being you." —*Thom, 55*

I was unemployed as I transitioned to my writing career, and that meant I had plenty of time to peruse the "job wanted" ads and wander through the love personals. I've found that in either search process—using classified newspaper ads or online sites—personal recommendations and just plain luck come into play.

"Say hello to your Dream Job! Say goodbye to your current boss! Apply for the opportunity of a lifetime!" Turn the page and employment come-ons compete with offers of romance. "Wife Wanted." "Renaissance Man Seeks Muse." "SBM hoping for his last first date!" "LOOKING FOR SOULMATE." "Mr. Right Now May Be Mr. Right."

## Singular Sensation #34

*Lose control.* Blow bubbles in traffic. Laugh hysterically. Eat a pint of your favorite Haagen-Dazs ice cream. Run in circles and spin until you're dizzy. Unwind and momentarily give up control.

Whether desirous of a mate for work or play, the potential partner publishes their laundry list of essential qualifications. Only serious applicants need apply. Review the random sampling of employment and matchmaking advertisements below. Can you guess which is which?

1) "Looking for extremely energetic, ambitious, motivated individual...if compassion is one of your attributes...must be outgoing, athletic, and have a good sense of humor...urban, cool, stylish...age: 18-25 yrs...Multicultural."

2) "You should be honest, trustworthy, and open-minded, not wedded to any particular political or intellectual dogma. You should be able to 'hold your own' in erudite discussions on art, literature, and music and equally adept at changing diapers and reading bedtime stories should there be a 'late delivery from the stork.'"

3) "Never will selling yourself be more important...a unique opportunity to learn and grow...No competition. Each person supports each other...enjoy the lifestyle you've always wanted."

4) "What can I say but I want it all. Bake a cake and twirl your butt around a dance pole. Shout it out at the laundry, shout louder in the bedroom."

5) "You can party...have beautiful candles...light up your own life and others...warm atmosphere of a home...your dreams come true..."

**Quickie Fact**

In 2003, close to 30 percent of single adults in America had never been married. *U.S. Census. Current Population Survey (CPS) 2003.*

6) "Do you naturally build trust with people you meet? Do you always live up to your commitments? Do you possess a *great* personality? Strong relationship building skills are essential."

(The employment ads are 1, 3 and 5; the personals are 2, 4 and 6.)

Over the last year and a half I discovered that I did not want to commit to any individual or corporate entity that wanted to commit to me for a long-term relationship. This all adds up to no ring on my finger and no reason to deny my creative musings. I'm starting to believe the two things are related.

In the end I've decided there's only one thing that separates me from my peers in pairs or corporate couplings: two words. "I do." As in I do promise to work weekends and to love, honor, and obey.

### Dateworthy Dish, Not Marriageable Main Course

Are you one of those dreary singles lamenting the staleness of life on your own? Then you need to meet feisty and fast Priscilla. At thirty-one, if Priscilla were a bumper-sticker it would say: "Fabulous for Play!" In the mating game, she's on the hunt for the ultimate playmate, not lifemate—and she wants a high endurance model built for speed. She says she's forever single because members of the opposite sex "just couldn't keep up." Priscilla says to just ask her college mates. "It's always been a very, very simple thing for me. I'm looking for somebody to play with. And then they say, 'You probably missed him because you're going too fast.'" Even as we talk in her French-themed home accessories store, she's moving close to the speed of light as she rearranges merchandise. She loves her life, where "I play as hard as I work and work as hard as I play." Why not be all that you can be and get the most out of living on your own? Heck, one can have as much fun as two or more. You can be living proof of carpe diem! Didn't you invent the saying?

In both her work and love lives, Priscilla values her independence, and right now she's only responsible for feeding herself and

> ### Singular Sensation #35
>
> *CEO, You, Inc.* Who would you choose to help you run your company? What skills or information do you lack? Corporations have the benefit of a board of directors. Recruit your own board that you can turn to for advice when making large-scale decisions. Two, three, or four heads can be better than one.

her cat. An entrepreneur at heart, she knew she couldn't do an office job. After a succession of employment situations, she opened her own shop in a trendy Northern California suburban neighborhood. Reveling in the luxury of not being distracted by a spouse, kids, or even friends who happened by—the pure joy of living in the zone—she focused on achievement and measurable success.

*Quickie Fact*

A study by four British universities published in the *Sunday Times* newspaper found that the higher the woman's IQ, the less likely she was to be married. Could it be that smart women make smarter choices?

Like most happy singles, she's focused not on what's lacking in her life but on enriching her days with as much joy as she can handle. By concentrating your immense amounts of time and energy on pursuing personal interests and goals, you will attain soul satisfaction. Priscilla is so boisterous and outspoken, it's hard to imagine her as a sheltered Chinese child. She was raised in the Mormon Church and still remembers the elementary schoolyard chatter: "What do you want to be when you grow up? I want to be a mommy and have children." She rolls her eyes and continues, "That never occurred to me. I think I came without a clock." And then she yells with sudden inspiration, "They've got banks!" I think she's referring to sperm banks but before I can ask, she's off on another subject.

Pushing her wire-rimmed glasses up on her nose, she explains all about "The LOOK." She's not afraid of the look that says, "How come you're not married, Priscilla?" Or the close second, "How come you don't have a child, Priscilla? Are you some kind of deviant?" There's a clearly pronounced natural progression in

*but i'm too _____ to be married!*

## The Single Best Attitude

Try living beyond your means. As in, you mean to be a good salesperson. How about stretching to reach that farthest shore by meaning to be the storeowner? What would it take for you to venture outside your current box and live beyond your means? Do you need a degree? Go back to school. Do you need a better image? Start paying more attention to the way you look. Do you need to dream? Take the time to let your mind wander away from the life you're living into new possible scenarios. Get a life outside your comfort zone and you might find yourself in an incredibly rich U-zone!

Chinese culture, she explains. "You do your schooling, you get married, you have a child. All of sudden you didn't do that—why not? Are you a money-hungry person?"

Priscilla ignored the cultural clues, religious demands, and peer pressure that surrounded her growing up. Being the black sheep of the family, she's raced to indulge her own grownup fantasies of adulthood. As a solitary family unit among your relations, I'm sure you've faced some disapproving stares, embarrassing comments, or downright uncomfortable dinner dates. It's not the end of your world; you've laughed or cried and gotten on with your life fantastic.

Yes, she believes being single is a choice. "I'm not saying I'm hot stuff, but yes I could just go up there and get married," she says with a toss of her blunt-cut bobbed head. She just doesn't see marriage as an option for herself. Her ninety-seven-year-old Chinese grandfather teases her that he can't die happy until she gets married. Priscilla's sly standard rejoinder has been, "Man, Grandpa, you're going to be the oldest man on earth."

# Steal This Life: The Romance Resume

**You've probably heard the saying that the best predictor of future actions is past behavior. Or the definition of insanity: doing the same thing over and over again, and expecting a different result.** Maybe our love life resembles our work life more than most of us care to admit. If we've never dated anyone longer than two weeks, shouldn't we look for a starter boyfriend before we attempt a full-on long-term relationship? Or maybe you're really "sex-only" material possessing all the desired prerequisites: charming, attractive, smart, disease-free, and seductive. Go ahead—create the perfect one-night-stand-winning resume.

## The Romance Resume

Name/Online screen name

Photo (CURRENT, not ten years ago)

Personal website/Email address _____

Address                                                    Age _____

Current Status:

____Single                              ____Single and available

____Single and not looking              ____Married (how long ____)

____Divorced (how long ____)            ____Separated (how long ____)

____Other

Gender preference ____Male ____Female ____Both ____Other

Mission/Object of desire:

Availability: ____LTR ____STR ____Friends w/benefits ____Booty call

*but i'm too _____ to be married!*

Sex Partners:    Male    Female    Other

AIDS/HIV Status:    Positive    Negative

Your past bed partners would describe you as:

    Selfish, driven by own needs    So-so

    Novice, but fast learner    The holy grail of generosity!

Personal Bests:

Most Romantic Date    Favorite Pickup Spots

Best Pick-Up Line    Signature Cocktail

Best Karaoke Song    Favorite Position

Special or Unusual Lovemaking Skills

Relationship History:

Long Term    Short Term

Who ended the relationship? Me    Them

How?

By email    By telephone

By letter    In person

Marriage proposals/engagements (describe in detail)

## Paid to Party

Tired of always being "The Girlfriend," twenty-seven-year-old professional model Stephanie decided to go it alone for a while. The Barbie look-alike has had more than her share of offers to become lifelong arm candy. Now she's been single for the past couple of years and loving it because "I've always felt I was holding myself back. I had offers to travel but I wouldn't do it because I didn't want to leave my boyfriend behind."

Sound familiar? Think back on all the times you've dared not rock your life's boat because you were tethered to family or friends. Not wanting to leave the safe harbor of current relationships shouldn't keep you from venturing out and making new ones. The beauty of living single is the endless possibilities

## Note to Self

Answer the question: what would you do if you knew you would not fail? Make plans to do it now. Tomorrow is one day too many and never is always too late.

for forming new attachments while nurturing the old ones. Now Stephanie goes wherever she wants as a promotional tour camera girl for an outrageous hot hunks video production company. Her job, if you can believe it, is to travel around the country, visiting friendly college towns, spring break hot spots, and infamous party locations like Florida's South Beach to film young men willing to flaunt taut biceps and rock-hard bodies. I asked if there were any particular qualifications needed to snag this single girl fantasy gig. Gorgeous? No problem with nudity? Congrats, you're in!

And while this atypical job situation is not for everyone, it has allowed Stephanie to totally embrace her sensual self outside the confines of a committed relationship. And she has been able to set "no sex" boundaries in a professionally consistent manner in free-for-all sexual situations. Anticipating the obvious, Stephanie is quick to dispel any fantasies. "They think you're going to flash. I let them know that's not going to happen." A curvaceous 5'3", she generally dresses in jeans and tight T-shirts with a heavy camera belt around her waist. "I can't dress too sexy. I attract the guys with my hair and makeup, and I wear four-inch platform heels or boots," she says describing her off-camera wardrobe.

Stephanie travels with a crew of hunks of her own, six guys aged twenty-one to early thirties who drive the bus, choose the locations, and ward off any unwelcome advances from rowdy fans. "It's a tour bus like the ones a rock band would tour in. The name of the company is plastered on the outside of the bus." Stephanie's home on the road for three to four weeks at a time has a lounge, refrigerator, microwave, and a narrow hallway with bunk beds for the crew. The back of the bus is equipped with a king-sized bed, bathroom with shower, TV and stereo, and plenty of mirrors on the walls.

She gets to play director creating her own exotic fantasy entertainment. Without input from anyone else, Stephanie basically creates the film scenarios for each shot of the sixty-minute videos. Coaxing college guys into stripping, streaking, or soaping up while stroking their egos is the main focus of her evening, which rarely begins before 5 p.m. and often ends well after 3 a.m.

And although some would consider this a fantasy job for a single woman, Stephanie's success in her work is due in large part to her ability to exist outside societal norms. And she's living outside her own personal comfort zone as well by opting out of forming personal attachments. Going beyond what feels safe and comfortable for each of us is how we change and grow. I'm not suggesting you run off and join the circus,

## Note to Self

Today, sample change. Use the new mini paint pouches offered by manufacturers to sample a new wall color for a room in your home. Pick a few colors for the price of a pint. Splurge on a new handbag, scarf, or pair of earrings and sample a new fashion trend. You might like a little of the gypsy look but not want to invest in the entire caravan style. Small changes allow you to move ahead one step at a time.

but consider that some area of your life might be ripe for transformation.

Stephanie's certainly enjoying her roadie lifestyle (she was home only two months out of the last year), and she's not anxious to get hooked up anytime soon. She's not interested in seeking male approval or balancing the two-headed beast of trust and jealousy. However, meeting scads of attractive guys does have a downside. "I always have to tell myself not to get too attached. Because I'm so used to having a regular guy, I find myself acting like a girlfriend. But it's in my best interest to stay single."

## Steal This Life: You-nique Travel Finds

**When traveling for work, incorporate some fun. Visiting a new city? Look for love and little luxuries in the aisles of the neighborhood stores.**

Foreign pharmacies make the best beauty "super" markets. You can find a mind-boggling array of "I-can-never-find-this-at-home" lotions and potions, a bevy of bathroom elixirs, and tons of new tonics to try in your hotel room or when you get home. Load up on cool stuff!

Hit a local flea market. Skip the concierge and chat up the locals. These outdoor markets are worth hunting around for and usually have the best souvenirs at the best prices. They are also great places to meet other wandering souls like yourself.

Shop in a local grocery store. Every culture has a taste all its own. Purchase spices, nuts, and loose teas to fill your kitchen pantry. You can also find great gifts for friends that won't break the bank.

For now, Stephanie is content to live her sometimes-scandalous single life. "I just think a single girl should be able to do anything a single guy can do without being labeled," she announces matter-of-factly.

## The Single Best Attitude

Glass half full or half empty? The answer is yours to decide. Don't let your parents, friends, siblings, church, colleagues, or favorite bartender make this decision for you. It's too important. Go with your gut. You've only got one life to live. Make sure the life you live is the one of your own choosing. Plenty of people before you will admit to taking the path of least resistance to law school, married with children, the family business, or some other predetermined destiny. Why not follow your bliss away from the altar down the river and through the woods of "I'm making it up as I go along"? If that's the path you choose, you're bound to discover your true passion along the way.

## Singular Sensations

**#36** *Instant message.* When you turn on your cell phone, what do you see? An anonymous greeting? Why not personalize your phone's opening message to read "Hello, Gorgeous!" "I am a Goddess!" or "Bow to the Queen"? A little self affirmation—and a secret reason to smile—goes a long way.

**#37** *Play your song.* Is there one song that always seems to brighten your mood, make you grin, or start your booty wiggling in your seat whenever you hear it? Well, that's your song! Burn it on a CD, program it into your iPod, always have it available to make you feel smart, sexy, fun, or just plain ol' alive when you need it.

**#38** *Fair trade.* Stretch your dollars and increase your knowledge by volunteering at the next professional conference or event you'd like to attend. Programmers are often looking for non-paid assistants to keep things running smoothly. Just remember to mind your manners and don't crowd the paying guests.

## The Last Word

**Being single is a choice. As in you choose to be you, satisfied and solo. The options are not marry or die.**

1. You are not obligated to hold on to a good man. Letting go is perfectly acceptable behavior.
2. Ignore peer pressure and encourage single-self expression.
3. Explore living without limits. Move beyond your comfort zone in some area of your life.


but i'm too _____ to be married!

# Chapter Six

# One Night Stands and Other Hostage Situations

I'd be lying if I didn't admit that a great deal of single life revolves around sex. The opposite sex. The lack of sex. Getting great sex. Sex with your ex. Sex with friends. Sex with the guy next door. Sympathy sex. Sex with a stranger.

At work, we daydream about sex. Over drinks with friends, we compare notes about sex. On vacation, we indulge in spring break sex. Sex at his place, your place, any place.

And with all the sensual aerobics, we don't even agree on what is sex. Oral sex. Anal sex. Tantric sex. Yet we all want it, need it, crave it. Life's fire and desire. S-E-X.

There are a hundred places, excuses, and thrilling combinations to have sex when you're single. 'Cause when you're married, every single person knows there's just sex with your spouse.

A quick wink, flirtatious deep kiss, held-too-long hug, and

you find yourself living dangerously in that bond that can happen when you're not ready or too ready for a lustful encounter. You're on your own to effect this rescue.

It was lust at first sight when I met Darryl, my delicious fantasy-come-true experience. A sexy musician with a buttery voice for singing old-school soul ballads. Breath-stopping sex, late night panty-dripping conversation, and on-call sex, I called and he was on it! He's still on it, actually—my seven-year itch that never goes away, no matter how much we scratch...I've been held hostage by his skillful caresses on random evenings for the past 2,617 days. I have gone willingly, seduced, been seducer, and actually craved being held in his arms in the six-by-six space of his well-worn mattress. No bars, but no escape.

## Quickie Fact

Population Reports estimates that at least seventeen billion condoms are needed worldwide every year to cover the sexual activity of unmarried men. Population Reports is published by the Population Information Program, Center for Communication Programs, The Johns Hopkins School of Public Health.

It's truly the best tell-only-your-best-single-girlfriends sex, performed with the most gorgeous genitalia. I once said that to a married woman I knew and she said she didn't think she'd ever seen gorgeous genitalia. I have that rarest of gifts when you're single—sex on call, sex on tap, no strings attached, burning and twisting, grunting and groaning kind of sex, as regular as I want it to be. Maybe I'm hostage to my own desires—I can't focus on the marriage manhunt because I'm too content with milking the cow. This is a definite take-no-prisoners situation. Where's the hostage negotiator?

I used to tell myself, stop this madness! How can you expect to find a real man while you're screwing a boy toy? Yet, he's definitely incredible Mr. Right Now material. And I'm not interested in having Prince Charming rescue me from my sensual indulgences. For now my mind and body are free to roam.

## A Lust Story

Who can predict the laws of attraction? No doubt you've experienced that unexplainable physical chemistry that happens between two individuals. Why not enjoy it for what it is, a fleeting passion or undeniable lust for another? You're single and you have choices.

> ### The Single Best Attitude
>
> It's misleading to call them "laws of attraction" because really there are no hard and fast rules for physical chemistry. There will be times when you fail to turn on the switch of a member of the opposite sex. Don't change your clothes, your hair, or your zip code in desperation. Chances are it doesn't have anything to do with you. His switch might be broken.

"You know what? Mark—I loved his smell," Flavia, thirty-two, says as she explains her deep attraction for a thirty-something law student. "OH MY GOD! I couldn't not touch him, the chemistry was soooo strong." The exuberant Brazilian catches me off guard with her amusing anecdote of "love at first smell." She never understood what people meant when they talked about being attracted to someone's scent. "I'm like, what do you mean, 'armpit smell'? Until I met Mark. The smell coming off of his body drove me crazy!"

Even though she knew this wasn't going to be a match made in heaven, she couldn't resist the urge to mate. "The reality was he wasn't that smart. He wasn't that good looking. He wasn't good in bed. He didn't have that much to offer. What the heck is going on?" Flavia admits to being led by her nose straight to the bedroom. She doesn't try to make the relationship more than it is. Flavia is clear that Mark is mating, not mate, material.

"Have you never met someone whose smell you just love? Not the perfume, not the cologne, not the sweat, just the smell," Flavia whispers. "I never understood until I met Mark. It's the most powerful thing."

## Note to Self

The next time someone pays you a compliment, don't get flustered and start in on self-deprecating repartee. The appropriate response is to say, "Thank you very much." And to truly believe the good press you're receiving.

### Singles Click: How Do You Know You're Good In Bed?

A very unscientific survey of nicely naughty singles shared their secrets from between the sheets.

"Your partner never wants to wash the sheets because your scent is all over them." —*Deirdre, 33*

"The neighbors complain." —*Bill, 40*

"You see it on the bathroom wall." —*Tanya, 22*

"Isn't it self evident? It should be self evident." —*Aaron, 32*

"Well! Because he keeps on coming back for more." —*Teresa, 32*

"It's not just when he wants more, that's easy. It's when *you* want more. When you feel confident and excited about doing it and it's fun, not just sexy. When you've gotten good at the basics plus you're looking forward to mixing it up a little bit every time." —*Adrienne, 29*

# Steal This Recipe: Award-Winning Morning-After French Toast

**Only serve this if you want him or her to come back for seconds. This French toast tastes as soft, sweet, and sensuous as your skin the night before.**

*Ambrosia Batter Ingredients*

Loaf cinnamon challah bread

2 eggs

1/2 cup whole milk

1 T. orange zest

1/4 cup maple syrup

3 T. Frangelico liqueur

1 tsp. pure vanilla powder

1 tsp. fresh ground nutmeg

2 T. butter

*Condiments Climax*

1 banana, sliced

Maple syrup

Chopped walnuts

Slice four one-inch thick slices of cinnamon challah bread; set aside. In a large mixing bowl, whisk the eggs. Stir in the milk and orange zest. Continue to stir while adding the maple syrup, Frangelico, vanilla, and nutmeg. Dip the bread slices into batter, making sure both sides are covered. Allow the slices to soak up batter. Remove slices and set aside. Heat two tablespoons of butter in pan over low heat. Place slices in pan. Cook toast slowly over low heat, turning frequently. Repeat with remaining slices, if necessary. Remove toast from pan. Arrange on plate so slices lazily overlap each other. (Like your bodies did the night before.) Cover with sliced bananas, sprinkle with chopped walnuts, then drizzle with warm maple syrup. Feed each other succulent mouthfuls and save the leftover syrup for your next tryst!

> ## Singular Sensation #39
>
> *Yoga:* You want me to put my hand where? The rhythmic stretching of yoga helps strengthen barely used muscles. Now when your bodies twist in passion, you'll go for more of that tingling sensation, wherever it is.

"I'm always concerned about pleasing my partner. My report card is how well I make the other person feel. Even for a one-night stand." —*Ernie, 44*

"No complaints." —*Alanna, 23*

"I have fun and I laugh and the woman I'm with is laughing and having fun, so if you can be having fun and orgasms you're probably good—your biggest problem is falling out of bed laughing...a hundred orgasms and a few laughs." —*Gary, 52*

"When you get a second opportunity." —*John, 31*

"One, response. Two is just because I know. I just simply know." —*David, 37*

How do you know *you're* good in bed?
Quick! Write it down:

_____

Now tack it up somewhere as a reminder of your ultra fabulousness!

### *Where Singles Fear to Tread*

Topping the list of places you're most likely to find a shame-faced or scared single: the HIV/AIDS clinic. As I walk up the steps of the community clinic I feel like I'm attempting grand larceny in broad daylight. I'm sure (aren't I?) it's just my imagination that all eyes are on me, and that they know who I am and what I've been doing. Undeterred, I enter the bland waiting room, which has about as much appeal as my dentist's office on the morning of a root canal. I stroll up to the counter, sign in, and receive a reassuring smile and a number (the test is anonymous) from the sweet-faced woman behind the desk.

Great news! It'll take less than one hour before I get my HIV test results back. Okay, so that cuts down on the agonizing weeks spent waiting for the results, like I did years ago. But then I suddenly realize that I'm not sure I'm ready for a life or disease to be decided so quickly. I mean, what if they get it wrong?

Still, I sit and wait my turn, and within a few minutes I am called in for the procedure. The lab technician administers a simple blood test by pricking my finger. I'm sent back into the waiting area where I mentally make a list of every person I've ever slept with. I slice and dice the list in my head: partners in the last year, previous six months, casual unprotected sex, and instances of sex with possible condom malfunctions. I negotiate with God. This really is too much stress for something so frivolous as the pleasurable exchange of body fluids.

My number is up and I'm escorted into a crammed office to meet with a counselor. He's young, maybe twenty-five. He pulls out a long form and starts asking questions that sound like an interview for a porn flick. "I need to document your sexual history for purposes of government funding. Would you answer a few questions?"

## Quickie Fact

Men and women around the world have had on average 10.5 sexual partners. Would you reveal your sleep number? 2004 Global Sex Survey Report by Durex

"Sure!" I chirp, unaware of the barrage that would follow.

"Are you heterosexual? Homosexual? Bisexual?

"Have you been tested for HIV in the last six months?

"When was the last time you had sex?

"Do you use drugs? Do you share needles?

"Are you currently in a long-term relationship?

"How many partners have you had in the last year?

"Do you engage in sexual activity with transgender partners?

"Do you use protection? Do you always use condoms?

"Do you engage in oral sex? Do you swallow?

"Do you have anal sex? Do you use lubrication?

"Do you engage in sexual activities where you are tied up?"

I try to keep things easy and conversational. Reversing roles and pretending to calm his nerves keeps me from climbing the walls. Just tell me, already! The counselor completes the questionnaire and excuses himself to go get my results. I don't envy him his job. He's tried to get an accurate sexual synopsis so he can put my test results in the proper light.

Me? I haven't stopped praying.

The counselor sits down with a solemn look on his young face. The envelope, please! No, it's just a simple index card with my number and a check mark in the "negative" box. My whole body sighs with relief. I know I dodged a bullet.

The rapid testing result has a high accuracy rate but he counsels me to return within six months for a follow-up test. We continue our chat and I, who can think clearly again, ask him what he has learned from his draining job. "I'm not sure what I've learned, but I'm always surprised, because so often I'm counseling people and they come back negative, which is hard to believe in light of their sexual practices, and then someone else will test positive."

He pauses. "What surprises me is the randomness of everything, which is why I don't work at the clinic full time."

I pocket a few of the free condoms scattered on the desktop, thank him for his time, and get the heck out of there.

### Respect This Four Letter Word: Safe

I wondered as I was collecting interviews for this book, did it matter if you were single because you aren't allowed to get married? Because gay people do not have the choice to marry, their lifestyle provides valuable lessons in how to be safe, sexual, and single. So I was intrigued when a close friend of mine suggested I interview his gay ex-lover, saying, "I love him, but he'll never settle down."

At thirty-five, Powie confesses that he has perfected evolving one-night stands into relationships that don't lead to lifelong commitment. Until now, between family and lovers, he hasn't been alone since he emigrated to the United States from the Philippines eleven years ago.

Powie's parents accepted his sexual orientation and acknowledged the fact that he wouldn't follow the traditional path leading

**Singular Sensation #40**

*The power of touch.* Pamper yourself with regular massages. Practitioners at massage schools offer great rates. Hands on one's body can soothe tense and sore muscles, increase the production of serotonin, the body's feel-good neurotransmitter, and just make you feel spoiled...which is exactly what you are!

**Note to Self**

No excuses. Get tested.

to marriage and children. "In my mom's eyes, I would never be married because I'm gay. Yeah, because the Catholicism is so strong they only view marriage if it's approved by the church," he says in a quiet voice of resignation.

The **Single** Best **Attitude**

FYI: You should be on a need-to-know basis with your body. You definitely need to know the status of your sexual health. Make it your policy to know whether you are living in sickness or in good health.

Today, well-dressed in a lightweight knit shirt and linen slacks with trendy square-toed, black leather shoes on his feet, Powie exudes casual chic. His fashion sense, coupled with his exotic good looks, scream heartbreaker. So far his romantic life has been pretty successful. He's a member of the boyfriend-of-the-month club with no deadly hangover. Most of his exes, who got careless after the breakup, are HIV positive. Powie is HIV negative and attributes his good health to being a very conservative gay man.

In monogamous relationships, Powie waits the recommended six-month period in which he and his partner both test negative for HIV before engaging in unprotected sex. That's a better record than most heterosexuals, who admitted in a casual online survey to engaging in casual, unprotected sex as much as 30 percent of the time.

It's been a crazy afternoon of soul-baring conversation. Just as the interview is about to end, I ask Powie if these random intimate moments are enough. Doesn't he ever get lonely?

"Lonely being single, you mean? NO," he says, laughing out loud. And he utters the words I've come to hear more than once,

"No, I'm alone but I'm not lonely." If you really think about his words, I believe you'll find yourself agreeing with Powie. When our lives are really clicking and humming along, having a partner is the icing on the cake. And sex is the sugar high. Emotional and physical partners are not a guarantee against loneliness. It's not the required presence or the quantity of our interactions that keeps lonesomeness at bay; it's the quality of the company.

### Singles Click

"I miss that meaningless sex. No-strings-attached-don't-care-about-the-person sex. That's the best!" —*Holly, 38*

## Steal This Life: Be Safe, Not Sorry

**Relationships. Ever think about all the people you interact with and who they know? Your colleague at work who knows a close friend of yours who knows the guy who plays on your softball team who knows that guy you occasionally sleep with?** All of these individuals have you as a common denominator in their personal network. Take out a piece of paper and begin an intersecting daisy chain of the relationships in your life. Now assume each of these people is having sex with the person directly linked to them. How many "degrees of separation" can you document before there is a break in the chain? If this exercise were real, most people's sexual history would contain a missing link or two.

"I'm not into the one-night-stand thing, but I do love to go out dancing. The sexual energy on crowded dance floors is amazing. One time, I was out dancing with girlfriends when I accidentally backed up into the guy behind me. I was tipsy and decided to rest by leaning back against him. He was dancing with another woman. I was dancing with my friends. But we linked hands and did this grind thing against each other. I never even turned around to see his face. But it was one of the sexiest experiences of my life." —*Deirdre, 33*

"Sex isn't casual for me. I'm incredibly sensitive. I totally merge with people in sex. I can't just do casual sex. It messes up my psychic space." —*Sally, 43*

"I only have had random sex. I don't have that person who knows me on a personal level or anything. It's like very random. It happened on vacation in Florida. It happened when I was visiting home with this friend of an ex-boyfriend. Big, bad mistake." —*Leah, 22*

## Note to Self

Get physical without being sexual. I love it when kids throw themselves at you with their arms open wide, fully abandoning themselves to their feelings of the moment. Give someone you care about a spontaneous love hug and experience the healing power of touch.

"I'm not a slut, but I definitely don't feel like I have to be married to have sex with someone. And if I want to go out with a friend of mine who's a guy and have a really fun night and end up spending the night at his house and having sex with him, I don't think that's a sin or a bad thing. I think we all have sexual needs.

"I have a friend, one friend in Chicago, who I connect with. He

doesn't want a girlfriend for the same reason I don't want a boyfriend. We go out. We have fun and we sometimes have sex. There's no commitment. No gotta call you tomorrow. We care about each other as people. But we both feel it's completely unrealistic to be in a relationship. I enjoy sex. I'm not going to lie. So it happens once in awhile and it's fine. I don't feel bad."
—*Brooke, 22*

"What's that stuff about 'The One' anyway? I don't know if there's such a thing. I think there are many ones. I think it depends on where you are and what you want." —*Flavia, 32*

## Singular Notion: Basic Instincts

Monogamy is not normal. Recent research in the animal kingdom confirms that the desire for multiple sexual partners is natural. Even many species of birds that were thought to have a happy nest have been revealed to fly the coop on occasion. It's almost impossible to find a species that doesn't cheat. Homo sapiens created marriage to rein in our biological needs, among other reasons. But for those of us who want to experience our full selves, singlehood is more in line with our true nature.

## *Singles Sex Haiku*

*The Quickie*
*Sex alone is fine*
*But two bodies are more fun*
*So, my bed or yours?*
—*Deirdre, 33*

## True Confession Time: For One Night and One Night Only

I looked forward to my "what happens in Vegas stays in Vegas" weekend with my girlfriends. I admit it: I was hoping to experience the naughtiness of Sin City's most successful public relations campaign to date. As we rode in the limo from the airport, I suggested we find the female equivalent of the Mustang Ranch in Las Vegas. My traveling companions said "No way!" and the topic was firmly closed.

The weekend proceeded with the usual shop till ya drop excesses, late dinner at the hottest new celebrity chef restaurant, and dancing to '70s tunes in a casino club. Then, Saturday night we flirted with two twenty-something cuties, Pete and Mike, at a bar. At about 1 a.m. my girls claimed exhaustion and returned to our suite at the hotel. But heck, dressed, pressed, and made up to excess, I was in no hurry to call it a night, so I accepted the young studs' invitation to hit the club scene.

"If you lose me, use your key," Mike says with a meaningful nod at Pete as we wait in line with the well-dressed crowd. Pete, a new Las Vegas resident, is staying with Mike, his best friend who's visiting from out of state and has snagged a room on the Strip.

> ### Quickie Fact
>
> Our parents may have warned us against them, but 45 percent of those surveyed globally admitted to a real life one-night stand. No strings flings are a happening thing! *2003 Global Sex Survey Report by Durex*

We pay the $25-per-head cover charge at the exotic-themed dance club and slide past the doorman into a steamy, erotic, pulsating world. Scantily clad dancers in day-glow outfits gyrate overhead in cages. We grab cocktails and head for the dance floor. Hundreds of slick bodies wet with sweat melt into a sensuous rhythm on the crowded upper level. The music, a fusion of trendy hip-hop, salsa beats, and blaring bass notes whipped us into a closer-than-close frenzy. Bare-chested drummers accompany the digital music as trapeze dancers hang from wires overhead.

Pete leans in, barely brushing my lips with his and says, "Do you want to leave?" I pretend not to hear so I can think about his question. I don't know. Do I want to go with him?

"Do you want to leave?" Pete repeats, this time with more emphasis, as he looks straight at me with his sparkling blue eyes.

The Single Best Attitude

Be happy. You're single and chances are you're healthy and having sex. And sex outside of marriage is still legal—and very enjoyable. My concern is it can be lethal. As single adults we can choose to be intimate with any number of partners. The reality is that sex today requires knowledge of not just elementary school subtraction and addition but the multiplication tables as well. You may know your partner but you may never know his entire universe of sexual partners. Don't mistake committed sex for risk-free sexual intercourse; choose to be safe. Sex can be just as much fun when you're not in harm's way.

"Yes," I hear myself say. Pete immediately grabs my hand and leads me down the stairs out of there. In the cab on the way to his hotel, he's a bit nervous and I'm a bit amused. I'm thinking, wow, I'm going to get lucky in Vegas and I didn't have to lose a dime in the casinos!

## Steal This Life: Save Sex. Have Safe Sex.

Variety is the spice of life the old saying goes. And having sex with a variety of partners is one of the benefits of being single. But like other indulgences, we must act responsibly if we want to continue to enjoy our pleasures. Don't let the fear of contracting STDs, being anti-oral, or unfamiliar with the latest sex craze keep you from jumping into bed. Practice, embrace, fall in love, champion—just do the safe sex thing.

- Celebrate Condommania! Go beyond the basic cover-up and explore the growing variety of lubricated, ribbed, colored, flavored, and sized condoms available. Don't be shy, ask boy friends which they prefer and why. Get tips from the sexperts; visit sensuality retailers online and off and ask about the best in their protection selection. Always check the expiration date before you use them—yes, there is an expiration date.

- Call Good Vibrations stores and get their condom guide. www.GoodVibes.com, 800-289-8423

- Host a sex toy party. It's a great way to be the first on your block to experience the best sex capitalism has to offer. Visit www.passionparties.com or www.pureromance.com to find a representative in your area or inquire about in-home demonstrations at your local adult sex toy store.

- Do try this at home and in a few other places. Make this the year of living your wildest fantasies. Make a list of the top ten, twenty, or one hundred fantasies you'd like to try once in your life. Then enlist sex partners whenever possible and appropriate in passion play.

## The Last Word

**Being single is a choice. So is having sex. Make it fabulous.**

1. Opportunity knocks at the bedroom door. You have the option of letting it go unanswered or opening it wide to a variety of partners and experiences.

2. Choose to be safe.

3. It's okay to choose to commit for an hour, a week, or a lifetime. The choice is up to you.

4. Don't let sex be something that happens to you. Good sex happens with your permission and full attention.

# A Year of Living Exquisitely Single

## January

> *"I am only one, but still I am one."*
> —*Helen Keller, a spirited single woman*

- Skip the New Year's resolutions you weren't going to keep anyway and draft a personal mission statement. These will be your words to live by in the year to come! Post them where you can see them every day.
- Hit the after-the-holiday sales! It's the best time to pick up ornaments and décor for the outrageous holiday gig you'll host next year.

- Be sex savvy. Your pre-orgasm checklist should include a sexual health checkup. Take an HIV/AIDS test. After unprotected sex, it can take as long as six months for HIV antibodies to reach levels detectable in a blood test. Know your status.
- Chase the blues away with a mini-vacation. Take a winter break and head for the sun or hit the slopes. Go after the fifteenth when there are fewer crowds and the kids are back in school.
- Plan to date. Make a list of all the places you've been meaning to visit to meet exciting singles. Call your friends and remind them you're not with el jerko anymore. Now that you're a free agent, get your gear together. Three things you'll need to know before you hit the social scene: your favorite drink, your best karaoke song, and one clean joke or one dirty joke—you choose. Plan the work, then work the plan!
- Dedicate yourself to trying something new each week. Need ideas? Pick up one of Lynn Gordon's fifty-two-card decks: *52 Things to Try Once in a Lifetime, 52 Ways to Simplify Your Life, 52 Relaxing Rituals, 52 Cheap Dates,* or *52 Ways to Nurture Your Creativity.*

### *February*

> *"To love oneself is the beginning of a lifelong romance."*
> *—Oscar Wilde, a very single-minded married man*

- Celebrate V-day in your own special way. Valentine's Day is a great excuse to gather together all your single friends or other friends and family you care about for a love fest. Plan a "Think Pink Party" or set an exotic mood with an evening under the warm glow of red lights. Have a potluck and invite guests to bring red foods—red bean chili, red lettuce salad with raspberry vinaigrette, and red velvet cake—yum! Just remember, couples don't have a lock on love. It's something we all can share.

• Attend some of television's biggest events. Sign up to be a member of the audience at www.seatfiller.com. Front seats at the hottest Hollywood nights are available for singles, not couples.

• Take advantage of last-minute travels deals. Now would be a great time to apply for or renew your passport. One can never take too many quickie European vacations.

• Rainy day blues? Stay indoors with other singles and take a cooking class. Break out your new skills and gourmet delights at a spring fling party.

• Spend an evening being starstruck. Host an Oscar Night party! Set the mood with a black-tie invite—literally, cardboard black ties with the invitation scrawled in metallic inks on the back. Rent a projection screen so that the party has that larger-than-life feel. Order in high-class munchies, take bets on the contenders, and tell everyone to dress like their favorite Hollywood Era: silent screen, '30s glamour, '90s grunge, or twenty-first-century spectacular.

## March

*"If you want to sacrifice the admiration of many men for the criticism of one, go ahead, get married."*
—*Katherine Hepburn, a single super heroine on and off-screen*

• Stir up your own brand of March madness. Host a SexSmarts trivia game party. You'll never laugh so hard or learn so much.

Sample questions are online at www.smartsco.com. Play boys against girls and determine once and for all who's better in bed.

- Get a head start on spring cleaning. Return all those overdue library books and DVDs. Practice feng shui and clear out all that clutter. They say that improving the flow of energy will bring you love—and money.

- Skip spring break and break for fun at spring training this year. Get a sneak preview of the baseball season by heading to Arizona or Florida to play around with the boys of summer.

- Energize your bedroom. Get rid of the television and create a sanctuary for sensual fun and relaxation. Evaluate your bed. Do you need to replace the sagging, sad sack of a mattress? Would a luxury mattress pad or down bedding improve the situation? What colors do you want to fall into at night or surround yourself with in the morning? Dress your bed in a richly patterned duvet cover or a soft single hue to suit your mood. Indulge yourself with three-hundred-count sheets (or dare I suggest ultra-luxury 990-thread-count Egyptian cotton dream sheets?). Add scents and your favorite mood music. Now you've created a personal paradise for you that's worth sharing.

- Spend some time with your sex toy collection. Doesn't thrill you anymore? Want something new and different? Get some adult education. Visit a neighborhood sex shop and get news you can really use. (See the resource list at back of the book.) Good Vibrations and Condommania stores nationwide have helpful, knowledgeable, and friendly staff who won't make you feel like a pervert. Required reading: *The Good Vibrations Guide to Sex* by Cathy Winks and Anna Semans and *Sex Tips for Straight Women from a Gay Man* by Dan Anderson and Maggie Berman. Go ahead, arouse your curiosity.

## *April*

> *"I'm single. I'm skinny. I still can't find a man."*
> —*Sarah Ferguson, Duchess of York, on being royally single*

* Host a Mad Hatter's Easter Egg Hunt. Invite friends over for a chocolate-inspired brunch. Serve chocolate chip pancakes and dark fudge muffins and invite everyone to wear fantastic whimsical hats. Hide chocolate- and egg-themed treasures around your place. Spice things up by adding amusing finds, such as chocolate pasta and egg-themed spring earrings.
* When the fifteenth rolls around, adopt an attitude of gratitude when you file your taxes. As a single filer you don't have to deal with the marriage penalty tax and only your John Hancock is required to seal the deal.
* Get a makeover. Refresh your look at a local makeup counter. Treat yourself to a whole new palette for spring. Remember to throw out old dried-up mascara, empty lip gloss containers, and stale shadows. Wash your makeup brushes periodically to avoid infection.
* Refresh your car as well. Get in the habit of getting your automobile detailed. It'll have that brand new care smell without the $30,000 price tag.
* Spring comes to New York. Go and enjoy sex in that city. Visit the Museum of Sex; it's a fascinating tour of sex throughout the ages. www.museumofsex.com

## May

*"The ultimate lesson all of us have to learn is unconditional love, which includes not only others but ourselves as well."*
—*Elizabeth Kubler-Ross, Swiss-born psychiatrist and author of the groundbreaking* On Death and Dying.

• Enjoy Cinco de Mayo. Celebrations are happening throughout the country. Host a cocktail-making competition among your gang of merry margarita contestants. It's a great excuse to do tequila shots and make new friends over chips and dip.
• Don the shades and make like a film star or would-be director at an independent film festival. There are close to two thousand festivals worldwide where you can preview the next blockbuster before it hits your local cineplex. Checkout the Get Shorty Film Showcase and Tour, which celebrates the best short films under five minutes; SCI-FI-LONDON dedicated to science fiction and fantasy film; or the MADCAT Women's International Film Festival which exhibits independent/experimental films by women. Visit the www.filmfestivals.com for worldwide festival database. See you at the movies!
• Enroll in summer school. Try a classroom in an unusual setting or explore a dream-come-true discipline: sign up for a pastry class at a culinary academy, digital painting at a fine arts college, or a writing seminar with a bestselling author. Lessons learned could stir new passions and interests!
• Become the ultimate joker. Stand-up comedians will strengthen your funny bone at San Francisco's Comedy College.
• Take a ride on the wild side at a Harley-Davidson rider

education course in your city. They even supply the bikes. Go cruising at www.harley-davidson.com.

- Have you always wanted to be a surfer girl? Surf Diva, based in La Jolla, California, offers your-round classes that introduce women of all ages to the sport and spirit of surfing. Hang ten, baby! www.surfdiva.com.

## June

*"Oh, I'm no one's wife, but I love my life."*
—*lyrics from that singularly successful musical* Chicago

- Non-brides unite! Recruit beautiful and zany bachelorettes for a "Runaway Bride Race" to support a local charity. All runners are required to wear veils and the obligatory white dress when crossing the finish line. Afterwards hit the showers at a local spa for an afternoon of well-deserved pampering.
- It's the perfect time to join a volunteer effort to clean up the nation's beaches or help provide "Christmas in July" to a needy family. Remember, the happiest people on earth care about someone besides themselves.
- Purchase tickets for a hot hot HOT show. Plan to attend the sizzling Erotic-La, world-renowned for introducing latest sensual products and concepts in the world of erotic entertainment. Visit www.erotica-la.com.
- Ready for summer fun? Time to take a bi-annual AIDS test. Just make it a habit and do it!
- Mid-year check-in: read your horoscope and see how the year's progressing. There's still time to make a change. The eerily

accurate www.astrologyzone.com provides in-depth monthly forecasts. Or for more vivid insights into your personality, visit www.colorstrology.com.

## *July*

*"If you are single, there is always one thing you should take out with you on a Saturday night—your friends."*
—Sarah Jessica Parker as Carrie Bradshaw in HBO's
Sex & the City

- This Fourth of July, celebrate your independence! Invite single friends over for a "Freedom Party." Have guests come prepared to share their stories of hilarious dates, first kiss maneuvers, and horror stories of online encounters. Or include a burning ritual around the BBQ. Write down things violating your freedom (personal fears, old habits, values you've outgrown) and toss them in the flames.
- Explore starting a new business to supplement your income and support your quest for financial freedom. Not up for being your own boss? Evaluate your spending and start saving for something big: retirement, a new home, or a holiday shopping spree!
- Spark your social life! Create your own personalized social calendar. Sign up to receive announcements and invitations from online sites, message groups, and local professional organizations, museums, etc. Bookmark Craigslist.com; they have event calendars for several cities around the world. Some others: SocialDomain.com, DateMyFriend, HurryDate, 8minuteDating, and www.EventMe.com.

## August

> *"Liberty is a better husband than love to many of us."*
> —*Louisa May Alcott, author of* Little Women *(Before the* Sex & the City *foursome, there were the four March sisters.)*

- It's cool to go back to school! This month many colleges start classes with weeklong festivities for returning students and new freshmen. Become the best bud of that little niece or nephew and accompany them back to campus. Hang out at the campus coffeehouses and graduate student parties and shop the bookstore. Life-long learning is a good thing.
- Is your wardrobe dateworthy? Toss anything frayed, stained, that you haven't worn in the last year, doesn't fit, or does fit but doesn't make you look super hot. Shop the sales with assistance from a personal shopper. It's a great investment that'll offer a fresh approach to creating a new you.

## September

> *"Leap and the net will appear."*
> —*Zen wisdom for aspiring singles*

- Celebrate National Unmarried and Single Americans Week. For more information visit www.unmarried.org.
- It's the end of harvest time at the vineyards. Have everyone over for a Mighty Fine Friends and Mighty Fine Wine tasting party. Ask guests to bring a bottle of vino costing a certain dollar amount. Cover the wines with sexy silk ties or plain paper bags. Wine snob or novice, it's now all about taste.

- Try a fall foliage tour. Autumn colors begin to paint the eastern states.
- Go house hunting instead of man hunting. Who knows? By year's end you could end up snuggling by your own hearth without a broken heart.
- Grab your single friends and head for the great outdoors! Plan a Wild Women of Wonder Slumber Party! Invite your closest friends to spend an evening under the stars exploring the joys and strengths of female friendship. Send out personalized invites with a tribute to each pal's special quality or talent. Then, at night over a "tribal council," toast with champagne or marshmallows the extraordinariness of each person present.
- Want to really hear the call of the wild? Contact your local zoo or aquarium. Many animal sanctuaries offer overnight programs.

## October

*"How many cares one loses when one decides not to be something, but to be someone."*
—*Gabrielle "Coco" Chanel, maven of individualistic style*

- It's National Orgasm Month. During the only month that begins with the big O, celebrate the fun and health benefits of giving and receiving pleasure. It's a great month to sign up for adult sex education at Erotic University at their Los Angeles campus or visit their virtual campus at www.eroticuniversity.com.
- Go trick-or-treating in your best costume ever! Some ideas:
    *Clever.* Kiss the cook, cheating husband, martini, fireman, Super Dave 4.0 (he does the same costume every year, just keeps

revving it). And don't forget: superheroes are always in style!

*Cute.* Movie stars, such as Audrey Hepburn—sleek Sabrina, sassy Holly Golightly—or Harrison Ford—adventurous Indy, wisecracking Han Solo. Make sure to pick a character that no one expects from you!

*Seductive.* Live fantasies—French maids, Mardi Gras mermaids, sassy schoolgirls, and frisky firemen. The ever-popular cat woman—not every woman can or should pull this one off, so know if you're purr-fect.

Props are key. Wands, paddles, whips (fetishes are huge!). Dress up as a schoolteacher with a ruler, a cop carrying handcuffs, or for a twist, an artist with chocolate body paint.

Strut your best stuff. Face, cleavage, legs—just don't try to show everything at once. Leave the whore/hooker/hoochie mama costumes at the store or in the trash.

No mask. Don't paint your face or wear a mask unless you're Zorro. They need to see gorgeous you if they're going to kiss you.

## November

*"I am the master of my fate: I am the captain of my soul."*
*—William Ernest Henley, British poet and the singular inspiration for the character of Long John Silver in* Treasure Island.

• Start your own "family" tradition. Host an Orphans Thanksgiving. My own tradition began with couple of engineering graduate students who weren't going home for the holiday. There were two enterprising guys, a large house, and many friends who would also be hanging around the campus. A few phone calls turned into a telephone tree mobilization of food, alcohol, and games for an all-day feast for a couple dozen "orphans." Cindy's rosemary turkey was served side by side with Monica's mom's greens, and my roasted garlic mashed potatoes; store-bought sweet potato pies joined Herek's chocolate bread pudding for dessert. Now each year a revolving cast of characters all come together to give thanks for the year past and the dreams ahead.

- Impress your friends and steal a guy's heart with an old favorite from across the pond: English Trifle. All you need is a deep glass bowl to show off the layers. I like to use something fun, like miniature clear champagne buckets or an usual crystal vase. Then layer pound cake soaked in rum or sprinkled with Marsala wine, raspberry preserves, and rich vanilla custard pudding. Top with whipped cream and decorate with more raspberries and mint leaves.

- It's time to get serious about holiday shopping. Compare lists, desired loot, and your budget. This is not the time to stress out, robbing Peter to pay Paul to make Bill happy. Unless you own a bank, chances are you can't give joy to the entire world. And are you on your list? Revel in picking out the one gift that's from you to you. Or, give yourself the gift of surprise throughout the year: join a chocolates, flowers, teddy bear, wine, cheesecake, book, pizza, coffee, candy, potato chips, cookie, fresh fruit, board games, jams, gourmet foods, pranks and gags, teas, cigar, music, spa, bath soaps, salsas, nuts, or pasta of the month club. Put the schedule away and then surprise yourself with a present every month just for being you! 'Tis better to give...and to receive.

- Take a drive in the country. Collect homemade jams and chutneys to spread on warm morning toast or savor in bag lunch sandwiches. Or bring home a few exotic, color-rich gourds and group them in clusters around your home for the holidays. Add a few simple votive candles and autumn leaves for a cozy winter's eve centerpiece.
- Indulge in a guilty pleasure. Get a 1 ½-hour massage. Yes, you deserve the extra thirty minutes. Stay in bed all day with someone...or a good book. Both can be equally satisfying.

## December

*"The privilege of a lifetime is being who you are."*
*—Singular author Joseph Campbell*

- Make and follow an end-of-the-year checklist. At the top of the list: all the really important things you need to finish up this year. Then save yourself the stress and date the list for following year. See, you're already ahead of yourself!
- Plan a New Year's Eve bash with friends. Pool your cash, rent a space, hire a bartender, get a caterer, or order premade delicacies from the gourmet supermarket in town. Hire a student DJ and art students to do the décor for over-the-top fabulousness. Dress your best and enjoy yourselves. Keep the guest list private, so you can create an intimate and memorable party to bring in the New Year.
- Do something stereotypically silly. Stop taking yourself so seriously. Loosen up. Flirt with the bartender at a well-known singles bar, buy something sweet with your bus fare and walk home, dye your hair an outrageous shade of purple. Oh, go ahead—it's

the last chance this year to be totally silly and self-indulgent! And your last chance this year to forgive yourself and then forget the thing ever happened.

* Dream Possible. Plan a once-in-a-lifetime holiday. Vacation somewhere you can't pronounce the name of. Plan a weekend away at home and indulge in your greatest fantasies. Cook a really complicated gourmet meal and invite another home-alone friend over. Participate in the magic of the holidays by creating your own new tradition. Focusing your energy on you will make you feel as special as the season.

# STEP THREE
## Claim Your Space

# Chapter Seven

## Individual Upkeep: Oil Changes, House Payments, and Dinner for One

I've often thought about what it takes to keep me alive and humming happily along on this planet. You know what it is? The Art of Self-Keeping, and the most successful singles have mastered it. I'll use myself as an example. I live in a completely remodeled two-bedroom flat. The contents of my closets rival the styles in most specialty boutiques. Alas, I have so many clothes I could wear a different outfit every day for at least two years. I own no fewer than ninety pairs of shoes, eighteen of which are black and twenty-eight of which are flip-flops for my tropical moods. When I feel it's necessary, I indulge in full body massages, imported chocolates, and South Sea island vacations. And my social life? Not too shabby.

Do I consider myself high maintenance? You betcha! But I can't worry about that because I'm busy creating my life, as I should be. After all, if you don't pay particular attention to the care, feeding, and amusement of you, you can be sure that no one else is going to pick up the slack. That also means that if life isn't what you expected, you're on intimate terms with the person who can change things in a heartbeat: YOU. Self-awareness is the foundation of quality self-keeping.

And it's never too late to start. As part of my recent twenty-fifth college reunion, each alumnus was asked to submit a page for the class book that was distributed among former dorm mates. The single-page memoirs were to summarize our accomplishments and include any wisdom we'd learned in the past quarter-century. When I faced the empty page on my desktop screen, I found that my life's wisdom often centered on elements that fulfill me as a single woman in a couples' world. The things I've discovered I can't live without:

Air

Good books

The unconditional love of family and friends

Engaging conversation

Spirit

Laughter

Disappointment

Work I love

Sand between my toes

Sex

Bikram yoga

The sound of running water

Fine chocolate

The things I've discovered I most definitely can live without:

| | |
|---|---|
| Limits | A man |
| Obscene amounts of | Health insurance |
| money | (doing work you love |
| Instant messaging | keeps the doctor away) |
| (nothing is that | Fear |
| urgent!) | TiVo |
| An office | A retirement plan |

I've posted the list at eye level in my home office as a reminder of the good things in my life. I suggest you do the same ...in your posting place of choice, of course. Self-keeping—it begins and ends with you.

## Steal This Life: The Essentials Exercise.

Take out a sheet of paper. Make two columns. Label one column "Things I Must Have" and the second "Things I Must NOT Have." Keep the sheet handy and add items at your leisure. You might surprise yourself and restock your life's pantry with delicious, fortifying new things.

## Good Housekeeping Does Not Require Husband Keeping

New Orleans single girl Giselle, a forty-eight-year-old financial analyst, definitely takes care of her personal business. A tall,

## Pleasure Passes

1. Happy New You! Do one thing that makes YOU happy. Please yourself and no one else.
2. Bathe in champagne. The bubbles will make you feel tingly all over.
3. Take a nap.
4. Do something, anything, naked.
5. Experience something for the first time.
6. Go window shopping for hot hunks at the mall.
7. Give in to the urge to splurge.
8. Sign up for a striptease class.
9. Give yourself a second chance. Grab a missed opportunity.
10. Eat chocolates for breakfast.
11. Introduce yourself to the next guy who catches your eye.
12. Run away for the weekend and don't tell a soul.
13. Expect a miracle. Believe in magic. Dream.

café-au-lait-skinned beauty, Giselle flashes a mischievous smile as she settles in to talk. A sexy Southern lilt sneaks into her speech as she casually describes her life as a never-married woman.

"I like my space. I like living alone," she explains. "I'm not one of those people who need to have somebody there all the time. I like my own company." Amen! She's right; you should be the best company you can keep. Everyone else is just a diversion and sometimes an unwelcome one at that!

A homeowner and domestic diva par excellence, Giselle prepares a home-cooked meal for herself just about every evening. She sets the table for company—her own—with her best linen, fine silver, and delicate china plates. A dozen roses and candlelight complete the warm and inviting dinner for one.

One night, a friend of hers, Carl, called unexpectedly from the airport and asked to camp out on her sofa. When he arrived, Giselle was cooking dinner and had just added a second place setting. Carl exclaimed, "Oh, you're doing this for me?"

"No," Giselle calmly corrected him. "This was happening whether you were here or not."

Giselle is a big believer in taking excellent care of herself. Her grandfather once told her, "You have to learn to take care of yourself, because a man is a bonus in your life. He's not a permanent fixture."

## Singular Sensation #41

*Grab your silver spoon.* Remember the special cup, plate, and spoon you had for your first meals in the world? Visit the best home decor store in town and select a place setting just for you. Once a week set the table with "your" china, light candles, and enjoy a great meal. Savor your own company.

## The Single Best Attitude

The more you know, the more you'll know how to do. You won't have to wait around for things to get done on someone else's timetable. And there's everything right with catering to yourself. Dinner alone should not consist of a rushed meal consumed standing over the sink. Your life is special because you're in it and not due to your supporting cast of friends and neighbors. Make it your personal mission to live the life you want. You only get one life to live so plan accordingly. Do for yourself so you don't have to worry about being disappointed by someone else. You are not alone. You always have you and you're great company. Don't take yourself for granted. Others appreciate what you have to offer. You should too. Treat yourself to your good home cooking at least once a week. Don't just save the best for friends.

Granddad's words have proved prophetic. At one point Giselle was in a relationship with a man named John. They had been together for nine years and she felt it could go on forever. John was changing the oil in her car one day when Giselle commented, "Y'know, you need to teach me how to do that because when you're not here, I'll need to know how to do it." She now says, "I'm glad I did that because now I have that information and I do change my own oil. Because John is not here anymore to do those things." The garage down the street changes my oil, but like Giselle I like being self-sufficient.

Giselle likes to do things because then she knows they're done right—and just as importantly, they're done her way. You too can guarantee things are done your way; just be in the know about the things that count in your life. Don't rely on others to make sure your car gets serviced, you've got fresh flowers at home, or vacation plans are made. Determine what you want and then do what's necessary to make it happen.

## *Home Is Where I'm the Head of the Household*

You can buy a home on your own. Invest for yourself and in your future. Don't wait for someone else to make this timely decision. One single woman who delayed buying her first condo said sarcastically, "My boyfriend kept saying, 'Honey, don't buy a house now, wait 'til we get married.' We never did and now I tell him he owes me $100,000 in lost equity." Make the financial investment in the roof over your head and you'll always be glad you did.

"I needed to take care of myself. It's an investment in my future. I signed the papers today, and man, I felt so empowered,"

### *Steal This Book: Create a Self-Keeping Journal.*

**Any good personal valet or manager of an upscale home keeps a house diary. It's the record of the all-important events in the lives of the home and its occupants, and it's the key to the smooth running of the household. Adopt this practice for yourself and your abode.**

You can start by documenting simple things, like your home move-in date or mortgage anniversaries, the landscaping plans for planting spring perennials, inevitable automobile repairs, water heater maintenance, annual doctor's visits, and wardrobe updates. Insert a list of your favorite service and repair people: the butcher, the baker, and the Italian shoemaker. And don't forget the phone numbers! Trust me—this will become an invaluable guide for the necessary keeping of yourself and your haven.

says Corinne, speaking slowly and deliberately in my ear. She's a twenty-four-year-old California girl transplanted to the slow, sweet greenness of North Carolina, and I've called her to talk about the fear and excitement of buying her first home.

For Corinne, who has lived with her twenty-six-year-old boyfriend Jack for the last five years, this is a bittersweet accomplishment. It takes courage to make a major step alone when you're in a serious relationship, and Corinne bought the house with her own money. She wants children and Jack doesn't, so the house is her "exit clause." If they haven't resolved their issues in three years, she'll have substantial financial equity to begin a new life truly single.

"I had to separate my heart and mind to go through this process," she says, reviewing the experience. "Jack and I work together and then come home and live together. We're together at night, on the weekends..."

Corinne knew the combination of her substantial salary from a high-tech start-up, the historically low interest rates, and the favorable Raleigh, North Carolina, real estate market made this a most opportune time to take the plunge. And yet, as she admits, "I wasn't ready to take it to the next level with Jack. There were so many deep unresolved issues."

Bravo to Corinne for doing what's best for her. She recognized

## Note to Self

Making choices in your life equals gaining control over your future. The clearer you are about the choices you make in life the more control you have over the outcomes. "I choose to get a new job" may get you working. But "I choose to get a new job in marketing with the trailblazing electronics firm in the next state" will get you closer to your dream job. Next time you're making a decision, no matter how small, clearly define your choice.

that satisfying the needs of their love and her money might require making opposing decisions. Corinne stopped putting her life on hold and started building her future, one with or without Jack. You can't be single and happy if you're constantly living for someone else who does or does not exist. Moving on with her life in the context of the relationship meant acting singly to take a big step.

At one point, Corinne confides, she almost fired her agent. The agent was driving Corinne and Jack around to look at houses. Corinne was in the back seat going over listings when she glanced out the car window and asked her agent to pull over so she could look at a house.

"Oh, no, you can't buy this house. It's on the corner," tossed the real estate agent over her shoulder, not even slowing down. Jack agreed, saying, "No. No. I can't live on a corner." And while Corinne now admits they were both right, she demanded they pull the car over, and then she admonished them. "Neither one of you gets to make that decision. That's my decision. I'm buying the house!" I laugh at her audacity, and am also amazed at Corinne's sense of self, and the ability of someone so young to stand her ground.

## Note to Self

Dream big. You know the saying, "Go big or stay home." What's your big, over-the-top, crazy goal in life? Write it down. Develop a plan to make it happen. Ignore the naysayers and open the door wide to your success.

## Quickie Fact

At some point in their lives, 85 percent of women can expect to be financially responsible for their own home. The life expectancy of women in the United States at 79.8 years tops that of their male counterparts by more than five years. *Centers for Disease Control, life expectancy study, 2003*

## The Single Best Attitude

A home of one's own. What does that phrase mean to you? Are you content with your tiny rented apartment, or do you long for a real house with room for you to grow? One of the biggest myths of adulthood is that single-family homes require two or more occupants. Banish the thought! As an unmarried woman you are a "single family." Discard the make-believe marketing of home-builders defining families as happy couples and adults with kids. Repeat to yourself, "I deserve to own a place of my own." If you're willing to work to achieve your dream, nothing can stop you—not even outmoded ideas of who qualifies to call a house a home.

Once she took ownership of the home-buying process, Corrine never let go. When she finally found the house her heart fell in love with, she made an offer despite the fact that Jack, who would now be her tenant, wasn't pleased that the property lacked a garage. The almost two thousand square foot, three bedroom, two bathroom, older home has a wood-burning fireplace, sunroom, and botanical gardens that were planted by local university horticulture students. Doesn't that sound good? Four months later, she and Jack are packing boxes for the move. She doesn't know how long they'll live in the new house together or when she'll "flip it for the cash."

The hardest part of the process has been trying to forecast romantic and financial futures. "I structured the mortgage so if I had to, I can pay it by myself. And I don't know if by buying this house, I've turned something off in Jack," Corinne says softly. And yet, this is the biggest commitment she's made in her life, and she's proud of being able to make it on her own. I'm proud too as I smile and hang up the phone. This is the house that Corinne bought.

Buying your first home will be one of the scariest, most stressful, and most head-over-heels exhilarating decisions you'll ever make. The important thing to remember is you can do it by yourself and you should do it for *your* self.

## A Table for One Can Be the Best Seat in the House

There's nothing standard about Courtney. When a pal heard I was writing a segment on eating out alone, she practically yelled, "You've got to interview my friend Courtney! She works really weird hours, so she often eats out by herself."

Courtney is the news copy desk chief at a metropolitan newspaper and at age thirty-one manages a staff of twelve on the 3 p.m. to midnight shift. She says it's a good, challenging job where there's "lots of head scratching" involved in creating attention-grabbing headlines for front-page stories.

And when it comes to dining out alone, Courtney lives by the old saying that strangers are just friends you haven't met yet—which is important, because her newspaper career has taken her to many locations where she was without friends or family. She recently moved to the San Francisco Bay Area from Monterey, California, where she spent a year building a new personal network of friends. As an avid sports fan, she'd spend each week watching *Monday Night Football* at a different watering hole.

"Frankly, I wasn't going to the bars to be picked up. Just to be out in the world, hearing conversation, and being around people," Courtney says, surveying the passersby from our patio seats. Some nights she didn't want to cook or spend another night home alone, so she'd enjoy a slow-paced evening sitting at a bar,

## Steal This Dream: Be Home Buddies.

**Are you single and looking to stretch your home-buying dollar? Why not consider holding property as Tenants-in-Common with siblings or close friends?** Be sure to consult an attorney who can inform all the parties of their rights and responsibilities of such an arrangement. A clever single in California seeking two single female co-investors placed an ad on Craigslist.com, the world's largest community-driven website, and moved two steps closer to buying the home of her dreams. Here's her ad:

"Alameda TIC Partners Needed ASAP

"Greetings! Have you been looking for a place to buy in this, hmmm, interesting real estate market? Are you a creative thinker open to possibilities? My name is Sally and I am a single woman looking to partner with others to have a home in Alameda. I would love to find people to partner with me to owner occupy a historic property in a Tenants-in-Common (TIC) situation.

"If you are qualified to purchase at least $300,000, have stable income, and have access to a down payment BUT cannot find that perfect place to call home in Alameda, send me an email. I have been looking since January. Hopefully, you too have been out there and have some idea of the challenges faced with being a homeowner in the Bay Area. Together we can get more for our investment so consider this an invitation to do so!"

Great digital resources for home buying and cash-keeping:

www.myfico.com: Get FICO scores and credit reports as well digital role-playing scenarios for repairing your credit.

www.freddiemac.com: Great home-buying assistance for first-time buyers.

www.ftc.gov: A source of information on credit issues for homebuyers; the Federal Trade Commission's website.

chatting up the bartender, and solving a brain-twisting crossword puzzle. And she'd always end up talking to the people around her. She sips her coffee and explains, "It's a matter of choices. I can either stay home and wait. Or, I have a better chance of meeting somebody if I'm out by myself than if I'm sitting at home."

Yes, you've probably found it difficult to meet new people in your kitchen unless they were there putting out a fire. And that one time the Oakland Fire Department dropped by unexpectedly we really had no time to chat. Go ahead and take up doing crossword puzzles or doodling in public as a way of expanding your social circle.

Courtney has even taken her personal brand of connecting out on the road. She traveled to Europe by herself a couple of years ago. She'd gone there previously with a boyfriend, but all she really remembers is "He and I did this. He and I did that." Courtney was itching to do it on her own to prove to herself that she could. One evening she just said, "Screw it! I'm going to Paris!" then went on the Internet and booked a Lufthansa super-fare ticket.

Once she got past her initial fear of being alone in a foreign city where she didn't speak the language, Courtney moved on to

*individual upkeep*

graciously dining alone in softly lit Parisian cafes. She admits that being a writer helped. She took along a journal and loved having the solitude to record her thoughts and the confidence to dwell among strangers in an unfamiliar place. She'd write, look around, and engage the waiters in conversation.

Don't let the fact that you're not a professional journalist stop you. You can still record your thoughts in a luscious journal you picked up in that little shop around the corner. It will give you something to do with your hands and a sense of purpose while you're looking at your beautiful surroundings. Now when hunger pains strike, you won't be afraid to satisfy your craving for spaghetti carbonara at the little Italian place down the street. Her ex, the confident, Armani-suit-wearing architect, once admitted to her that he would never eat out sans companion. But Courtney firmly shakes her head and states, "There are times when I would rather be eating alone than out on a date with somebody that I wasn't interested in. The free dinner just isn't worth it." I'm sure you know exactly how she feels.

> ### The Single Best Attitude
>
> My dime, my rules. You might well consider this mantra the next time you're shelling out your hard-earned cash. If you feel like having it your way, ask. If you don't ask, you certainly won't get. Instead of disappearing into the tablecloth when you're dining out alone, try sitting up straight and acting like a queen on her throne.

When Courtney and I first met we headed to the nearest Starbucks where she quickly ordered a "venti iced Americano—all ice, no water, with one Sweet-n-Low and a *tiiiiny* bit of whipped cream on top." The barista took the order without blinking and

Courtney said with a shrug, "I very much believe in getting what you want. I'm paying for it; I should have what I want."

Take a page out of Courtney's book. Single doesn't mean your wishes don't count. Especially simple wishes like dressing on the side, steak medium rare, and first cocktail served promptly. Makes sense to me.

### Taking Yourself Out
### *Get Dressed*
Now's the time to forgo the comfy sweats, oversized T-shirts, baseball caps, or your ex-boyfriend's jacket. Don't wear anything that will disguise the beautiful person you are. You're taking yourself out to dinner, so dress for the occasion. After all, you never know who might be sitting at the next table: your future boss, new best friend, or—egads!—ex-boyfriend. You owe it to yourself and everyone else to be presentable at a fine dining establishment.

> ## Quickie Fact
>
> A lot of us singles own a home of our own. According to recent figures from the U.S. Census bureau, 55.2 percent of all singles have purchased a home—and a higher number of single women own the roof over their heads than their male counterparts.

### *Flirt Like a Fiend*
As you peruse the menu, pause to gaze around the room. Let your eyes light quickly on the cutie at the bar. When the waiter stops by, ask him to tell you about his favorites. While you're at it, smile, laugh, and flirt with that waiter. This allows anyone who's interested to see how charming you are.

### Use Your Imagination

Don't leave home without it when dining au solitaire. See that tall, handsome stranger? Let your mind wander. Where is he from?

## Steal This Idea: Join the Jet Set!

**"I said if I'm going to be single, I'm going to make the very best of it," states fifty-year-old Elaine Lee, author of Go Girl: The Black Woman's Guide to Travel and Adventure. And for her, the best thing about being single was indulging her love of travel.**

Flush with excitement from a whirlwind visit to the City of Lights, Elaine went straight to see a financial planner when she got back from Paris. Her dream was to retire in two years and see the world. They charted out a plan and two years later, she spent her fortieth birthday in Rome, the first stop on her solo trip around the world.

How'd she do that? Elaine suggests planning for the trip well in advance of your departure date. You'll need to think about paying travel expenses and the income lost while you're on the road. Look for ways close to home to build a nest egg. Elaine converted her garage into a studio apartment and banked the rental income to fund her trip.

You might consider getting a roommate or refinancing your home. Downsize your lifestyle. Research the best and cheapest plans for recurring expenses like phone and utility services. Start a grocery club with friends and buy home necessities like toilet paper, laundry detergent, and paper towels in bulk. Where you've got the will, you'll make a way!

Why is he alone? Is he on a business trip? Is that a briefcase full of money he's grasping tightly? Hardly, but it's fun to make up stories about the world around us and exercise our gray matter. Just like when we were kids, a little bit of make-believe can go a long way.

> ## Note to Self
>
> You can leave home without a "him." Take yourself out every once in awhile. Out to lunch, out to dinner—out of the country. You'll be glad you did.

### *Relish your meal*

Enjoy the visual feast placed before you. Gently raise your fork to your mouth and wrap your lips around the succulent morsels of food. Breathe. You've left behind meals in front of the TV or standing over the kitchen sink. Relax and settle your butt firmly in the chair. This is a special moment. Don't rush it.

Yes, it can feel strange or uncomfortable to sit in a restaurant by yourself, but tell yourself you deserve the best table in the house. (Because it's true!)

## Singular Sensations

**#42** *The secret ingredient.* Do you have a special spice you add to your favorite dishes, a skincare secret, or an eye-opening makeup color that makes your brown eyes beautiful? Why not trade secrets with a friend? This information is good insider trading.

**#43** *Be a home chef.* Flex your culinary muscle and shave your food budget by preparing a weekly dinner menu. Hey, it works for cruise ships and restaurants, why not your private castle? No more "what's for dinner? I'll do takeout" excuses. You'll look forward to shopping with purpose and those specially prepared meals for one. Now when you do takeout, it's your choice!

**#44** *Avoid do-it-yourself drama.* Hit your local hardware store and have fun creating an à la carte tool kit to suit your needs and ergonomic comfort. It's all about having the right tools for you!

**#45** *Make-believe money.* Paid off your car or your credit card? Pretend the bill still exists and pay the money instead into a savings account. You're used to doing without the dollars; now do something that's a real investment in your future.

**#46** *Make the right move.* When choosing your next place to live, visit the neighborhood at different times of day. Inquire at the local police station about any unlawful activity that's taken place nearby. Meet the potential boys and girls next door. Do your new home homework.

**#47** *Give yourself a raise.* Need more cash? Review your current job responsibilities with your boss; maybe you deserve a raise. Check the company website for current openings that might fit your skill level. Companies love to promote from within. Moonlight on the job. Can you take on additional tasks for more money? If you don't ask, you certainly won't get.

**#48** *Have a haven.* Home ownership is within your grasp. Many cities and companies and government institutions offer first-time-homeowner programs. Know before you say "no" to owning your own home.

**#49** *Getaway essentials.* Pack an in-flight bag for long cross-country flights. Toss in a warm, ultra-soft shawl that doubles as a blanket against the chill on board and a stylish wrap once you land. Dry air will affect your skin; carry a small tube of an ultra-rich hand cream. Dab it around your eyes and cuticles to keep your skin feeling fresh. Fresh fruit, water, and a high-protein food will keep you snack happy and healthy!

#50 *Variety is the spice of life.* Each season try something new in the looks department. Change your hair color or hairstyle. Add a variety of sunglasses frames to your repertoire. Collect colorful handbags. Between outlet shopping, Internet resources, and your favorite second-hand store, none of these options needs to break the bank. It'll keep you looking fresh.

## The Last Word

**Being single is a choice. As a result, no one else is privy to what it takes to make you happy. So indulge yourself!**

1. A spouse doesn't necessarily make a house a home. Your tender loving self-care absolutely does.
2. Have the courage to act in your own best self-interest. Don't let someone else's best intentions guide your life.
3. Don't be afraid to go it alone. If you need them, there will be people all around you.

# Chapter Eight

## Going Public With APOs
### (Independent People Only)

To date or not to date? That is the question when one is forty, fifty, and beyond. 'Tis cheaper on the purse and easier on the ego to retire to the sofa with a glass of wine and a bag of chips than to venture out and face the slings and arrows of retreads, rebounds, and rejection.

From talking with friends, I've surmised it's a new dating game for the thirty-six million Americans aged forty-five years or older who are on the loose. They inform me that as a member of the Over Forty Club, I'm playing by new rules.

Steve, a forty-four-year-old Jewish financial consultant, confirms the existence of this line in the sand. "There's a whole different dating timeline, scenarios, rhythms, that are part of being in the over forty club," he explains. "You get to a certain age and people have different expectations of a relationship, maybe you don't go at the same pace or have the same rules," he continues.

Also the over forty club usually includes another element of surprise: children. "I'm sick of women with a bunch of misbehavin' kids they're draggin' along. Too much baggage for me," says Eric, a sales executive, as he leans back and spreads his arms for emphasis. "You go to a bar, you don't know if they're single or not. Interested or not..." another frustrated over-forty male dater confides.

The good news is we may be over the hill but we're not dead on the other side. The bad news is we stop believing we're Cinderella and entitled to a date at the ball.

A couple of years back, I definitely felt like one of the forgotten toys at Christmas. No one was picking me up. In my twenties and early thirties, I'd been way too aggressive with men, confident in my power to attract the best of the opposite sex. At thirty-four, I retired to the state of matrimony. When I was single again and in my forties, it seemed I couldn't get a date if I was the last single girl on the planet.

> ## Singular Sensation #51
>
> *Adopt a second date rule. Most of us are too nervous, too clumsy, or just too out of practice on our first date to make or grasp a fabulous first impression. Give yourself a second chance.*

I started looking around. I found I had plenty of single friends and colleagues who, like myself, had a "look thirty but is forty" appearance, weren't having much dating success either. Carol, a lawyer in Hoboken, New Jersey, complained, "I'm too tall, too blonde, too smart. Everyone tells me I should move to California where the guys love blondes." At forty-two, Carol finds herself "geographically misplaced" and has just about given up on increasing her social status to a party of two.

What's my excuse? I'm sure my lack of interest in my appearance and in making a appearance was partly to blame. Most evenings I could be found with my nose between the pages of a really good book, rearranging my apartment, or spending quality time with *moi*.

When running errands I left the house in my no-fuss uniform of long, multi-colored braids and baggy, mismatched, paint-spattered sweats. When I joined a male friend for an early morning workout at the gym, he asked, "Uh, you're wearing that?" My defensive

> ## Singular Sensation #52
>
> *Play grownup.* Get a department store makeup makeover before you go out on the town. Be polished up by the pros.

reply was, "We're only going to the gym." No wonder I wasn't meeting anybody.

Somewhere along the way I think we go from expending as much energy as possible to look good to getting dressed on autopilot. As youngsters we're gym bunnies with supercharged nails, hair, and clothes. In our middle age we've moved on to career, convenience, and comfort in sixty seconds flat.

As the dating game progresses we morph from being the flavor of the week to believing we're only giving or receiving a bad aftertaste. And if we don't date, we don't DO anything to engage the opposite sex. When was the last time you and a group of gal pals hung out at a club just to see what's shakin'?

When we're younger there seem to be so many opportunities to interact with the opposite sex: work, house parties, clubbing, hanging out with friends. Any one of these activities might lead to a one-on-one evening to get to know someone better. As we age and our social circles shrink, we're less likely to venture out on our own. Especially when we feel that all the forty-something guys are on the lookout for anything under thirty wearing a skirt.

Lately, as a recent visitor to dateland, I've been anything but a casual bystander. I've figured out that there are great benefits to being over forty while flirting. I do know now what I wish I'd known then—and it's not too late to work it! Look at yourself. You're more confident. You know who you are and what you can do. You can hold your own in an intelligent conversation and put the opposite sex at ease with your quick sense of wit. At your age when it comes to relationships, you still rock—and you know when to roll with it.

## Steal This Life: Mastermind a Makeover

Don't get stuck in a rut. Every now and then I take the opportunity to remodel my life. You know, open the gym door more often, the refrigerator door less often. It could be something small like hair and makeup—okay, those are big. Or it could be something even bigger like hair, makeup, and wardrobe. Or career. Or trying out different living situations. The point is, I seriously question whether the choices I've made in the past are still appropriate for my future. Because as I grow, shift, change, age, I find that sometimes the "rooms" I've created for myself at home and at work may not fit my lifestyle or the goals I want to achieve. Sometimes I find I need to shrink some spaces and enlarge others to fit it all in.

I'm in makeover overdrive. I've changed my hair, dumped baggy for tailored, and banished black from my wardrobe. And there's nothing like getting out of the house and hitting the see-and-be-seen party expressway. Dating is like playing any sport, I've discovered. You don't always have to play to win; sometimes, you just want to enjoy the game.

## One Is Always Enough

When I decided to interview other singles, I never dreamed I would come across someone as fascinating as Frederick. At seventy-eight, he's lived a single life that's been so incredibly exciting and fulfilling, he's never really had time to think about getting married. Imagine that!

Many people would envy the trail of whirlwind travel, foreign intrigue, and

> **Note to Self**
>
> A lot of singles are still going strong after a lifetime of solo living. Ask them for their secrets to solo living success. Chances are, if you ask they'll tell you how to enjoy the best this life has to offer.

secret affairs pursued by Frederick. From the start, it seemed fate decided that Frederick would always be single. After a tour of duty in the army, Frederick went to college on the GI Bill. He majored in accounting and while at school worked at a secret radar laboratory, where employees translated intercepted Russian messages. After graduation, Frederick quickly took a succession of jobs that required him to travel 100 percent of the time. He began what was to become a lifelong habit of living on an expense account.

"So that started my life of traveling, of not having, you might say, roots," Frederick explains, settling back in his well-worn

## The Single Best Attitude

Loneliness, boredom, a lack of love or self-respect—those are reasons why many crave the safety and comfort of marriage. Some believe that outside the realm of coupledom lies a vast wasteland littered with take-out cartons and bitter, bad-date dish sessions with friends.

But your life will be what you make it. Like Frederick, you too can be courageous in your career choices, as well as in your adventures of the heart. It couldn't have been easy, a young man alone traveling through the tradition-bound '50s, '60s, and even '70s. Like you, I'm sure he endured many a whispered barb, impolite joke, and rude question about his single status. I admire Frederick's strength of character to go his own way unapologetically. I encourage you too to have no shame in your game.

leather chair. "That affects relationships, because how can you have a relationship?" It seems that early on Frederick realized there was a choice to be made. He had no desire to compromise his lifestyle with the demands of marriage. In today's ever-changing global society, the wealth of job opportunities is staggering. Balancing work and personal goals requires an honest assessment of what you want out of life. Frederick has enjoyed the road he's taken because he was willing to let go of traditional family values and follow his interests.

He has no regrets. "It was an absolutely WONderful life!" he booms, throwing his arms wide. Eventually Frederick found himself in New York with a great job and a generous expense account. He was a regular at the 21 Club and other posh spots. He got the best tables and was surrounded by big names—the Kennedys, Tom Brokaw, George Steinbrenner, and modeling magnate Eileen Ford.

And of course, with the unofficial keys to the city came the introductions to the city's most glamorous women. Frederick was often set up on blind dates. He jokes, "Married women can't stand a single man—'I have a friend you should meet.' Friends who might even be married."

Obviously these experiences were available to Frederick because he was available to take advantage of them. Over the years he hasn't had time to get bored or to become ambivalent about life. His cutting-edge antics demanded a level of excellence. That's the great thing about being on your own; you have time to focus on what interests you and to achieve world-class skills. You too could be scaling Mt. Everest during the day and attending black-tie cocktails parties 'til the wee hours.

"To me, it was a handicap," Frederick says of marriage and children. While he was enjoying himself at a resort for the weekend, his married colleagues were flying home Friday night to the kids and chores. The fact that he was usually alone during his travels has never bothered him. "I have never been lonely in my life. I live like I'm going to live forever," Frederick says, stretching his long legs.

### Advice for the Newly Single

My brother Dwayne got divorced at age forty. I knew he had never planned it to go this way. When he was a little boy, his goal was to grow up, get a job, marry the perfect girl, and raise a family.

Well, three out of four ain't bad.

I wrote him a letter when his divorce became final so I could put a few myths to rest. Here's an excerpt from that letter:

Let's review the "Six Things You Think You'll Hate About Being Single."

Thing #1: **One is the loneliest number.** That's true…except when you're Number One. Ask anybody who's the best at what they do. Tiger Woods and the Dali Lama both have a following. You now have all the time in the world to focus on improving yourself and getting to know yourself better. Become the extraordinary person I know you can be, and before you know it, you'll have your own tribe. I can hear the crowds chanting now: "You're number one! You're number one!"

Thing #2: **I'm bored.** Well, get out there and get back in the game! Cruise the personals and sample the profiles of lucky single people like yourself. Scroll the Web to look for a new love interest— you'll find it highly entertaining. Once you've scanned the dating field, ask a few ladies out. Your mantra: "Make new friends."

Thing #3: **I do everything by myself.** This one is not a myth; you *will* do a lot of things by yourself. The point is to love the one you're with. Be selfish, not lonely. Treat yourself to a stroll around the block or a trip around the world. Enjoy the privileges of your new life. For example, you live by yourself, so that means everything is right where you left it. No more playing "who hid the remote?"

Thing #4: **I hate eating alone.** Well then, don't. Meet friends at your favorite restaurant or invite them over for pizza or take-out Chinese. Otherwise, yes, there will come a time when you eat alone at home or out at a table for one. But the good news is, no more old-fashioned bland TV dinners! Now your supermarket freezer offers an array of gourmet singular sensations for your microwaving convenience (and don't forget that deli down the street). Also, those fancy restaurant chefs cook single dishes as well as full-course meals for five. The bonus is your meal comes faster because he only has to prepare one delicious masterpiece for your table. When you're really hungry, that's a plus.

Thing #5: **Movies are meant for two.** Oh, please. Where else can you be alone in the dark and *not really* be alone? And usually there are plenty of single seats scattered throughout the theater, so even on a blockbuster opening weekend you can probably get a great seat. No irritating whispers of "What did he just say?" in your ear, either. And with ticket prices so high these days, this is definitely a case where less is more.

Thing #6: **Yours, mine, and ours.** Not anymore. It's all mine—or yours, as the case may be. No more wondering why you're overdrawn at the bank. No more fighting over who made the last ATM withdrawal. Your credit card limits are your own. You are the master of your money universe.

Yes, I admit it—it will be hard going out that first time alone. There's no denying the obvious. But like learning to ride a bicycle or kissing a girl the first time, you may feel awkward in the beginning, until your head is spinning, your heart is beating fast, and you're grinning from ear to ear.

Love, your one and only,

Big Sis

## The Midlife Mating Game

What's this? A Singles Expo? When the invitation landed in my email inbox I decided to venture out to see what an official gathering of the unattached looked like. It was the Wednesday before Thanksgiving, so I was expecting a large crowd. What I didn't expect was a room filled with middle-aged singles. At forty-five, I keep forgetting that's where I am on the timeline. When I look in the mirror the smiling face of my youth smiles back. You, too, can't believe how time flies and still feel like a kid at heart. Don't lose that feeling.

## Steal This Life: Why Don't You Steal Away

**...to a weekend in Manhattan or a relaxing beach getaway?**

Sometimes getting away from "it all" can mean your married friends and annoying roommates. Skip the usual advertised travel specials offering the discriminatory double occupancy prices, and check out companies that cater to single fare travelers. Connecting Travel Network, www.cstn.org, is a Canadian-based non-profit organization that assists globetrotting singles. They list trips with No Single Supplement Charge and provide travelogues for those of us with wanton wanderlust.

It's easier to grab a low fare seat for one than for two. Check out www.cheapair.com. And want to know which airline has the best accommodations for your sassy single bum? Get the plane truth on airline seating at www.seatguru.com. The site shows specific airplane schematics for most major airlines, and gives specific information on actual aisle, seat, and legroom measurements.

So go ahead, be selfish. Leave when you want and plan an uncompromising itinerary of guilty pleasures or languid leisure. Travel by yourself, for yourself. Enjoy the freedom and independence of taking yourself away from it all!

I'm pretty surprised when I walk into this singles gathering and I'm greeted by a forty-and-over crowd with crow's feet, comb-overs, sports coats, and sequined dresses, lined up for the pasta buffet. It's definitely not my scene, but I don't head for the exit. I realize that while fifty may be the new thirty, in some places this is what forty-five looks like. I want to know how these singles swing the solo life.

So I'm on my way to the ladies room to boost my attitude when I overhear Karen expressing her joy to a friend about the men in attendance. I had to capture her relief and exhilaration at seeing the men at the event who were older, balding, and paunchy.

> ## Singular Sensation #53
>
> *About the boys.* Every once in a while remind yourself of what you like about the opposite sex. You don't want to turn into a sex-starved scrooge or a bitter man-hater. Just because they're not Mr. Right doesn't make them all wrong. Appreciate their humanity.

Karen is a lively fifty-four, with soft brown, shoulder-length hair pulled back in a barrette. "I belong to Bay Area Linkup, another place to meet people, but they're so much younger. I actually felt like a den mother at one event," she says, laughing, her brown eyes sparkling. She's dated younger guys, but she's excited about the men milling around in the next room because "we've got more in common. You know, I've got a belly, they've got a paunch."

I never thought I'd miss six-pack abs or firm biceps, but maybe Karen's got a point. As you age, don't you want to be with someone who's feeling the same effects of gravity?

Later in the evening, I see Karen circulating in the crowd. Her trim figure in a tailored turtleneck and knee-length skirt is meeting with much approval. After an almost thirty-year marriage,

## The *Single* Best *Attitude*

How great is your life? Miss shakin' the latest cocktails or dancing 'til dawn? Just because you're older doesn't mean you're dead. You can have a swinging social life at any age. There are age appropriate venues where you can mingle with others who share your passion for sailing, wine tasting, and dancing to the oldies—which includes any music where you can understand the lyrics. Okay, so you're not that young anymore. But you're still as young as you feel, and who wants to go through puberty again? You may not be able to do now what you could do then, but you've perfected a few new tricks worth showing off. You've finally figured out what clothes make you look ten pounds thinner and can dance without looking like a contortionist. So, don't let a defeatist attitude keep you from being seen on the scene.

Karen wasted no time diving into the dating scene after her divorce. But she's in no hurry to leap back into a serious relationship. "I see all these people and they're, like, desperate—and I'm not desperate," she says simply.

In fact, Karen follows the 100 Hour Rule. She lays out the finer points for me. "It means that when you meet a man you have to engage in social intercourse away from home. He can't come over and watch TV." I can't believe my ears. Nothing physical for the first one hundred hours? It seems like eternal wisdom to me. Get to know them before they get to know where all your body's flabby bits are.

"It takes some of that 'static cling' away," Karen explains, creating her own sex slang. "You have to be social before sexual. It's something men can understand. They can do one hundred hours. I don't know about 105," she's quick to add. And just in case you're wondering, phone time doesn't count. It's gotta be in-person face time.

As a second-time-around single and an older, wiser bachelorette, Karen knows to go slow in the fast lane. She has expanded her social horizons, which now include whale watching and glow-in-the-dark miniature golf. "I got out and all of a sudden, it was like, there's a world out there," she says in a wide-eyed whisper.

So, this is what it's like being over the hill and back on the block? Karen laughs and shouts, "It's not over 'til it's over!"

## Note to Self

Everything is better the second or third time around, when your confidence soars because you know you've got it right. Tonight spin a few of your favorite tunes and dance like nobody's watching. Celebrate being on your own like it's the very first time.

I like Karen's attitude and positive spin on the over-forty dating scene. No need to rush into anything; you've been here in first date territory many times before. And you're not desperate for companionship because at this point in your life you've amused yourself many times before. Join her in believing that the best is yet to come and you'll more than likely find it's so.

### Menopausal Male Stickiness

It happens to the most seasoned of us, not just the novices. For every "perfect" date there's an equally perfect dating disaster. But the one thing we singles learn to excel at is handling a bad date with grace. Because one thing's for sure: most of us get better as we age. The rest just get older.

I was at a conference reception, networking and looking for potential interviewees for my book-in-progress. As I was standing at a table with several attractive female managers discussing the dating scene, a fiftyish-looking black gentlemen sauntered over. He flashed a smile at our circle and introduced himself. He was a

## Steal These Guys: Partnership Beyond the Passionate Pair

**"Just because you're single doesn't mean you don't have partners." Ann G., 56**

I like Ann's thinking. You don't need a spouse. You can choose great people to take good care of you: a good mechanic, travel agent, hairdresser, florist, handyman, lawyer, accountant, real estate agent, personal shopper, house painter, and the essential movers and haulers. Pay them well and they'll love you for life.

tall, handsome, toffee-colored man who looked very much at ease in his dark designer suit.

"Welcome," I said, and quickly returned to the conversation at hand. Toffee (that's what I'll call him) listened as I peppered the conversation with questions about the single lifestyle. I confirmed names, telephone numbers, and possible meeting places with some of the women. Unsolicited, he tore the corner off a sheet of paper, quickly scribbled his contact information, and slid it across the table.

Several days later I called Toffee to leave a well-rehearsed message about an interview date. I didn't want there to be any confusion about who was in charge...*me!* But after a couple of rings, he startled me by answering the phone.

He had an appointment, but he wouldn't hang up until I promised to be home at 8:30 that night, so he could call me back. "Sure," I replied, flattered by his interest. So flattered, in fact that

I didn't even notice that just that quick, he'd taken control.

It was 8:30 on the dot when he called me back. "Good. You're there," he purred into the phone. We talked noncommittally for about an hour, then I hung up, thinking that he definitely had possibilities. A black professional, divorced man, obviously close to my age. An adult.

An hour later, Toffee called again. He suggested we get together *that night.* It was after 10 p.m. and I was thinking, well *this* is a little quick. But I tried to just go with the flow, so I agreed to meet him at a neighborhood bar. *Wrong move!* I should have listened to my intuition, and the next time Mr. Wrong shows up, so should you. Don't take for granted the warning signs of your skin crawling or your brain scrambling. Trust yourself. You have intution; you know you'll regret this.

### One Liner

"I'm much too young to get married. I still want to sow my wild oats," boasts forty-four-year-old Jackie, an attractive British blonde. "With menopause you either go one way or the other with the testosterone. It either all goes or you get this like...*rush.* I'm getting the latter," she says, throwing her head back with a delighted laugh. "I feel like a teenage boy. It's great!"

At close to 11 p.m. we rendezvoused at a working class beer joint. We slid into a booth and that was when the first alarm went off in my head. Not only did he sit on the same side of the booth, he was so close that he was almost in my lap. "You know, it's so great we could get together tonight. We're both lonely and we're heeeere," he drawled while sliding his hand down to stroke my hip.

I interjected, louder than I intended, that I *wasn't* lonely and that, while there were times in my life when I had been lonely, this was *definitely* not one of them. But it was like he never even heard me, because the next sentence out of his mouth was, "You know, I'm a really good lover."

Huh?

I'm amazed that even at fifty, some men still haven't figured out that if you tell a woman you're good in bed that translates as "I'm absolutely horrible in bed." This is not an occasion to toot your own horn.

I think Toffee sensed he'd made a misstep, because he promptly paid the check and we headed for our respective cars. He offered to follow me home. I admit that I can be naïve at times; I thought he was just being nice. I said yes. However, my cell phone rang once we got a few blocks away from the bar.

"I want to come up when we get to your place," Toffee said, his purr back in action. I squashed that idea in a heartbeat with a firm *no*. "C'mon, just think about it," he begged.

I hate it when men beg. Especially after telling me how good

## Steal This Life: Your Personal Date Book

**Convert an ordinary date book into an extraordinary record of your conquests and defeats. Take notes in your Date Book about who made the first move, what you wore, where you went, what you did, and if the earth moved. An honest self-critique of your dating style will help you improve your succulent social skills.**

they are in bed. Somehow, I thought that when men got older, they got wiser. Boys will be boys, I suppose, even beyond age fifty.

## Sex 101

When I'm out with friends, I have some kind of torrid sex radar. I enter a room and immediately I pick up on who's having great sex at home. In contrast, my married women friends can enter a room and within ten minutes tell you which guys have money. It must have something to do with survival in each of our chosen environments, I've decided. *Sex and Happiness, An Empirical Study* published in May 2000 confirmed my suspicions that the amount of activity in your bedroom rather than your bank account contributes more to your happiness. "See?" I tell them, "I'm focused on what really matters."

> ### Quickie Fact
>
> Of the 3,501 single men and women aged forty to sixty-nine years surveyed, 37 percent said they were having sex at least once a month. Hey, they're not getting older, they're getting laid. *Lifestyles, Dating & Romance, A Study of Midlife Singles* by AARP Magazine.

By the time most of us have left high school we've figured out that it's not rocket science but chemistry that counts. And we never skip the lab homework. Somewhere along the way the sex haze clears and we lose touch with our bodies and possibly everyone else's. Time for a refresher course on "Good to Great in Bed."

So, what's sexy now? Secrets will always be sexy. Having one, keeping one, or telling one, mystery wins out over the total reveal every time. So whether it's the tattoo on your hip bone or how you like to be kissed, always remember to save something

## Quickie Fact

Most Americans consider self-confidence one of the sexiest things about a person, ranking just below eyes as the most attractive feature. *2004 Global Sex Survey Report by Durex*

for later. Whispering your most intimate thoughts in someone's ear is bound to get a fire started.

**Take Time to Seduce Your Senses**

*Touch.* Slinky is sexy. Wear a belly chain underneath your clothes. Have a jewelry store size a custom chain to slip just below your waist. The feel of the cool metal against your skin will remind you of your sexiness all day along.

*More touch.* Self-sensual massage. Get out the oils, dim the lights, and explore what makes you feel good all over. Focus, go slowly, vary the pressure of your fingertips, and pay attention to what makes you tremble.

*Sight.* Scenes are sexy. The ones you play in your head. For sizzling inspiration check out one of these smoldering films:

*Bound*

*In the Cut*

*Love Jones*

*Body Heat*

*Nina Takes a Lover*

*Unfaithful*

*Bull Durham*

*9 ½ Weeks*

*The Thomas Crown Affair* (The original or the remake)

*White Palace*

*Smell.* Scent is central. The more sexually active you are, the greater the quantities of chemicals called pheromones, the "sex perfume," your body releases. Drive him crazy au natural or create an aphrodisiac experience using a collection of personal fragrance notes. Spray yourself and your pillows for delicious dreams. Make a scent all your own at The Body Shop stores.

*Taste.* Buy fine chocolate. Let it melt on your tongue. Then bite into it. Savor the burst of flavors in your mouth. Try this experience with ripe fruit, rich liqueurs, or your favorite dessert.

*Sound.* Tantric sex focuses on the breath. Try focusing on the sound of inhaling and exhaling of your breath. Then add the vibrating rhythms of a tantric CD. With practice, you'll experience mind-blowing orgasms, alone or with a partner.

### The Pleasure Principle

And finally and most importantly, believe in the Pleasure Principle. Make a commitment to do it till you're good at it. You'll achieve an intense amount of pleasure from participating in an activity at which you excel. And of course the more often you're doing it, the better you'll get at whatever it is.

## Singular Sensations

**#54** *Clothing exchange game.* Once a season have your friends bring over their unworn wardrobe items. Then pull out your favorite board game. Instead of awarding points, award chances to pull from the clothing pile to the winners. Don't forget to include some "free passes" for the unlucky players.

**#55** *Enjoy the finer things in life.* Every once in awhile elevate your taste level. Splurge on a great bottle of wine. Sample the caviar at a gourmet deli. Order the cheese plate at an upscale restaurant. Live the luxe life.

#56 *Be joy crazy not boy crazy.* Celebrate the people, places, and things that bring true pleasure to your life.

#57 *Progressive dinner.* Friendships near and dear provide the perfect excuse for a moveable feast. Plan a dinner party where each course is eaten at a different person's home. Appetizers at Alice's apartment, salads, main course, and dessert to follow at each of your pads. *Bon appetit!*

#58 *Personally yours.* You're special and you know it. Now you can show it by personalizing your T-shirts with your favorite sayings, monogramming your towels, and TiVoing your favorite television programs. Think about how else can you say "this is mine!"

#59 *Singular collectibles.* Become a collector of anything that catches your fancy: comic books, black dolls, or antique pins. Study the history of your chosen passion, so you're an informed buyer. The thrill of the hunt will fuel your self-expression.

#60 *Separate your work and personal lives.* At your next social engagement hand out personal calling cards. Revive the old-fashioned practice of exchanging a card with your hobbies and interests listed beside your personal contact information. Project manager by day becomes the renaissance woman or professional raconteur by night.

#61 *Are you lonely tonight?* Prepare a Personal Loneliness Emergency Kit for yourself. Include items guaranteed to change your mood such as a prepaid movie pass, the address of the nearest Build-a-Bear Workshop to make yourself a new best friend, a huge hunk of your favorite chocolate, a book you're dying to read, and the phone number of your favorite club diva. Open whenever necessary.

**#62** *Love your body.* Shower by candlelight. Use a gorgeously scented shower gel and a luxurious bath mitt. Play soft music while the light dances off your glistening body. Take time to scrub all your curves reflected by the soft glow. Go beyond your typical five-minute watering routine.

## The Last Word

**Being single is a choice. Your life is what you make it. Make it something terribly good. Invite envy.**

1. Don't let your routine run you. Break out and discover some new wonderful habits.

2. Over the hill is not the same as in the ground. Pick up the phone. Surf the Internet. Open a newspaper. Just get out there!

3. Try as you may, you won't always be able to avoid misbehaving John Doe. Recognize him for what he is and graciously move on.

4. Your sex life is yours to enjoy. You're not just getting older, you're getting better, too.

# Chapter Nine

# Managing Milestones Without Marriage

Time is a precious resource, isn't it? Do you treat it that way? Does time pass more quickly when you're single and slow its pace when you're married? Or does time that's measured in hours sometimes weigh in as heavy, silent moments when you're alone? I think one of the beauties of being single is that there are many instances in which time seems to stand still—moments when you're suspended within your own thoughts or you really can't think of a thing that needs doing, so you just...*sit*. And then there are situations where time zooms by much too fast, like the first kiss on the first date with the dude you met at the supermarket.

Although your family and friends, depending on their perspective, may see you as a spousal failure or irresponsible rogue, it's important to note that you're not lined up in anticipation, waiting for your turn at "real life." Just look at reality television; single life

> ## Singular Sensation #63
>
> *Potluck plates.* Visit your local pottery studio and create original dinnerware that doubles as an invitation to get together. Invite your friends to coffee with a mug inscribed with all the details or a dinner plate which invites them to bring their own plate to your house for a monthly feast. The personalized pottery will serve as a reminder of your next gathering.

is the real world. You're just as fierce a memory maker as your clockwatching couple counterparts. But for each of you, that inner tick-tock sounds a different alarm.

There's no surer sign of the changing times than birthday celebrations. Chances are, when you were young your family and friends gathered 'round to help you mark growing another year older. Now that you're in your thirties, forties, fifties, and single, how do you celebrate your birthday? One of the rites of adulthood is the passing of the torch on traditions. As a free agent you're left to create a cohesive thread through your life. Don't leave it to chance; become the memory chip for your life. You are now responsible for storing and creating the moments and memories that have special meaning for you.

Of course your very important, not-to-be missed moments may look different, but that doesn't make them any less treasured. Don't tell me you don't keep track of…

- when you reached our perfect weight goal
- the last time you had a date
- the best presentation you ever made on one hour's sleep
- when you bought your first brand new car
- when you savored your first kiss
- the cross-country road trip with your best college buddies

- when you got lucky at the semi-annual shoe sale at Nordstrom
- when you suffered the worst breakup ever
- when you lost your job—and the six months, two weeks, three days, seven hours and twenty-three minutes it took to find a new one
- the time you drank that way too expensive bottle of champagne way too quickly
- when you received a love letter
- the last time you had sex

Life happens one moment at a time. Hallelujah for all those big little moments!

If a tree falls in the forest and even one person is there to hear it, the tree makes a huge sound. So it is with your life. If you are there to witness your little laugh-out-loud comedies and tearjerker tragedies, they matter. How you spend your days becomes how you spent your life, and it's important not to let the years go by unnoticed. How will you choose to record the days of your life?

## Is Marriage a Mandatory Milestone?

Definitely not. Many of you have managed to accomplish other loftier achievements like attaining a graduate degree, meeting a non-profit's fundraising goal, becoming a single parent, or living overseas in a country whose name you can't pronounce, proving it's not necessary to cross the marriage hurdle to make something of one's self.

Todd certainly agrees with that assessment. He's traveled much and at forty has no plans to get married. At 6'3", he caught my eye at an upscale networking party because he looks so much like Marriage Guy—you know, the guy that every girl with the tick-tock in her ears is looking for. A full head of brown hair frames a pleasantly attractive face with deep hazel eyes. Todd's average build is clad in a perfectly acceptable muted color shirt and dark pants. There's nothing flashy about him, just a welcoming smile and an easy manner that immediately puts you at ease and starts your nesting radar humming.

"I sympathize with the women who have to deal with me. Because it's clearly about me not wanting to be married," Todd

## Steal This Life: Singular, Sensational Scrapbooking

The next time you're on a hot date, far-flung vacation, or out for dinner with friends, click away with the digital camera and grab mementos: bar matchbooks, napkins, business cards, color postcards, travel brochures, dinner menus. Then, instead of throwing your photos into a box to be forgotten, pull them out and create an album pièce de la resistance using your party favors, photos, and more creativity than you ever knew you had.

Don't play it safe! Add witty lines like "we come here way too often," or, "I'd like to make him breakfast in the morning," or, "look at Mr. Right Now!" or, "Hey, I was on the rebound," for a no-strings-attached record of your flirty fun adventures.

Blackmail, anyone?

candidly admits when I ask him if this issue has ever confronted him. "Turning forty was a milestone because it really made me start to think, 'Well do you have to get your life together and start to do something now or not?'" He's got a sexy job as an interior designer for upscale home electronics systems. His younger brother is married and has begun reproducing the family gene pool. Is Todd all grown up with no place to go but down the aisle?

Not hardly. He's not about to be pushed into someone else's direction. "You don't have to do anything you don't want to do because of society, because of whatever," he says throwing his hands in the air for emphasis. "You don't have to get married. You don't have to have a family." At his age most of his friends are holding a woman tight with one arm and a toddler with the other. Why is he really footloose, free, and forty?

Todd admits he's really very picky. "I'll be honest—I have a whole laundry list of qualities that I'm looking for in a person. They have to be smart—intelligent, common sense—attractive, they have to be secure on their own, you know, a sense of self, they have to be slightly outgoing, motivated, but not too flighty or a social butterfly, they have to be…" And he knows that list stands between him and the love of his life. At thirty they may have just been word play, but at forty the qualities he's looking for seem to be carved in granite.

So contrary to popular marriage myths, there may not be anything magical about any given milestone. Todd believes that "it's just all about when you as a person feel that being in a long-term relationship is more important than the luxuries of being single."

## The Single Best Attitude

At any given age, it's all about what's right for you then. So when and if you're ready to share the sheets permanently with someone, you'll make that bridal registry. If it's at thirty then it's at thirty. If it's at fifty, then it's at fifty. And if it's not on your list, you don't have to pencil it in. Last time I checked there were still plenty of mountains you could climb, medical cures only you can discover, and you're late for your date with world peace. So break all the hooking up rules and establish your own measuring stick for your life.

### Creating a Circle of Life

"I think about all the things I've been free to do as a single," asserts Kathryn, a never-married, fifty-two-year-old former Madison Avenue ad agency founder cum international marketing specialist cum consulting strategist to *Essence* magazine and now a nonfiction writer. She's definitely living her single life large and in charge.

Even though she grew up in a wonderfully loving two-parent family and displayed Type A achiever traits in almost every endeavor, Kathryn doesn't take marital success for granted. "I feel so comfortable being single that often I think, how do you really make a marriage work?" she asks in all seriousness. "How do two people really grow and stay together, not grow apart but still fulfill their own interests and individuality? So it's puzzling. Marriage is probably a really nice thing, but I just haven't figured it out yet."

I definitely understand what she's talking about. How many times have you thought to yourself about other people's relationships, "I wonder how they do it?" And then quickly refocused on the abundance of your solo lifestyle. Kathryn has chosen to focus her energies on enriching her life as a single parent. Her parents joyously cultivated a tradition of family celebrations, from Sunday dinners with extended family members to Thanksgivings in Philadelphia with her mother's family to piling in the car to drive around and see the Christmas lights in Manhattan to the annual arrival of orange- and grapefruit-filled crates from her Bahamian grandfather in Florida. Kathryn hadn't figured out how she would replicate the experience of "family" for her daughter, she just knew that was her priority.

Kathryn's inspiration came one day when she came across an article about celebrating the holidays as a single parent; she read the article in one of the 79-cent family lifestyle magazines as she waited in a grocery store checkout line. She learned that the important thing is to reconcile your reality with all those ad images of happy families at Christmastime.

You, too, should reexamine your family traditions as an inspiration for creating moments of celebration in your life. You've got to establish traditions that make sense for you as a single person. Putting your personal stamp on the holidays will bring anticipatory joy rather than feed the "woe-is-single-me" blues.

So Kathryn and her daughter started a tradition of baking edible holiday creations. They beautifully wrapped them in cellophane, presented them as gifts to friends and family, and offered them as treats at their annual holiday party. "We would decorate the home

## Note to Self

Mark a special occasion by celebrating with a few of your friends. It could be as simple as getting together for drinks on the first Friday of every month. Or note the anniversary of the beginning of your friendship. The important thing is to make it a consistent timeout for tradition in your lives. Try it and you'll all feel very special because you're acting like you are.

## Steal This Life:
## Fine, Fabulous, and Forty

**"You're invited to attend Paula's Fine, Fabulous, and Forty Birthday Party,"** the invitation read. Paula, who had never married, threw all that wedding reception energy and cash into throwing herself a beachside bash for her milestone birthday. She hosted a catered reception at a private club complete with a live jazz band. It was a once-in-a-lifetime event.

Don't wait 'til you're tying the knot to celebrate your marvelous self. Flaunt your party planning skills and host a night to remember for family and friends. They'll toast you and shower you with incredible gifts all the same. So choose to celebrate you!

with all different kinds of Christmas tins. Rum balls would be in one, ginger snaps in another, and cutout cookies in another," Kathryn recalls, painting a warm picture of the twosome's holiday spirit. "So part of the joy would be the people finding themselves at a certain spot in the party and then they'd open a tin and just be delighted."

At your next holiday party, create your own consumable Christmas treasure hunt. Decorate colorful holiday tins, scatter them throughout your home, and label each one "Eat me!" or " Open now!" à la an *Alice in Wonderland* adventure.

Kathryn reminds me of how the richness of tradition adds to our experiences, even the solo ones. "My choice has been to live life to the fullest. I have an enormous amount of love even if I'm not in a committed relationship. My friends get my love. My space gets my love. I get my love."

You can make memories throughout the year. All it takes is the wish to share your love with those around you and the desire to re-imagine the warm gatherings of your youth.

## You'll Scream for This Creamy Cocktail

"It's something I've known all my life—my father and my mother met in 1943 and he was shaking those cocktails. My father shaking the Brandy Alexanders is part of the rhythm of my life," Kathryn says, reminiscing as she pours the chilled creamy beverage into my waiting glass.

So of course when Kathryn was old enough to throw parties that involved alcohol, Brandy Alexanders were an intrinsic component. The drink became The Famous Charles Leary Brandy Alexander when she realized how many friends planning to attend her parties would ask, "Is your father going to be making Brandy Alexanders?" Her dad was one cool cat!

## The Single Best Attitude

Don't lose track of your life. Create traditions that honor and support you in creating a home of your own. Personal rituals connect you to family and friends in a meaningful way. Rejoice in your personal sense of family. For example, bond with the people you love at your annual spring open house. Making an entire Thanksgiving dinner yourself might not make sense. But sharing the joy of cooking with others fills your home with the scents and sounds of the holiday just like when you were young.

## Note to Self

Remember you. Leave behind something that says you were here. Plant a tree. Tutor a child. Have a plaque inscribed in your name for a community fund. Don't let your life end without a trace.

### The Famous Charles Leary Brandy Alexander

1 part crème de cocoa (sometimes hard to find, but generally available in liquor stores; choose the dark version rather than the clear one)

1 part brandy

1 part heavy cream (you can use Carnation canned milk, but I prefer organic heavy whipping cream or half & half)

A hearty scoop of Haagen-Dazs Vanilla Ice Cream (add to taste; the more the creamier!)

Shake heartily with ice, strain, and serve (the secret to the creaminess is in the shake).

All parts are equal parts. Enjoy!

## *The Last Dance with My Father*

I was recently reunited with a popular college classmate, the forever-cute-as-a-cheerleader Sasha. She still has her mega-watt smile and bright brown eyes, which mask her true age of forty-seven. She proudly admits being a daddy's girl and was devastated by his loss several years ago. Her ongoing close relationship with her mother and network of close friends supported her during his long illness and death. Sasha found out there's no need to walk this road alone. You can let your friends share the burden. When the going get tough, you'll be grateful for all the attention and tender loving care.

While Sasha worried about her parents, they worried about leaving their only daughter alone and without a partner. Her mother said to her in a quiet moment, "I really hope before I close my eyes you'll have somebody to be in your life." At the time Sasha's mother was facing living alone for the first time in her life, having gone straight from her parents' home into a married home of her own.

Sasha tries to calm her mother's fears by discussing the family of friends she has chosen to be her support network, among them a close friend who talked her through the scary bits during the wee hours of the night. "She'd call just to say, 'Hello, how's it going?' but I knew what she really was asking is 'Do you need a shoulder to cry on?'" Sasha says, remembering their heartfelt conversations. "It was if I was the front guard for the battle yet to come for her as well." At one point her refrigerator was stacked high with casseroles and precooked meals from well-meaning church members and close friends.

She counts herself lucky to have people who cared about her enough to keep her connected to her own life. Her friends got her

## Fantastic Fun at Fifty

Celebrate reaching the big 5-0 by joining The Red Hat Society, a group of over three hundred thousand women worldwide who get together in local chapters to demonstrate that fun begins at fifty. Celebrate the marvelous milestone by joining in mischievous mayhem! And yes, you really do have to wear red and purple—*together*—when you come out and play with these ladies! Get the scoop in *The Red Hat Society's Laugh Lines: Stories of Inspiration and Hatitude* by Sue Ellen Cooper or by visiting www.redhatsociety.com.

*managing milestones without marriage*

## The *Single* Best *Attitude*

One of the most uncounted advantages of single life is the wealth of friendships and intimate relationships you possess. You are not limited to having your needs met by one single person. Society does not predetermine to whom you should turn to for solace or seek out in celebration. You are free to choose the individual you feel most in sync with at that moment. You've been there for them and now they want to return the favor. Don't waste the riches at your doorstep. Especially in times of trouble you would do well to remember you have friends just waiting for you to call their names. Don't be too proud to beg for their help. Shout!

involved in acting at a local playhouse and singing in the church choir. "I'm lucky. I didn't lose my life," she realizes. Sasha's story reminds us that there can be more than one important relationship in our lives. Make it your goal to replicate the constant connection between the group of friends portrayed on popular television shows such as *Friends* or its black counterpart, *Living Single*.

Now that Sasha and her mom are both single women, they often travel to exotic places together. "It's so much fun taking her to these off-the-wall places. My mom's eyes sparkle like diamonds," Sasha giggles. You can delight in seeing the world through someone else's eyes besides your own.

In your forties, it's wonderful if your parents are still alive to share your life but your own life is filled with commitments and responsibilities. The media has a nickname for adults who have families of their own yet are also responsible for the care of their aging parents as well; the Sandwich Generation. With a wry smile, Sasha refers to herself as a member of the "open-faced sandwich generation." And she explains that it's been difficult to balance her devotion to her parents' long-term care and her own personal needs. She wouldn't trade this dilemma for the world, and feels lucky to have had a social network to help lighten the burden.

And yet, she believes the real reason she's not married is because she's chosen to spend the last few years with her parents. "So if there's one regret that I have about not getting married it's the dance with my dad," she says as her fingers idly trace a pattern on the tablecloth and her slender braids slide forward to brush her cheeks.

As I listen to Sasha's life story, I realize she may have dreamed of marriage but she never took a step towards accomplishing the goal. "[Marriage] was something I thought I wanted, but looking back I guess I have to say it wasn't a priority. Gee—that's not very comfortable," she says with a self-conscious laugh.

"But I don't think it's an immutable choice," she says with a wink of an eye. "I mean, I can change that at any time." Yes, that's the power of choice; if you change your mind you can always make a change in your life. Being aware of your singleness as a choice means you can alter the course of your life if you choose. Singleness is not necessarily permanent and never fatal. The power is in your hands.

### Home Blessing Ritual

Moving into a new home or decluttering or remodeling your current living space not only represents a physical change, it also is a reflection of our inner selves.

## Note to Self

Once a month call a friend you haven't spoken to in forever. Connect and catch up on each other's lives. As one of my friends reminded me at a recent meeting, "Life is too short and we're all dead too long." Make the call—it'll revitalize your friendship and your life.

## Steal This Life: Blessed to Excess!

**Single people go through life's ordinary and extraordinary ups and downs like married people; they just often do it without others to share their experiences. But it's important to take time to recognize the joys and mourn the losses inherent in our every day lives.**

Whenever I move into a new home or office or leave a job or begin a new endeavor, I christen the space with the personal best wishes of friends and family. Hey, if the launching of the *Queen Mary 2* deserves breaking open the champagne, why not that new deck you built last summer or the new home office you just organized? Your friends and family will love any excuse to help you celebrate your new addition!

Cultures across the world have various traditions regarding living space. For instance, in the Chinese feng shui tradition, the connection to one's home is held on an emotional level. Feng shui practitioners view everything in life as interactive and strive for the balance characterized by the yin yang symbol. Thus, placement has extreme importance—from how the living space is situated in the landscape to how things in the interior are placed. Now, onto your ritual:

### What It Is:

The blessing of your home has five steps.

The first step is GREETING your new, remodeled, or decluttered living space. The second is the NAMING of your space; finding a name that honors the essence of your home. Third is

INTUITIVE; imagining or sensing what type of energy your home has held prior to your living there and what it symbolizes for you. Fourth, and sometimes most important, CLEARING of the space with the use of some of tools listed below. And lastly, bring your own INTENTION to the space: let it know what you plan to do there, i.e., entertain friends, create a personal sanctuary, start a business, etc.

## What You'll Need and What You'll Do:

• Candles and incense; choose your favorite colors, sizes, and scents
• Bells or tingshas (Middle Eastern meditation bells used for clearing blocked energy)
• Bowl of salt water to clear negative energy
• Charm of some sort to decorate your new home (examples: crystal, chime, or window ornament)

Begin by greeting and naming your space. Once inside, walk around the structure and listen to how the space speaks to you. Does it fill you with joy? Inspire new beginnings? Resonate with a sense of anticipation or contentment? Some of you may feel comfortably shouting out loud, "I'm going to write my first book in this den," or whispering, "This will be my place of peace."

To begin space clearing, place the bowl of salt water in a central place and direct all energies that need to shift or be cleared to transmute into the bowl. It is important to clean your space from top to bottom before beginning the rest of the ritual.

Create an altar space by clearing the desired surface and spreading a beautiful cloth across it. Altars can live anywhere, and they don't have to occupy a lot of space. Select a location that calls to your spirit and make that the altar's *permanent* location. Add items that hold special meaning for you, like seashells from your favorite beach, coins to bring prosperity, or photographs of loved ones or desired spaces. Add candles and light them.

Light the incense and walk around every area of the house with it. Follow this by walking around again and clapping your hands or ringing the bells or tingshas. The happy sounds will wake up the good energy. Once you feel that your space is cleared—and you *will* feel it—much like when you greeted you space, face your altar and proclaim your intentions. Offer a token or charm to the altar to represent your gratitude.

### New Year's Eve: Blindly Following Tradition

"New Year's Eve never lives up to its top billing, especially if you're single," Miller warns me as he prepares dinner for us in his new loft kitchen.

I'm sipping a glass of Chardonnay and lounging at the dining room table, contemplating plans for welcoming another year. I know Miller's right. A) Trying to find the sexy and sophisticated dress that makes you look drop-dead gorgeous, B) securing the invitation to the more-fun-than-you-ever-thought-possible end of the year party, and C) scoring a great kiss at midnight, is damn near impossible. But it did happen to me once...and a chance reconnect with my friend Jackie gives me hope that maybe lightening can strike twice in the same life.

A week ago, the telephone rang and I picked it up to hear Jackie's lilting British accent announcing, "I love my girlfriends to death, but I'm not spending another boring New Year's Eve with girlfriends. I want to be around some guys!" So this year, we've vowed to find the ultimate singles party and hang out till dawn. Miller pooh-poohs our plans as his skillet starts to sizzle and the mouth-watering aroma of Asian spices wafts into the air. I refill my glass and consider the options.

New Year's Eve is one holiday that always seems to over-promise and under-deliver. It usually leaves me feeling frustrated, because shouldn't singles be taking over the streets? Shouldn't we own this celebration of the last sanctioned barhopping, let-it-all-hang-out night of the year?

Take matters into your own hands. Plan ahead and book a private party for close friends at a local hotspot, a girlfriend get-away at a luxurious spa, or a quiet evening of reflection at home. Don't wait till the last minute and then bemoan your lack of evening entertainment. You could pull out the stops and make this your own special night to celebrate with a chosen few year after year.

"So, how did you spend your best New Year's?" I ask Miller, now curious. He's quite the foodie, and has eaten at the best restaurants on both coasts. I'm sure he has an entertaining tale of final day frivolity. "The best time I had on New Year's Eve was a blind date," he responds, rather matter-of-factly. He had planned to spend the evening sitting home alone, but a friend called up and asked him to escort a young lady for the evening. Miller said, "Why not? Nothing ventured, nothing gained."

That blind date turned out to be the brass ring at end of the year. The woman was beautiful, intelligent, and witty. The two couples attended parties, danced their way into the early morning hours, and capped off the evening with a visit to a late-night pancake house for breakfast. Miller and his date shared an appropriately discreet kiss at midnight, and wound up dating for several months after their propitious encounter.

## The Single Best Attitude

Are you a member of the "same old, same old" club? Trying to defy the definition of insanity: doing the same thing and expecting a different result. Put your imagination to work and go for an "I never would have thought of doing that" experience. You could bring a picnic lunch to work instead of eating in the company cafeteria. Attend an opera in a language you don't speak (it's not too scary, they have subtitles). Make your vacation a working vacation and lend a hand to a non-profit in an exotic locale instead of lying on the beach. The point is to change your response to an ordinary life question like "what's for lunch?" to achieve a stand up and cheer result.

## Birthday Breakthrough

Julius, a forty-year-old corporate human relations executive, celebrates each annual reminder of the beginning of his life by taking a self-inventory. "It's the time to really invest in yourself," he says. This exercise from Julius is really about making a plan to fully realize your potential. There might be certain countries you want to visit, or certain cultures you want to learn more about. The opportunities are always there, but until you make a plan to take advantage of those opportunities, they'll remain untapped.

Julius offers his sister as an example. She's always wanted to live overseas in Spain. On her birthday, she and Julius sat down and discussed how she could make that happen. During the planning process she remembered she had a friend looking for someone to be a caretaker for her house in Spain for year. She formulated a plan and was able put the pieces together for a workable overseas sojourn.

Oftentimes, Julius says, the opportunities are there all along, but defining a personal goal puts them in context and gives them meaning. "The whole point is to document, memorialize, and write this stuff down!" he stresses. It doesn't have to take all day; you can still blow out the candles and cut the cake. Just set aside some quiet time to reflect on where you're going in life. On your special day, take the time to ask yourself (and be sure to write the answers down!):

- What kind of person do I want to be?
- How do I want to live?
- What makes me happy?
- What do I want my life to look like five years from now?
- What's the one thing I would do if I knew success was the only outcome?

Julius's final words of encouragement are the icing on the cake. "Things happen because you make a plan. It's really about being the best person you can be as *you* define it."

## Note to Self

Freshness counts for things other than bread and cereal. Don't wait until the new year begins. Where can you make a fresh start in your life today? Clear the air with a colleague, bite the bullet on a failed plan, or throw out a clothing size you no longer wear. Admit it. Your life could use a little freshening up now and again.

**It's Your Birthday! It's Your Birthday!**

Pretend it's your birthday. What do you want to do with the rest of your life? Write it down and live it!

_____

_____

_____

_____

_____

_____

_____

_____

_____

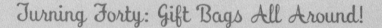

### Turning Forty: Gift Bags All Around!

When my friend Tish celebrated her fortieth birthday in Las Vegas, each party guest received a gorgeous silk brocade handbag filled with "the day after the night before" goodies: a little book for numbers, single use facial scrub, embroidered Do Not Disturb satiny eye mask, ear plugs, Alka-Seltzer morning relief tablets, vitamin tangerine drink powder, scented "wash away your sins" towelette, four vials of lubricant eye drops, and a slammin' party CD with her own version of Viva Las Vegas inspiration.

sweet snacks for middle of the night hunger pains. Stash in a closet or corner 'til guests arrive.

#74 *Away for the weekend.* Skip the end of the year madness or plan a weekend away anytime of the year. Get a map and draw a two-hour drive-time radius and a two-hour air-time radius. Pack a bag and visit a not-so-far away spa, interesting neighboring city, shopping destination, or beautiful beach. Welcome the year ahead with a weekend away.

#75 *Become a calendar girl.* Create a special calendar for the new year with photographs of your past thrilling experiences and worthwhile achievements. Your terrific girl-of-the-month pictures will inspire you throughout the coming year.

#76 *Rockin' Rolodex Party.* Need to restart your career, find a great gardener, or get an introduction to the president of your local chamber of commerce? Host an information exchange. You provide the munchies, friends bring their PDAs, old school business card files, and personal address books. Trade cards and contacts to improve your lives.

## The Last Word

**Being single is a choice. Track your nontraditional choices. Remember to make memories memorable. Record the everyday and extraordinary events of your life.**

1. Marriage is not a mandatory milestone. You still have more than enough to celebrate.

2. Celebrate your life. Let your singleness inspire your sense of tradition. Honor your sense of family.

3. Life's a bumpy road. Reach out to your friends for support.

4. Rethink annual anniversaries. Experiment. Explore. Enrich your celebrations.

# STEP FOUR
## Embrace
## the "L" Word

**Be the Love of Your Life**

# Chapter Ten

# Hooking Up and Hanging Out:
## The State of the Date

Date: the four-letter word singles and some married folks as well dismiss with a roll of the eyes. Many of us haven't experienced a date in a while. In California, the state with the highest singles population, a survey commissioned by *San Francisco* magazine found that singles in the potentially date-rich San Francisco Bay Area had fewer than five dates in the previous year. In fact, more East Coasters said they were out having fun at least three nights a week than any other region in the country according to the Yahoo! Personals National Singles Week Survey in September 2003. The chances of being asked out on a dream date seem about the same as any televised matchmaking ending in true love.

Maybe the problem is that no matter who the participants are, they've forgotten what they should be doing. Webster's dictionary simply defines a date as "a social appointment." The

> ## Singular Sensation #77
>
> *Prioritize your personal life.* Don't leave filling your social calendar to the last minute. Seek out opportunities to meet new people and be open to spending time with new faces. People who like people get lucky more often.

authors of the infamous dating advice book *The Rules* stated that the man must make the appointment no later than Wednesday for the privilege of seeing you during the weekend. In our time compressed lives, good luck on *that* coming to pass.

Dating is the new horror story. It seems as though now no one knows how to behave as dating disaster stories proliferate on the Internet. Dating assist companies are springing up everywhere offering advice on ways to meet, people to meet, places to meet, and 24/7 meeting time. There's plenty of evidence around us of new kinds of hooking up: reality show dating, speed dating, group dating, dating in the dark, online dating, celebrity blind dating, video dating. There is an abundance of dating sites, dating coaches, dating self-help books, dating shows, and the recent phenomenon, the "dating wingman" to help navigate the scene.

We're suffering from mating paralysis. Everything's up for discussion: with whom, who asks and how, who pays? "That wasn't a date, you were just hanging out," my female friends say, arguing the technicalities. "He has to pick up the phone, ask you out, and pay." Other women I've met at singles events are not so specific. Said one woman, "A date. That's where a guy picks you up...or you can pick him up and you go somewhere, right?"

It's all part of the growing D-Day Dilemma: what can you do to nurture your dating life?

## Date to Be Determined

Irene is a sassy forty-four-year-old human resources professional who's very committed to having an active social life this year. "I've got a profile on Match, Yahoo!, eHarmony, and J-date," says, ticking them off on her fingers as she rattles off her list of date-seeking sites. I'm amazed. I ask how she keeps up with them all. She admits that it's very difficult. "You're into it when you're into it and then you're not. I go on a rage. You do it for a few days, and then you stop cause it's exhausting." She stops talking and catches her breath. "It's a numbers game, like sales. How many no's do you have to go through before you get a yes?"

Sounds like a lot of work to me to acquire companionship for an evening. "So what's a date?" I ask, curious about her standards. "A date is when some guy comes to your house dressed nicely and picks you up and takes you out and you go out for dinner," Irene explains in no-nonsense manner. Like Irene, you should set personal standards for being in your company. You're not obligated to

### The Single Best Attitude

You're dressed to impress and he shows up in a dirty T-shirt and torn jeans. What's up with that? Mixed communication. Yes, you want to enjoy his company but he needs to respect you. Don't be embarrassed to state what your expectations are up front. It's perfectly okay for you to have social standards for behavior, which resonate with your professional behavior at the office. Your best friend wouldn't expect her boss to wait patiently for her at a business luncheon when she arrives well into the first course. Why should you? You are not some bedraggled maiden who should be grateful anyone wants to be with her. You're the most fabulous you! It's your responsibility to clearly state what you expect in return for the pleasure of your company. After all, they can't read your minds. After that it's on them. Because as the saying goes, "I can do bad all by myself."

## Note to Self

Raise the bar. It's perfectly okay for you to tell someone, "We're meeting for lunch at 1 p.m. and I don't expect you to be late." Or the more gentle, "If you're late, I'll expect a call." If they aren't on time, then you leave. You're not required to accept the bad behavior of others.

hang out with him at his house to enjoy TV dinners and a Blockbuster video.

Even with guidelines there's still the opportunity for failure, Irene admits as she tells me about her last encounter. "Last night somebody showed up in blue jeans and he took me out for BBQ—it was really good BBQ—but you walk in, you order, it's all over your mouth. It was not a cool date."

And she's got strict rules when it comes to who pays. "Man always pays," Irene says without hesitation. "That's a new attitude for me. It wasn't like that all through my twenties and thirties, because I always thought you needed to prove something to them," she confides in me. "The truth of the matter is I'm a woman and I want a *man*," she raises her voice for emphasis.

And if a guy doesn't want to pay for the first date, Irene's not shy about kicking him to the curb. "I'm not in this to show that I can make as much money as you. We're women and we want to be taken care of."

### Hope Is Not a Strategy

"Hope is not a strategy," Tish strongly advises to her girlfriends who don't date. I couldn't agree more. If you want it to happen, you can't sit home alone whining. You've got to get on the field of play and throw some curve balls, girls!

"Cynthia's tried Table for Six and eHarmony, so I don't think Match is far behind. I know she's gone on there and searched," Tish says, tracking her friends' dating progress. "Celeste's out there looking, too. She just hasn't crossed over yet," she adds, referring to her girlfriend's inability to take the plunge and become a member of Match.com, Tish's current favorite dating assist program. "I don't get all the voyeurism." Are you sitting on the bench? Tish has plenty to say on the subject of how you can get in the game.

For starters, you could aim for forty-year-old Tish's Olympian social calendar. Just this week alone she's managed to fit in a business trip to Minnesota and meet three online suitors for drinks. We're sipping wine at a chic San Francisco bar. We move from a couch by the window to bar seats, where we have a better view of everyone…and everyone has a better view of us. Tish believes in being seen on the scene—always. Follow her strategy and you'll have the guys' eyes following you as you move around the room. Checking out the restaurant decor or going to the ladies' room provides an opportunity to meet and greet your fellow patrons.

She'll admit to dating Match men about twice a month,

## Quickie Fact

Who's on the playing field? According to the Current Population Survey on Marital Status released by the U.S. Census for 2003, the total number of single men is slightly higher than women between the ages of twenty-five and forty-four, the years most actively recruited by singles events. So despite the myths, there are enough good men out there!

## Note to Self

Tish's Biggest Tip: "Your first Match meeting is not a date. You're getting together to see if you want to have a first date." Take the pressure off. Realize it's a meet, not a lifelong match. You're not locked into anything. Breathe deeply and proceed to have fun.

## The Single Best Attitude

Have fun. Have Fun. And in case you missed it, Have FUN! The point is not to drive yourself crazy over who likes you and who doesn't. You're not in high school any more. Talk, meet, enjoy. Talk, meet, enjoy. Repeat as necessary. If it's not working with a particular person, don't beat yourself up. Move on to the next available and willing partner. There doesn't have to be a point to all of this. You can just enjoy what you're doing and being with one another for a few hours. You're single. You've chosen to be single. You enjoy your single life immensely. So loosen up and enjoy the man of the moment!

although that seems like a very low estimate by my count. She scores "Thursday night guy" relatively high. "I hugged him and felt his lats." She smiles, "Mmmm. I could have just seen him naked." Earlier this evening she met another young man but couldn't really tell if he was into her. And then there's "tomorrow guy," whom she's meeting at a sports bar to talk while they watch the last football playoff of the season game.

"Who winked at who first?" I ask, referring to Match's cute way of flirting with an emoticon when you see a profile that you like. "He winked at me," Tish says coyly. "Generally I'm not the instigator. Once in a while I'll go out and 'hunt,' but mostly I just respond to people." This is not a hard and fast rule. If you're comfortable making the first move, go right ahead.

No worries—Tish's click-thru rate on Match is a thing to be envied. She receives four to five emails a day from potential suitors and five winks on an average Match.com day. The more you log onto the site, the higher your profile on Match, and the better chances of being seen by surfing members of the opposite sex. It can be difficult keeping track of it all—I recommend taking notes on the guy's profile names, what the two of you talked about on the first call, and rating "Nah!" or "Yeah!"

A Match.com member since 2001, Tish has scored a couple of long-term relationships and figures that about 30 percent of her first dates lead to a second date. Caution: results will vary depending on your level of interest.

## Steal This Life: Advice from the Match Maven

**I asked Tish for her best bits on taking the byte out of the online dating scene. Read 'em and leap into love online:**

1. **The Picture.** You *have* to have a picture. Tish has three or four posted in her profile. "When I look at someone, if they have a few pictures I get a better feel for who they are—especially if I see them in pictures with their friends, their family, their pets." And please no, "model boy" headshots. "How do I know you didn't scan that in from a magazine? They're *never* going to look like that picture." Especially if it's not really them.

2. **The Screen Name.** Hers is "Badkitty." Okay, no snickering; it all started with a T-shirt. Tish says, "It's more important to have an intriguing name than an explicit one."

3. **The Money Box.** Tish doesn't indicate a salary range. "I don't talk about what I make with anybody. Why would I publish it online? I talk about it with my boss and my HR person." Enough said.

4. **Red Flags.** These clues are clear indicators of someone who is not worthy of your attention:

a. You're a guy in his forties and you've checked "never been in a relationship."

b. You list only one racial preference and it's not your own.

c. You're a woman in your late thirties and you've indicated you "definitely want children." Yes, I know it's rude, ladies, but guys don't want to be rushed.

d. All-time downer: someone whose profile reads, "I want someone who doesn't play games." Tish's response: "What the hell happened to you? If that's the best thing you can say..."

5. **What are you looking for?** "At the end of the day I'm not asking for anything less than I am. I'm not saying 'I have a college degree, but I won't date anyone unless they have a PhD. I make X but I won't date anybody that makes less than 2X.'" Tish is honest with herself and looks for a certain level of compatibility based on shared values and common interests.

## A Single Gal Has a Ball!

Once upon time, in a city across the bay, there was a single girl who was very pretty, worked very hard, and had very wonderful married friends. Every two years a very special party was held to benefit the San Francisco Symphony—the Black & White Ball. The single girl's female friends and their spouses, along with more than eleven thousand people, came from near and far to celebrate.

The single girl dreamed of partying in the outrageous, moving music festival on the arm of a tall, dark, and handsome gent in an Armani tuxedo.

On the afternoon of the big night, the phone rang. The single girl listened as Michael, her friend and fairy godfather said, "Jerusha, get dressed. You're going to the Black & White Ball tonight. I'll give you a camera and drop you off at the event." And just like that, the single girl, also known as me, Jerusha, found herself going to a ball! But alas, I had hundreds of outfits and piles of shoes, but no date. What was a girl to do?

> ## Singular Sensation #78
>
> *Party perfect fashion.* When you spot that to-die-for timeless dress on the rack at your favorite boutique—grab it! You'll save time and have no regrets when you receive that hip and haute invitation from your boss, best friend, or soon-to-be boyfriend. Be prepared!

Go solo! Undaunted, I dressed in my finest black and white attire: silk ruffled white shirt; black crushed velvet riding jacket; and black velvet trousers, accessorized by a pair of brand new white sneakers. As I headed out the door I grabbed my black velvet top hat festooned with a large white ostrich feather. At the bottom of my porch steps, a pumpkin-turned-sporty-Lexus waited for me. I jumped in beside Michael, who was playing chauffeur, and off we went.

I'll admit I was pretty nervous about going alone to a big black tie event in fashionably coupled San Francisco, but I couldn't find a last-minute hunk to dress to excess for the party of the year. I soon found out my dateless state didn't matter—loud cheers and flashing camera bulbs in praise of my outfit greeted me. I was beginning to feel like the belle of the ball.

The ball was held at twelve different city venues, where attendees feasted on hors d'oeuvres and chocolates, sipped glass after glass of wine, and danced to live swing, jazz, salsa, and rock 'n' roll. Boy/girl, girl/girl, boy/boy, anything went—I even met a young woman accompanied by her dog in a dashing black doggie formal!

I drifted through the layers of black sequins, white satin, and black tuxedos, only to discover many other unattached attendees in slinky gowns and black ties. I spotted a posse on an upscale boys' night out, a gang of girls with free tickets from the office, and a pair of forty-something dancing divas, Laura and Lori. "We're the only two mature, straight, black and white women from San Francisco. We're looking for Mr. Right here."

When I escaped to a quiet corner to recharge my batteries, I met a couple of brave singles that used the opportunity to meet for a blind date. They were working out ball logistics when I asked who fixed them up. The giddy gal replied, "My mortgage agent actually. No interest!"

At the top of the rotunda's breathtaking marble staircase, the San Francisco Symphony filled the spectacular dome's interior with stirring music and pageantry. The hall had been transformed into a great ballroom reminiscent of the court palace of Louis XIV. As I wove my way through pairs of waltzing couples, my eyes met those of a handsome stranger across the room. We moved toward each other, then without a word he took my hand. His arm encircled my waist and we moved in time to the music. I felt as if everyone else was moving in slow motion as we whirled around the dance floor. I'd come alone, and like Cinderella I'd found my Prince Charming—even if only for one night.

At midnight my cell phone alarm rang. My prince and I danced a parting waltz, then I raced back to BART, the Bay Area's rapid rail system, to make the last train at 12:20 a.m. All the way home I smiled as I relived my dreamlike party of one.

Oh yeah, about that prince—of course I got his number!

## Steal This Life: Black Tie Is Back

**Remember how much fun it was preparing for your high school prom? The fun of scouring the mall for the perfect dress and matching shoes? Ever notice how the tickets to those formal parties are sold individually? There's bound to be a handsome devil or two on his own hoping for the chance to dance with a beautiful woman.**

Conjure the magic by dressing like a red carpet starlet for one special night. Make a date for your town's society ball. Contact the event organizers to get a feel for the mix of the crowd, flow of the entertainment, and required dress. Then cajole your best friends into becoming a band of dateless divas hell-bent on an evening of all-out fantastic fun!

### *Options Are Meant to Be Kept Open*

Kate, thirty-three, a high-powered, Jennifer Aniston look-alike, keeps an open mind and an open heart as she moves forward in her stimulating solo experience. Follow in her footsteps and you will discover that while the door to marriage may be closed, there are many other doors which open up in your life.

Kate is the perfect example of a social butterfly as she floats

*hooking up and hanging out*

> ## The Single Best Attitude
>
> Think single and mingle. Open yourself up to meeting others. Smile, wave, and laugh with those around you. Don't let you arms hang limp at your sides. Talk with your hands with your palm raised upwards in a gesture of acceptance. When you're out in public, your body language speaks volumes before the other person actually hears your words.

from one opportunity to the next. She was a Los Angeles-based music industry executive before she networked her way into a career as a marketing guru for a boutique firm in San Francisco. She approaches her life as a single the same way she approached her career change.

"When you put yourself into a mindset that you're going to go out and meet people—and I really *do* believe it's a mindset—you're going to go out and meet people in general. And sometimes it's women and you end up being really good friends, and sometimes it's men," Kate explains. "I can look back from where I was a year ago and I have so many funny stories and great new friends. It's all a ripple of allowing yourself to be open to meeting people."

One such incident happened as Kate prepared to temporarily leave San Francisco. As she moved boxes out of her apartment, she encountered an attractive man who introduced himself. It turned out that he lived on the first floor.

There were maybe five units in the building. She'd lived there for two years and had never seen him before. Kate said to herself, "Just my luck I would meet this cute guy just as I was leaving the city!" They chatted and exchanged business cards.

There was no further contact. Then, when she moved back to San Francisco months later, Kate found the guy's business card as she rummaged through some boxes. She emailed him; he emailed back. The rest is the plot of a twisted romance novel. The duo dated briefly, then became great friends.

Undaunted, Kate feels sometimes you meet Mr. Right Now, and sometimes you make a friend for life. The important thing is to be out there, mingling at life's great party.

"In the last year I've definitely exercised my rights as a single. Definitely dated in all its various forms. I've been set up. Gone out and cruised and met people…all sorts of flirting and…the occasional one-night stand," she says, laughing.

Kate's actually surprised to still be single at thirty-three. As a young woman she was a "serial monogamist"; always in a relationship. "High school, college, even post-college, it's been boyfriend, boyfriend, boyfriend!" she states, bouncing the edge of one hand off the palm of the other for emphasis. And now she finds San Francisco itself is stiff competition for those seeking a long-term commitment, she says.

"People here are so busy and do so many things, myself included!" Kate moans, rolling her eyes. "There's Tahoe, there's this happy hour, there's this book club, there's museums, there's

## Note to Self

Get lost. Get in your car or on your bike and travel down roads you'd normally pass on by. You never know who'll you'll meet or what you'll find on your unplanned adventure.

## Singular Sensation #79

*The Best-Ever Girls Night In.* Host a different home sales production demonstration party each month at a different friend's house. They're fun and teach you something new; discover state-of-the-art items and potential money earning opportunities. Make sure to talk to presenters about their "low-pressure" sales approach. You want your guests to leave happy, not feeling their wallets were drained.

dance clubs—so much stuff going on and so many people here in their twenties and thirties that it's like sensory overload. People are always...wondering what the next cool thing is whizzing by!"

Hmm. Are we in danger of attention deficit disorder becoming the new cause for a lack of commitment? Maybe, but Kate has no plans herself to slow down. She's currently relishing her singles

## Steal This Life: Passionate Party Throwing

**Create an opportunity for marvelous mingling. Throw a fete, bacchanalia, or glorious gathering. For parties, my friends and I like the feeling of spontaneity. We get everyone together at unexpected times; midweek or late Sunday afternoon to extend the weekend just a little bit longer.**

Provide party food. Supply all the fixin's for shish kabobs—meats, seafood, veggies, fruits—and toss 'em on a grill. Light up the night with a million twinkling votives or corral clusters of neon light sticks as party favors and centerpieces. Invite an unexpected guest or two. People like to try new things and meet new people.

Keep the party moving. Have cocktails downstairs, dinner upstairs. Sprinkle large mirrors throughout the spaces; inexpensive door mirrors swathed in fabric work great. That way, you've set the stage for intimate dining where guests can see themselves and engage in a bit of dining voyeurism. Have dessert outside around a blazing fire pit—a dramatic climax to a cozy evening.

existence—and she won't give it up, even if she does find the man for her. "Why would I stop enjoying time with my girlfriends? That's something that's HUGE for me," she says firmly.

As we're leaving the building, Kate's cell phone rings. It's a call from a guy she just met. "Oops!" she says, with a twinkle in her bright blue eyes. "You just caught me in a 'singles moment.'"

## One Liners: Have Them at Hello

"He said, 'That's what you're drinking? You're crazy!' and then he bought me a glass of champagne." —Monika, 31

"'Your eyes have a smile of their own.' I like that one better than, 'Damn girl! You're the best thing I've seen since I looked in the mirror this morning.'" —Alanna, 23

"I don't use pick up lines—'Hey what time is it?' That'll get you talking to me. Won't it? 'Hey what time is it? What's your name? Very nice to meet you. My name's Jameson.'" —Jameson, 35

"'I've temporarily lost the use of my legs. I think I might need to stay with you tonight.' It's the funniest one I ever heard. I would fall for that." —Jessica, 26

Worst pickup line: "Where's your friend?" —Celeste, 23

Best pickup line: "Hi."

# Singular Sensations

**#80** *Have it your way.* Always ask for what you want. Make it a habit to state your preference at the supermarket meat counter, the hair salon, or when out with friends. Don't be shy. If they're interested enough to ask, you should be confident enough to answer truthfully.

**#81** *Upgrade yourself.* Every once in a while, take something you'd do anyway and bump it up a notch. Buy flavored coffee instead of regular, add fabric softeners to your laundry routine, or get an electric toothbrush to jazz up your morning manual routine. Your thoughtfulness will raise your spirits!

**#82** *The actor's studio.* Gather fun-loving online singles for an evening of video karaoke at a local hangout. Pair off and reenact scenes from your favorite movies. Take turns judging and award prizes for the best performance ever on a "first date."

**#83** *Taking online offline.* Once you've met online, keep from becoming a digital pen pal by moving the process along. Invite live conversation with Tish's favorite line, "I'd rather talk than type." Get their number first so you can call when you're ready.

**#84** *Having fun in the sun.* Get some rays but wear your sunblock. Buy multitasking cosmetics for beautiful look and beautiful skin. Choose facial moisturizers, lip glosses, and body lotions with SPF protection. On the outside, beauty is skin deep.

#85 *Pay it forward.* Have a big birthday or career anniversary coming up? Why not start saving now so you can splurge later. Each month put away a little something towards the big event. At the end of a year, three years, or five years you could make a big dent in those celebration expenses.

## The Last Word

**Being single is a choice. You're free to date. Be selective about who you spend your time with. Set your own standards.**

1. Hope is not a strategy. Take advantage of all the dating assistance that's out there.

2. Date yourself. Skip the movies in favor of a big night out on the town.

3. You're single. Mingle for maximum exposure and fun. You've got to greet someone new before you'll meet someone new.

# Chapter Eleven

# Living with Love as Possibility

Love makes the world go 'round—even in the singles world. There's just a lot more of it. We spend more time, energy, and money seeking it, falling for it, and nurturing it. Just because we're single doesn't mean love doesn't exist or isn't part of our routine. We live constantly on the edge of passion, tempting fate, however briefly we touch love. We're the aspirational consumer that keeps the "romance industry" churning out books, flowers, chocolates, and vacations for two. We're the potential they hope never is realized.

When you're living in the lap of loving relationships, you simply take that love for granted. How many times do you end a call with a friend with the phrase, "love you"? Or sign a letter, "love," and your name? I have a good friend who, each time I see him, hugs me and says, "Love you, mean it!" That little phrase reminds me that his love is not a throwaway sentiment. Who loves ya, baby? Count the many loves in your life. Beginning with your parents, siblings, extended family, close friends, colleagues, and spiritual companions, the list goes on. Romantic love is not *the* answer, it's just *one* of the many forms love takes in our lives.

## Don't Typecast Love

Once a year we're reminded that a certain kind of love is missing in our lives. On that day it's important to remember it's not the *only* love there is. It's not even the best kind of love. On Valentine's Day, open your heart to love in whatever forms it chooses to show up in your life. Unconditional love. Puppy love. Self love. Embrace love and you'll find she loves you back.

Host a champagne tasting gala for your single girlfriends. Celebrate the love you bring to each other's lives. Take turns toasting the amazing gift of one another in each of your lives.

Enjoy the thrill of starring in a romance novel that's all about you. *Medieval Passion, Pirates of Desire,* or *Western Rendezvous* are a few of the titles offered at www.booksbyyou.com, which creates personalized books. Settle down for a night of steaming hot chocolate and steamy passion!

Take a tour of the holiday's sweet spot: a chocolate factory. Venues Willy Wonka would enjoy: Toronto's Soma Chocolate; Manhattan's Jacques Torres Chocolate Haven; Scharffen Berger

---

## Singular Sensation #86

The four-legged love of my life. Keep yours healthy and happy with regular visits to the veterinarian. Want to keep costs down? View insurance options at www.petinsurance.com. Make sure to keep your pet's important medical records, test results, and vaccinations in a separate folder at home. Purrr-fect!

Chocolates in Berkeley, California; Maison Pralus in Roanne, France; Hershey's Chocolate World in Hershey, Pennsylvania; and Tasmania's Cadbury Schweppes Chocolate Factory.

Tally up all the money you're saving on flowers, candy, cards, and dinner. Vow to save it for a special "gift of love" for yours truly.

Find the look of love in unexpected places. This year exchange valentines with children and seniors. The kids love the funny ones and the seniors' eyes light up at the kindness of just being remembered.

This V. Day, celebrate U. Day! Be "the one" you want. Make a commitment to yourself. "I love me so I vow to get more sleep, say 'no' more often, and feed myself only healthy snacks." Say it and live it. Look in the mirror and promise, "I will always be 'the one' I want."

> ### Singular Sensation #87
> *Love your vegetables?* Eat them fresh from the farm. Make it a habit to shop at your local farmer's market. In many areas you can enjoy year-round locally grown produce. Be sure to ask the growers what's freshest right now. Get fresh food that suits your mood!

## Conscious Cuddling

At some point, you make peace with being single. You name the important parts of being you and claim this life as your own. For me that means being a bon vivant who indulges her love for cooking ethnic foods and entertaining children and adults. And in my best moments a creative genius who really shines in this single space. At thirty-six, Suzanne and her compatriots are contemplating living life on their own. They meet periodically to reconcile the stories of their single lives and their conflicted ideas about finding a life partner. When I emailed Suzanne to request an interview, she suggested I read her online personals ad before we met. It read:

I am...very committed to the spiritual path of self-exploration and growth. I want a deeply spiritual and emotional partnership, as well as incredible physical chemistry. This is not too much to ask for, is it?

Over lunch, Suzanne answers her own question with a sigh. "The problem with having this kind of consciousness is the higher you get, the more you expect from a male partner," she says. "I may be cursed to be conscious. I've grown on my own and I'm not willing to settle anymore." I laugh at the bit of irony. Most people would consider someone with Suzanne's California-girl looks anything but cursed.

Suzanne belongs to a group of single women in their mid to late thirties who meet monthly to explore the interrelationship of the feminine and the masculine. An often-discussed topic is "Why do we have this desire to partner with a man?" Another is "How active should you be in the search for a mate?"

It's healthy for them and for you to question long-held societal beliefs about marriage and partnership. In such a

## The Single Best Attitude

Today, focus on what you have in your life and not on the love you think is missing. Just because society measures us by our marital status doesn't mean we have to. Even those with spouses can't always claim they have the lives they've dreamed of. Acknowledge the ideas, enthusiasm, and passion present in your solo life. Hold on to the satisfying vision of life on your own. See clearly that you have all the things that matter most to you.

search for answers you'll find come to the realization that what's good for the many is not always the perfect choice for the one person who matters most in your life: you. And it's inspiring to be a single seeker on the road to discovering your happy-with-myself nirvana.

> ## Singular Sensation #88
>
> *Precious drops.* Splurge and buy yourself a single crystal water goblet. Drink like a goddess and you'll feel like a queen.

In her quest to date men of a similar persuasion, Suzanne frequently attends seminars and retreats at a meditation center in the Marin County foothills. When we meet, she has just returned from a weekend retreat that explored single life. The sessions focused on the stories that we—consciously or unconsciously—tell ourselves about being single. In the words of an age-old expression, "What a man thinketh, he becomes."

Suzanne admits to telling her inner self fairytales that lack the proverbial "happy ending"—and she thinks they might have contributed to her single status. "I fell into the trap a little while ago of thinking that it wasn't important for me to find a partner. I wanted to have a baby even more than I wanted to find a partner," Suzanne explains. She also repeatedly told herself that she wouldn't find her soul mate until she was older. (It takes time to find true love, you see.) Since this was the reality Suzanne created, she never let herself be open to that love in her twenties or early thirties. Instead,

> ## Note to Self
>
> Write your own obituary. Ponder how you would like to be remembered. Will it contain mentions of how you won the Nobel Peace Prize or the story of rescuing your elderly neighbor's cat? Will it recount your trek across the Italian countryside reliving the path of ancient saints? Write the story of your life and then live it!

she kept repeating her pattern of choosing men who weren't interested in committing to a creative life with a partner.

"I don't think people honor in our society [the] people who want to remain single," Suzanne says now. "I told myself that story as a form of protection against being one of the 'unchosen people.'" These days, Suzanne is writing new stories for herself. She has accepted the fact that she can have a full and happy life as a single woman and it won't be a "devastatingly lonely" one. Her definition of a relationship has changed as well. "I think that you can form a community. You can have a really full, rich life being single or having a series of different relationships instead of engaging in one that you tell yourself is supposed to last forever."

## Steal This Life: Clean Up Your Language

**Exercise your word power! Tell your story but cut these "trash you" terms out of your vocabulary. Take a red "magic" marker and draw a line through these words you need no longer use.**

| | | | |
|---|---|---|---|
| desperate | failure | old | lonely |
| alone | bored | insecure | fat |
| unattached | must marry | unchosen | shame |
| bitch | selfish | unlovable | slut |
| Mr. Right | unlucky | biological clock | settle |
| dumped | fear | grownup | the one |
| Why | aren't | you | married? |

During my conversation with Suzanne, we discussed the fact that many singles have decided their search for self takes precedence over the search for a mate. In particular, I've met many women willing to weigh lifestyle options well into their thirties.

These women want to give new meaning to the phrase "having it all": they want a perfectly realized self. The members of the latest "Me" generation may find that they are the first generation to get what they really, really want.

## *Can We Talk Kisses for a Minute?*

Right on the heels of the dating decline is the scarcity of the sought-after first date kiss. It's easy to forget how much fun just kissing can be. Kissing is an underrated sensual activity, and it needs to come back in style. People are jumping into bed so fast they're missing the exhilarating warm-up!

There's a TV commercial I just love. It's for a national cellular telephone company. The woman is doing everything in reverse order: eating dinner for breakfast, walking her dog backwards, and the final shot shows her on a first date, where the guy is about to order dinner and she flips the menu away and kisses him. After all, isn't the promise of an incredible goodnight smooch the reason everyone suffers through the uncertainty of the first date?

### *Passion Pen Letters*

A love letter is the most precious of all documents. The receiver savors its cherished insights, passionate praise, and honeyed truths, treasuring it in times of self-doubt and disappointment. Dust off your high school yearbook and reread those heartfelt declarations of love. Dig up treasured letters from old boyfriends, or treat yourself to published accounts of famous amorous writing. Relive your greatest moments of intense passion and deepest devotion.

## Singular Sensation #89

*Brand yourself.* Pick a terrific shade of lipstick that you always wear or a funky pair of glasses that shows off your eyes. Own your look and make a great first impression.

A great kiss is the expression of a pure connection. When our bodies align themselves and our lips lock for those precious seconds, it's like the sensual version of the Vulcan mind meld. A kiss can speak volumes about compatibility, dexterity, and creativity. A prolonged pucker has been known to shove a not-so-good-on-paper guy into the wow-I-think-he-may-be-The-One category.

And think of the wonderful variety! The Kama Sutra alone catalogs more than two hundred fifty different kinds of kisses between lovers. Because really, who enjoys monotonous smooching? Ease from the French kiss to the Eskimo kiss. Trace a tongue gently along the mouth's contours or nibble on the smooth, sensitive flesh of the inner lip. I once read about a "chocolate kiss" on a website soap opera, and was definitely intrigued by a technique that involves a person blowing gently on the ear of another, then making contact with a quick flick of the tongue. I say *definitely* try that one at home!

Maybe kisses *do* tell. The fleeting brush of lips often holds the promise of later passions. A guy's casual peck on the cheek surely lets a gal know she ranks right up there with his sister. And anyone who's suffered through a tongue thruster knows actions speak louder than words in the bedroom.

No matter how many personality quizzes you take or personal ads you write, a kiss dares to bare your true nature. Your eyes may be the windows to your soul, but sharing a kiss can fling

## Singles Click: A Stranger's Kiss

"I'm sure I made out with one of the best kissers in the world one night—years ago in a crowded club on Bourbon Street in New Orleans. The guy was adorable, with sleepy, sexy green eyes that I can still see, and he came dancing up and gave my friend a quick peck, then turned to give one to me. Quick flash of tongue—electric. He backed up and stared at me. I swayed on my barstool, like 'Damn! What was that?' and stared back. Without a word, we began a make out session that lasted a couple hours. Mouths and hands everywhere. People were walking by, staring. I didn't care. I've *never* responded to a man like that before or since. I just never wanted him to stop kissing me.

"Unfortunately, I can't help but compare all other men to him...and they are all found lacking." —Deirdre, 33

those windows wide open. You can even connect with someone if you don't speak his or her language—just let your lips do the talking. A kiss is the most intimate conversation our mouths can have without saying a word.

### My Personal Dream Catcher

One afternoon my enthusiastically in love friend Alexandra invited me over to her house for an afternoon of girls-gone-wild crafting. "You know, Jeri," she said with a twinkle in her eye. "In order to get your dream guy in your life, you've got to make him up.

You've got to create the perfect guy for you!" I was a little more than skeptical as she dragged piles of magazines on to her living room floor, grabbed a blank hardcover book and some pens, and then announced that we were going to create a dreamboat journal.

## Steal This Life: Flying Friendlier Skies.

**Why not take advantage of the airline that plays Cupid? Southwest Airlines, "the airline built on love," recently touted its open seating policy as the low-cost multitasking dating alternative.** Over the years, the Dallas-based airline, which calls the city's Love Field its home, has received thousands of letters and scores of wedding invitations addressed to top executives from couples who met on one of the airline's flights.

Its New York Stock Exchange stock ticker symbol is LUV and it calls its monthly company newsletter "Luv Lines." Their website even uses hearts to designate airfare specials and search "matches."

Some advice from dating experts on the airplane dating ritual include trying to make some sort of contact in the terminal, where small talk comes as easily as asking, "Isn't it a hassle to travel?" If there is a connection, then try to pursue it during the flight. If things do not look good in the terminal, do not bother the person on the plane. I'd always thought of their no-frills seating arrangement as a cattle rush at check-in. Maybe on my next flight I'll look for love in the air.

She instructed me to cut out words and pictures that grabbed my fancy: tall…dark…the perfect body…loves romance…loves to dance. The floor was littered with scraps of paper as I cut my way to the dozens of guys who could be the one. Next, Alexandra advised me to write in the book about what he looked like, sounded like, what it was like to be with him in bed, and without much prodding I was off in my own fantasy world. I clipped, glued, pasted, and reread my journal entries as she encouraged me to be more specific. By the end of the day, I had a composite of my dream guy.

"Now read this book every day for twenty-one days and then put it away," Alexandra counseled me. I faithfully followed her instructions. Unlike Alexandra, I wasn't looking for Mr. Right to show up. I've gotten my wish because a lot of other great guys have and whenever the well runs dry, I pull out this homemade charm and ask the heavens to start raining single men.

### Matchmaker, Matchmaker, Make Me a Match!

When and if you go looking for love through a personal matchmaking service, be honest and specific about what you want. If you prefer chocolate ice cream, vanilla will never taste quite right. Remember personal preferences are just that personal.

Definitely ask about the makeup of the organization's client base. How many men? How many women? You'll need this information to evaluate your chance of success with their database. But you need to dig deeper. How many of these individuals actually fit your personal wish list based on their age, race, profession, etc.

Finally, ask to see how successful they are matching people like you. Persons with disabilities, plus-size women, older women, educated women of color, and singles with passions outside the mainstream may need to seek out services which cater to their interests. The company may be very successful with middle Americans, but if you don't fit the mold, honestly evaluate your chances of success with the organization.

## Singles Click: Loving, Losing, and Loving

Being single gives one the opportunity to experience *le grande affaire*, the heart-stopping, can't take my eyes off you moment of connection that blossoms into a love for a limited time only. Go for the gusto! Love truly, deeply, madly. Colin, a forty-one-year-old never-married single says about his on-again-off-again love life that he's learned he's able to share his life. "I'm capable of letting somebody in. Capable of taking on risk," he says thoughtfully. And he admits he can be "just like a young teenage girl—yes, I've gone without meals for a few days."

Your broken heart can always be mended. And yes, whatever doesn't kill you will make you stronger—and with luck no one else dies, either. You strengthen your emotional muscles and experience a deep-end-of-the-pool connection with another when you love. Sure, you feel vulnerable and you're in a situation that's not under your control. But that's what love is at its best. Believe that it is better to have loved and lost—and to love again.

## Making Value Judgments

Beauty is more than skin deep. Love at first sight is often lust at first sight. Try looking beneath the surface the next time you're attracted to someone. Try to discover their best qualities. Often we confuse physical attributes with deeper, more long-lasting values. True love brings out the best in each partner. Circle the top five qualities below that appeal to you the most. Be careful, not all of these are the qualities they seem.

| | | |
|---|---|---|
| Kind | Romantic | Honest |
| Sexy | Courageous | Disciplined |
| Athletic | Intellectual | Compassionate |
| Perseverant | Inspiring | Charming |
| Enthusiastic | Strong | Integrity |
| Devoted | Content | Spiritual |

## Singular Sensations

**#90** *Live to love.* Take the time each day to do one thing you love. It could be hanging out with friends, reading a great book, or cooking up a storm. The important thing is to open your heart to the people and things you love.

**#91** *Fabulous flea market affair.* Hold a happy hour garage sale. Price everything in large print for easy reading as the sun goes down. Sprinkle twinkling lights around the tables for a festive mood. Here's to love at first sight.

**#92** *Mastermind your mission.* Mission statements represent the principles of and drive the success of *Fortune 500* companies. Borrow a tool from forward-thinking managers who post the corporate beliefs in plain view. Draft a personal monthly mission statement. Post it where you can see it easily at home and at work. Carry it in your wallet. Watch your words make a difference in your world.

**#93** *Argentinean Tango.* Spend an evening at these sizzling hot, south of the border dance classes. The widely acclaimed *Forever Tango* Broadway show has spurred more interest in this niche dance art. Practitioners swear that that the intense choreographed moves are passion personified. If you can't locate an Argentinean studio, begin with regular tango lessons.

**#94** *Find romance.* Spend an afternoon at the movies where you can live vicariously through the affairs of your favorite characters. Watching your favorite romantic comedy or yummy love story will warm your heart.

**#95** *Paint the picture.* Explore all your options in life. Don't close the door on the "next new thing" that comes your way. Throw a lot of paint on the walls.

#96 *Fabulous face time.* Catch their attention with your smile. It'll brighten their day and yours. Tooth whiteners will keep you dazzling. Show them your best and your brightest.

## The Last Word

**Being single is a choice. Expand your choices of love to include affection in all its many forms.**

1. Every life has a story. Take the time to really get to know yours. Make changes where necessary.

2. You can experience love as a single person. A spouse is not required.

3. Always remember to keep love in your life.

# Chapter Twelve

# Be Your Sole Support:

## Find Support for Your Soul.

"God bless the child who's got his own," my grandmother's phlegmy voice with its southern drawl still rings in my ears. Oh, I don't know what it was I was pleading my parents for this time, but it didn't matter because that was her constant reply to any nonessential request. It definitely motivated me at an early age to dream up neighborhood schemes to put some change in my pocket. By the time I got to college I had so many on-the-side money-making endeavors, I was constantly sliding into class on a wing and the clang of a bell.

On my own in my thirties, I set aside lawyering to pursue my entrepreneurial dreams of being a fashion designer, confident in my own talents and survival skills. My friends all dreamed of solo success as well, but they each definitely had a Plan B…and it usually involved boyfriends who would pay their bills.

## Quickie Fact

Does one live as cheaply as two? It depends on what you're counting. Solo men and women spend a greater portion of their take-home pay on shelter, but less on food. More of their hard-earned cash goes towards buying alcoholic beverages and electronic equipment—meaning flat screens TVs, high-end stereos, and wave radios—than those who live with others. However, solo dwellers aren't as fussy about furnishing their personal space or the car they drive.

Go figure.

My friend Molly, a fifty-something Welsh storeowner who imported trinkets from around the world, constantly worried about my hand-to-mouth existence. "Darling, my business doesn't have to make money," she purred as she wandered through her bazaar, admiring Moroccan rugs and stroking favored artifacts. "Stuart pays the awful bills and doesn't muck about. If you don't make it, who will take care of you? Have you thought of that?"

Actually, I had. My philosophical take on the whole thing was that it was the perfect time in my life to start a business. I didn't have a family to support. I didn't have a husband to convince that I was doing the right thing. I could work twenty-four hours a day, seven days a week if that's what it took, without someone nagging me to spend time with them. And if things didn't work out, the only person I had to worry about was myself.

I knew I was walking the tightrope without a net; I just believed that being single was the only way to try.

### Skip the Middleman. Buy Your Own Damn Ring!

Chances are if you're like most singletons, you're livin' large rather than taking charge of your financial resources. At forty-nine, Cheryl

Broussard, a once married, now divorced nationally recognized investment advisor, appreciates the truism that "money talks," but she also understands that today's singles are not always listening.

"The thing is," Cheryl says, "when you're single you really do have to think about what kind of lifestyle you want to live. Do I just want to live like this—living paycheck to paycheck? Yes, it's fun to go out to dinner every night and buy $300 purses, but at some point that's going to get old." Are you feeling guilty as charged?

Acting as part therapist, part financial guru, the best-selling author challenges her clients to address the emotional needs of their spending habits as well as the physical ones. As a top-earning single woman, she's been there and "basically, I find that when we live like that we're filling up the empty hole in our heart. We feel like there's nothing else and we've got to fill it up with stuff."

Today she advises singles to spend more time goal tending and less time impulsively spending. For example, once you make a plan and you're accountable to that plan, the dream of buying that condo is within reach. "You get clear, you get focused. And you don't buy those $600 shoes and you don't do the dinners out every night because you know what it is you want," she says excitedly.

## Singular Sensation #97

*Quick-change artist.* Make your pennies, nickels, and dimes count. At the end of each day, clean out your purse and empty the spare change in a jar earmarked for a special fund. At the end of each month, wrap up the change and deposit it into an interest-bearing savings account. At the end of the year, roll those dollars into a less-liquid CD. Make your money grow.

## The Single Best Attitude

Be responsibly single. Be financially self-aware. Maintain a lifestyle focus. Don't just think about money in terms of their dollars and your sense of not having enough. Make money a personal resource tool to achieve your goals. Respect yourself by committing to the financial decisions you make for your future happiness. Give yourself and your money more than a second thought.

Your dream of financial success starts to become a reality when you state your intention clearly. "I'm ready to buy my house now," one single woman client recently told Cheryl. That's the kind of thing that you have to say in your mind—you're buying a home now and those designer sandals later.

Your single self may lack the necessary financial foresight because you're not accountable to anyone. A dough disciplinarian like your personal financial advisor will ask all the hard questions like, "Didn't you say you want to do this but then you're doing that?" No more forgetting to balance your checkbook or leaving credit card statements unopened in the inbox. You'll learn to hold yourself just as accountable for your money as you would any other financial caretaker such as your bank or retirement plan. You wouldn't stand for them misplacing a few zeroes in your money market account, so don't let yourself off the hook either when your dollar amounts don't make sense.

Another habit to get into is stashing your cash. Cheryl is a big fan of investment clubs because they offer bonding opportunities *and* increasing financial rewards. She recommends building a financial portfolio this way because of the low initial investment, which can be as little as $25 to $100 a month, and the opportunity to earn while you learn. "I've heard of investment clubs that do real estate, stock market. I've heard of clubs that invest in theater plays," Cheryl says. Members of the club are each responsible for finding the investments. The sky's the limit when choosing your niche and you're doing it without a lot of risk to your own money.

Investment clubs build a more beneficial cash camaraderie than an afternoon of shopping. When you come together as a group, you've got someone you can call up and say, "Hey, what do you think about this? Should I invest in this? Or how do you feel about that? What have you heard about it?" The clubs are another way to build a support network that's often missing when you're single.

With friends like these, one really could get tired of dropping cash at the mall. I mean how many pairs of black pants, four-inch heels, and crazy croc leather handbags can a girl love? And how long will that love last when the creditors start calling?

Statistically, we're becoming a nation of singletons. We cannot afford to act financially irresponsible. Live for today, but put enough away for tomorrow.

## Note to Self

Next time you're tempted to make a big purchase, delay the decision for two weeks. Give yourself the opportunity to weigh spending the dollars against the fill-in-the-blank financial goal you've set for yourself. Let self-satisfaction outweigh your instant gratification.

## Singular Sensation #98

*Cheap thrill.* In style isn't always in the budget. Peruse consignment shops for great wardrobe and interior design bargains that can be altered to fit current trends. Your creativity will keep you fiscally fit.

## Steal This Life: Six Secrets of Single Income Success

1. **Create a dual income.** Mastermind a moonlighting plan. Home-based business opportunities abound. Why not multitask and bring in an extra paycheck by spending your evening as a singles event hostess?

2. **Return to college.** No, not to the classroom, but to the lifestyle. Remember when you made more happen with less? Remember the days when you were chipping in with friends rather than tipping big at restaurants? Cooking clubs, carpooling, and vacation sharing all stretch your dollars and your lifestyle.

3. **Hang out at the library.** You can browse the stacks for fun, educational, and *free* reads.

4. **Surf for savvy secrets.** Plenty of online sources offer great financial advice, much of it tailored to your lifestyle: professional singles, single moms, out-of-work singles, etc. Look for the profile that fits you best and take advantage of the brainy budgeting.

5. **Don't buy it, borrow it!** Companies and websites are springing up all over the place that allow you to be decadent on a budget. You can rent beautiful art for your house or borrow designer duds for a fraction of their cost.

6. **Don't be penny wise and pound foolish.** That cheap coat you picked up at a bargain basement sale isn't worth anything if it falls apart after one chilly season. Invest in quality over quantity

## *Money in the Bank Bingo*

Single life sometimes is all about the Benjamins—and not the
Tom, Dick, or Harry variety. But can you bank on yourself to take
care of yourself from now until next week…or forever? Cover five
squares in a row with quarters and you'll be right on the money,
honey! Or cover the board and become wealthy and wise!

| B | A | N | K | O |
|---|---|---|---|---|
| Budget Like a Billionaire | Take Notes | By the Numbers | Rethink Your Relationship | Your $$$ and Your Life |
| Be Fearless | Make Friends | Habit-Forming Freedom | Cash Out | No Limits Attitude |
| Convert Clutter into Cash | Know and Grow | Free Space | Annual Checkup | Make the Big Payoff |
| Mind Your Own Business | Toss Temptation | Time Is of the Essence | Shop Secondary Markets | Use the Four Letter Word |
| Don't Roam, Own Your Home | Healthy to Wealthy | Invest in Yourself | Personalize Your Portfolio | The Estate You're In |

You'll get money back guaranteed when you play Bank-O Bingo. It's hip to be square and here's how:

**Budget Like a Billionaire:** Donald Trump treats his money like the love of his life. He's keenly aware of how much his companies earn and spend. Doesn't matter if you have millions or a miniscule savings account, every penny counts; it's all your money.

**Take Notes:** Know where your paycheck is going. Begin by keeping a daily record of how much you spend on everyday essentials. By week's end you'll see how quickly lattes, lunches, and long island iced teas can add up.

**By the Numbers:** Digits make you crazy! Me, too. I love the online calculators in the toolbox at www.soundmoney.publicradio.org, which run the numbers for you. Say I'm making X dollars today; how long will it take me to pay off my credit cards or save for a monthly retirement income of X, and how much money can I save by taking a bag lunch to work once a week? Hey, figures are fun!

**Rethink Your Relationship:** Annually evaluate the services you're receiving from your bank, insurance company, and financial advisors. Make sure they still fit your needs and your budget. Cell phone and landline phone services should be monitored on a quarterly basis to take advantage of the latest plans.

**Your $$$ and Your Life:** Money can buy happiness, but only if you decide what makes *you* happy! Money is one of the greatest resources each of has to shape our life's style. Achieve your wildest dreams by making definite goals with measurable milestones. That will put a smile on your face.

**Be Fearless:** Don't let the fear of the unknown solo future or low money IQ stop you from taking action. Now is always the right time. Do one thing today that increases your net worth like learning a new skill or not splurging on another pair of black pants.

**Make New Friends:** Carpooling at least once a week saves gas. The Insurance Information Institute has found that lower car mileage (7,500 miles a year) will help reduce your premiums at most insurers. Think of other ways it pays to share.

**Habit-Forming Freedom:** Practice makes perfect. Adopt money-saving habits like drinking home-brewed coffee or cutting back on dinner out. Begin slowly and stick to habits which build your financial freedom.

**Cash Out:** Leave your credit cards and checkbook in the drawer at home. Only make purchases with cash. It's harder to let go of real paper money, and when it's gone, it's gone. Then there's nothing left but an empty space in your wallet.

**No Limits Attitude:** Indulge in blue sky daydreaming. Believe that you can succeed in changing your current financial situation. Don't let a current cash crisis paralyze your potential. If you can see it, you can be it!

**Convert Clutter into Cash:** If you never use it, wear it, open it—then you shouldn't own it. Turn your storage space, closet space, and garage space clutter into cash. Your neighborhood consignment shop will turn your unused items into their must-have inventory and earn you must-needed dollars.

**Know and Grow:** There's a wealth of financial resources out there. Attend classes offered by your local bank or credit union. Borrow books from the library. Interview financial planners and

> ### Singular Sensation #99
>
> *Get crafty.* Host a handmade-gift exchange. Invite your friends over and celebrate getting together by exchanging gifts made by your own two hands. Blend flavored olive oils, string semi-precious jewelry, or design mosaic-tile home accessories. No store-bought presents allowed.

search online. Do the homework that leads to homeownership or meeting your financial goals.

**Annual Checkups:** Review your credit reports provided by the major credit reporting agencies annually. Look for errors and signs that you maybe a victim of identity theft. Knowing how much credit you rate is power in the marketplace.

**Make the Big Payoff:** Commit to paying down your credit card balances. Start with the highest interest rate card first. Cancel unnecessary gas, department store, or duplicate vendor cards. Having a high number of open accounts, even with zero balances, can negatively affect your credit rating.

**Mind Your Own Business:** Women-owned business generated $818.7 billion in 1997 according to the last major survey by the U.S. Census. Shouldn't you be leveraging your sought-after skills or knowledge to create additional income for your piggy bank?

**Toss Temptation:** Additional credit card offers, sale flyers, and solicitations to buy things you don't need should go in the circular file immediately. No home-shopping channel or e-shopping if you can't control your urge to spend. Don't give into a tease!

**Time is of the Essence:** Establish a bill-paying ritual. Pay your bills at the same time every month in a comfortable place with stamps, envelopes, pen, and checkbook, or establish online accounts. Instead of having cause for anxiety, create an atmosphere of gratitude for the ability to take care of your financial obligations all by yourself.

**Shop Secondary Markets:** Everyone seems to have owned everything at least once. Take advantage of the bargains to be had on previously owned designer cars, clothes, and home furnishings. Skip the trash and find true treasures!

**Use the Four Letter Word:** Free! Turns out a lot of things in life are just that. Magazines at the library, opening weekend movie tickets, community concerts in the park, consumer product giveaways. Why pay for it when you can get it way cheaper than wholesale?

**Don't Roam, Own Your Home:** Buying real estate is still the smartest investment you can make in your future. Why? Not only does the value of your home appreciate annually, but your personal sense of well-being rises exponentially, too. The keys to your own home are the ultimate precious metal.

**Invest in Yourself:** $3.2 million. That's the earnings difference over a lifetime between people with professional degrees and people without, according to data released in 2002 from the U.S. Census. Complete that degree, upgrade your education to a professional degree, or take continuing education classes in your field. A little knowledge goes a long way toward increasing your earning power.

**Personalize Your Portfolio:** Variety is the spice of life and

> *Singular Sensation* #100
>
> *Picture your dreams.* Frame the best illustration, photograph, or print you can find that represents your ultimate wish. Set it on your desk or hang it in the living room over the sofa. Your art will remind you of your goal. And you'll live with your dream everyday until you make it come true.

## Note to Self

Try this exercise in self-reflection. Look in the mirror and repeat this affirmation: "I will always take good care of you. I've got your back. " Begin by expressing the intention softly, then increase in volume till you feel it's true deep within your soul. Make this affirmation a part of your morning routine.

the essence of good financial planning. Look to invest in a collection of interest-bearing or revenue-producing options. Investigate mutual funds, individual stocks, passive income earning opportunities, and interest-bearing accounts. Build a financial portfolio that serves your interests.

**The Estate You're In:** Most of us have more than we think we have. Between 401K plans at work, that cherished piece of art that has appreciated in the marketplace as well as our hearts, rare collectibles, and the common savings account, who gets it all when you're gone? Since the laws on inheritance vary state be state, it's important to make your wishes known.

### True Believer in Me

How often have you heard, "You can make your dreams come true." I've always believed it was true and Anna, a beautiful fifty-six-year-old single, has certainly lived it. She's achieved a life-long dream of becoming a professional artist. On a beautiful "lucky you live in Hawaii" afternoon, I'm sitting in her warm, wonderful Maui home "talking story."

"I came out here twenty-five years ago. There wasn't even a streetlight on the whole island," Anna begins, her bright brown eyes shining with the memory. "My first week... I found a place I could sleep down at the marketplace. I had a roof over my head. I was living on $3 a day," she says as I look at her in amazement.

After a winding road through several different fine art careers—scrimshaw artist, animal illustrator—Anna found her niche as a still life and landscape painter. Today she's at the top of her profession, commanding high prices for her brilliance with a brush. But not only was the road not straight and narrow, it was downright rough at times. Married at nineteen, Anna divorced three years later. She and her only daughter traveled the world together for a dozen years. Then at the suggestion of a friend, Anna decided to move to Maui by herself to pursue her artistic leanings.

"So that freed me up and I really became an artist, 'cause up to that point I had a partner. I was never alone. So I thought, am I ready for that? And you know, I didn't know how to be alone." I shake my head as she says this, as I realize the significance of Anna leaving her daughter behind. "This was the beginning of being single. The beginning of being truly unto yourself," she explains of her new life.

One year, she tells me, "Nobody bought my work. One single year. Not one single piece." I'm thinking most people would be freaking out or packing their bags for the next plane back to the mainland. Here she is with no family, just a few new friends, no job to speak of, and trying to do the art thing.

Not Anna. She robbed Peter to pay Paul's credit cards but she

> ### The Single Best Attitude
> Give yourself credit every once in awhile. You're happy living a life you're proud of. You've made some of your dreams come true and look forward to accomplishing more. Congratulations, you're doing a fabulous job taking care of yourself. Keep the faith.

refused to give up on her dream to support herself as an artist. "I thought, oh my God, what do I do? I'm not going to give up my dream. I've earned it. I started living on my credit cards. I had great credit. One credit card paid off the next credit card. The next month that credit card paid off that credit card. It went back

## Steal This Life: Maui Wowie!

**One nice thing about being in Hawaii is when you greet people, everybody hugs. You're always rubbing up against warm, brown bodies at the supermarket, at luaus, on the beach, and at the discos. And the exchange of a garland of flowers gets you lei'd.**

Anna shares the island's expansive view of relationships. "I'm not single, I'm with you. I'm completely with you right now. We're as close as anything," she says softly as we stroll out onto her deck. "Yes," I say, "but before I walked into this room..." Anna turns to face me and says, "No, I was in a relationship with my work. I am happily committed to my work. I wasn't single; I was with that. I have a relationship with it. I wasn't alone. There's no aloneness in that."

Her words remind me of the joy of growing up in Hawaii, where everyone is part of one giant "ohana," or family that includes the warmth of a stranger's smile and the swaying of the palm trees in the breeze on a deserted beach. We are always at one with each other and ourselves. And Anna says there can be no aloneness in that.

Add the aloha spirit to *your* life.

and forth for a year," Anna shuffles her hands as she explains her plastic money survival strategy.

Finally she got a break and a client ordered a triptych for $10,000 and all of a sudden she had a huge commission and a solid footing in her new career.

Listening to her words reminds me of my own struggle as an unmarried creative person. You always have the work for inspiration and you're always living on the edge. I think of all the little miracles and machinations that come together to make a space on the planet for my dreams and me. When my married friends announce they're going out on a limb to start a business, I always bring them back to reality; "No, you're not on your own, you still have a husband to pay the bills." They've got backup. We singles truly take a leap of faith and manage to lead lives filled with overwhelming success.

## Me, Me, Me! The Self-Serving Pleasure Principle

"Why *not* be single?" Lara challenges me, raising her glass of champagne in a mock toast at a mutual friend's birthday party. That should really be the question. With all the freedoms you enjoy, control you exercise over your life, and promises you keep to yourself, the joy of solo living is truly the last unexplored country.

Lara certainly enjoys the sense of ownership that comes from being completely in charge of her destiny. The twenty-nine-year-old high school dropout put herself through college, discarded a bad marriage, and worked her way up from an hourly night shift worker to biomedical sales professional. She's originally from a small, nondescript town on the outskirts of Chicago. She made her way west to California all by herself.

Right now, Lara's focus is completely on herself—and it shows. "Single—it's not just about sex, it's not about love…it's more about independence. It's about who you have to think of first. Ultimately, you're responsible for you.

"When you're single and you have to rely on yourself, you find out so much more about yourself," she continues, leaning forward and raising her voice above the din to make her point. "Where are your strengths? Where are your weaknesses? What do you like? What do you hate? If you're always thinking of somebody else and their feelings, can you ever really know what you would choose if you were on your own?"

Lara admits to being lonely sometimes, just like everybody else. But she compares being single to the art of meditating; neither is a couple's activity. When meditating, you're focusing on your breathing and your inner self. When you're single, you're forced to truly think about you. She believes when you're doing either of them right, you succeed in knowing yourself better.

> ## The Single Best Attitude
>
> Coming into your own is the great prize of adulthood. That moment when you really "see" yourself and "know" yourself for who you are. Recognize what's always been true about you. Have you always loved to paint? Been drawn to the color pink? Made children laugh? Honor whatever it is through your words and actions. Don't deny what you know to be true about you. Take the time to read your own mind and discover what makes you tick. If you spent as much time figuring out yourself as you spend worrying about others, your life would be an open book for you.

Like Lara, I had my Cinderella night at the ball and found my Prince Charming lacking. I married at thirty-four, and at the time I felt I had a strong sense of self. Yet as I look back at the years since my divorce, I find that I've been constantly reinventing myself, discovering hidden parts of my personality I never dreamed existed. As

**Note to Self**

Take a yoga class. Engage in an evening of quiet prayer. Relax in silence. Your rhythmic breathing and quiet concentration will lead you to the center of yourself. The focus on self will be enlightening.

they see the light of day, I amaze myself and my friends with my self-knowledge and newfound talents. I am also encouraged by the thought that I will always amuse, delight, and entertain myself.

## The Power of Choice

I bet you don't know how much power you have. The sheer force of your will keeps you moving through life. It's your bright energy, which inspires you, fuels you, comforts you, and applauds you throughout the hours of the day. It's because you think "I am" that you do and you go on living. Like the song says, you are woman and you are strong. It's that strength that never allows us to betray ourselves.

Sally, a forty-three-year-old recovering stroke victim learned the hard way about the strength in her singleness. "When I woke from the surgery, the right side of my face was totally frozen, my hearing was gone, but I was alive," Sally writes on her Web page. One year after the surgery she still had only 3 percent functionality on the right side of her face. Her well-respected doctor at Stanford said that she would never have any movement on that side of her face again. Sally responded bravely. "That's statistics. Statistics are based on experience, and I have power," she remembers thinking. She recognized that she had choice, free will, education, and a whole range of resources to draw upon in managing her recovery. She refused to accept his diagnosis and began the long journey to restore the beautiful face she'd seen all her life in the mirror.

**Note to Self**

Evaluate your health insurance coverage. Are you covered in the event of a major health crisis? Check out health plans on your job or review low-cost alternatives at www. covertheuninsured.org.

"I was just leveled. I was sleeping sixteen, eighteen hours a day. I slept that way for probably a good nine months after the surgery," Sally says.

The first year after the brain surgery, she could do two things a day. That was it.

And yet, here was a time when being single had its advantages. With her wry sense of wit, Sally points out that many people who had the same tumor she had didn't have her miraculous recovery. "They don't have the function that I have because they didn't have the time to do acupuncture every single day and they didn't have the time to do all the process work and the mirror work."

The result is that today I sit looking at the beautiful smile of a beautiful woman. There's a little softness on one side of Sally's face, but she's come a long way since the surgery five years earlier. "I didn't think it would take me…really, honestly, take me…five years to recover." She finally began to feel like a fully functioning adult about a year ago. She now works full-time, pays her bills, keeps her apartment clean, and has a social life.

Sally's dreams of having a family returned with the normalcy of her life. She's had to overcome heartfelt issues about her sense of attractiveness because of the facial paralysis. Men don't see her the same way they used to, and that's hard. And after attending a fertility conference, she cried for days. Her chances of becoming a mother at age forty-three were slimmer than she had imagined. She wondered, "How in the hell did I get to be almost forty-four years old and not have a baby and not get married?"

But now that she's living life ABS (after brain surgery), Sally is open to the many ways in which she could become a parent. "I don't know. Does the man come first? Does the sperm come first? Do I adopt a child?" she laughs loudly as she states her options.

As I leave Sally's apartment and walk out into the cool night air, I'm thinking about something she said: "Savor the moment, because the moment changes. It's not about what we don't have; it's about what we *do* have. It's about acknowledging that because we are single we have different choices."

## The Single Best Attitude

Always choose the glass that is half full. Let the power of positive thinking be your stronger better half. There's only one you, but as the one in your life, always expect miracles. Your unique combination of personal strengths and special gifts can outweigh a statistical collection of numbers. Believe and you can make it so. Choose to have faith in yourself and watch your life become a self-fulfilling prophesy of success. Choose to amaze yourself. Flaunt the power of one.

## Steal This Life: Learn How to Fly

**How about celebrating your brilliant choice to be single by making a limitless one? Learn how to fly through the air with the greatest of ease!** After all, circus tents are now popping up in major cities across the country. Choosing to be single can often feel a lot like living without a net. Metaphorically let go of the fears that keep you from truly celebrating your unfettered state. Why not start living life embracing the joy of being single? Come join the "daring young men and women" on the flying trapeze. Grab the bar and soar with other singles! Be fearless at www.trapezeschool.com and www.trapezearts.com.

### *Only One Is #1*

"Live like you mean it," I once saw graffitied on a bathroom wall. Okay, so I've heard life is not a dress rehearsal, but this scraggly handwritten message gets right to the point. C'mon, you made the choice to be single; are you making the most of it?

Deacon Tom certainly is. He's chosen a profession that forbids marriage in favor of a life devoted to serving others. In about a month he'll be taking his final vows to be ordained as a Catholic priest. Sitting at the big wooden dining table, his back to the window on this beautiful spring morning, he says, "I really do feel society puts more pressure on people to be married than are either ready for marriage or should be married." Amen! I certainly know what he means and I'm sure you've known a marriage not made in heaven.

### Note to Self

Post this where you can see it everyday: "Live single life like you mean it."

For Deacon Tom, religious life offers a satisfying way to live in community with others outside the bonds of marriage. When I ask him about being single in a married church, he responds, "I can tell you stories about living with ten other bachelors. We get up from dinner and we've got that kitchen clean in fifteen minutes. We have our chores. You name the bad habit and I've seen it," he chuckles with obvious delight. "In a way, I think it's the same way with married couples. You learn how to live together, except they have to fall in love with each other in order to get along," he adds.

Yes, you've experienced the joys and sorrows of communal living as well. You love your roommates but wish for more bathroom time, less dirty laundry on the floor, and more privacy. Yet you appreciate having someone to share the grocery bill and the latest episode of *Lost* with.

Deacon Tom spent his younger years honing the skills which would allow him to live with others. The fourth of nine siblings, he grew up in a close-knit Catholic family in the Park Hill neighborhood of Denver, Colorado. At forty-five, he's never been married despite being surrounded by plenty of role models.

"No, nope, never married. Dated a lot. Part of it was I moved around a lot. After graduate school I moved to D.C. for a little over a year, then I moved to New Mexico, then I went to Idaho when I was twenty-nine or thirty, " he says by way of explanation. Here he was the single guy in a town of about thirty thousand people. And he had this idea of the perfect girl. "I was looking for somebody probably never married. Outdoorsy but intelligent, you know, I had all these criteria," Deacon Tom

## The *Single* Best *Attitude*

Discover the sacredness in your single life. Stop and reflect upon the amazing gift of life itself. Adopt an attitude of gratitude for all the time, money, and energy you are able to invest in yourself. Experience the joy that comes with knowing you have everything you need. Challenge yourself to remember that being single is not *all* that you are. It's just a small part of what you offer the world. You fulfill many roles in your life. You're funny, talented, a driven leader, a loyal friend, a responsible adult and much, much more. And don't you ever forget it!

laughs at his own naiveté. "I started to realize as I got a little bit older, in my early thirties, that the field was getting smaller and smaller, especially in a small town."

Savoring the incredible freedom and independence of single life, he bought a house. He traveled extensively for work as a conservation advocate and took monthly vacations on his own. Bachelor Tom was really enjoying the single life.

Then in his early forties, Deacon Tom made the commitment to pastoral life. "It's a different life. People don't understand my life. It's often really difficult to have a conversation with close friends, family," he leans forward in his chair as he gestures expressively with his hands. "You won't get married. So they don't know what questions to ask." Your friends and family may not understand your life choice either. They ask the same questions repeatedly: "Why aren't you married?" "What ever happened to that nice person you went out with in college?" Deacon Tom answers their questions for all of you when he says, "Ultimately it's about what you do with your life. Not everyone is called to married life."

**246**

## Steal This Book: Cherish the Power of Prayer

**There are so many inspiring books on the market, but I always think the most precious words are the ones that speak personally to us. That's why I created my own personal prayer book.** It began when I found a beautiful handmade journal wrapped in silk sari remnants. In this beautifully bound book, I collect my favorite poems, quotes, images, prayers, and other bits of inspiration.

I note when I enter each piece of solace and wisdom. During the day I'll escape for a moment by lighting a candle before opening the book to any page. It's my personal peace from heaven on earth.

## Singular Sensations

**#101** *Mind over matter.* There's no magic formula for meditation. Quiet your mind and focus on what's in front of you: a spot on the carpet, a piece of chocolate cake, or the photo of something close to your heart. Be entirely in the moment, aware of your breathing, and sensitive to how you're feeling. Be here now.

**#102** *Pink power.* Everyone looks better with a rosy glow. Trying using pink light bulbs in your dining room. The soft color adds a warm glow to most people's skin tones. Sleep between pink sheets or add a pink piece to your wardrobe. The rosy color will lift your spirits. Flaunt the power of pink!

#103  *Less is more.* Take a break from multitasking. Do one thing and really enjoy it. Stop eating over the sink with a book in one hand and a fork in the other. The next time a friend calls, give her your full attention. Enjoy your life one thing at a time.

#104  *Day-to-day duties.* Make daily goals: get the laundry done, revise your résumé, or plan your vacation. Giving yourself a little personal challenge will boost your energy.

#105  *The art of housecleaning.* Investigate all the twenty-first-century labor-saving devices and new and improved household cleaning products. Create a cleaning toolkit with your favorite dirt-busters handy. Establish a home care routine for a dust-free abode.

#106  *Live together.* Reap the benefits of living with a roommate. Increase your circle of friends by networking with theirs. Choose someone for their companionship as well their good credit. Share the fun and divide the dirty work.

# The Last Word

**Being single is a choice. You can choose to support yourself wholeheartedly through good times and bad.**

1. You are financially responsible for your single self. Commit to making your money work toward your happiness. Respect your dreams and the dreamer.

2. Believe in yourself and your ability to make your dreams come true.

3. Protect yourself. Carry medical insurance for major medical emergencies. Write a living will to make your wishes known in case you are unable to speak for yourself.

4. Come into your own—now! Dig deep for self-knowledge. Never stop being your life's work.

5. There is great power in your singleness. Make power-driven, not "poor me" choices. The rich life you build will be your own.

6. Neither singlehood nor marriage is meant for everyone. Take *your* pick.

# Finally

# The Single Best Last Word!

So, is my single life the life I imagined it would be? I happen to think it's been much, much more. I always say, when I'm asked, that I've managed to work and play with really smart people and have more fun than I ever thought possible! I've bribed, persuaded, seduced, and paraded my glorious self into the life of my dreams...only better.

I've jumped whenever I've liked to the next job, the next person, the next lifestyle. I've lived a fast-paced jumble of minutes clinging to shrinking hours on a flighty calendar. I'm not sure how I got here, but I'm awfully glad I did. Because the alternative—misery and loneliness—just wasn't an option.

You have the right and the responsibility to determine your life choices. Choosing to be single is not the same as choosing to feel unwanted, unhappy, or undesirable. Your options could just as easily be *limited* to single equaling an amazing, incredible, tremendous life on your own.

My friends used to joke when I was attached that I was "the most single married person" they knew. Now that I am no longer married, they still comment on my *joie de vivre* and succulent, wild, wanton ways. My life has been an ever-evolving mix of close friends, competing personal interests, and delightful world travels.

Near the end of my marriage, my husband and I went in for counseling. I remember that during one of my solo sessions, the therapist asked my greatest fear about getting divorced. "I would be alone," I replied.

He laughed and said, "Jerusha, you may be single, but you will *never* be alone."

And you know what? He was right.

You, too, are never alone when you're living *la dolce vita*, solo!

# Solo Living Resources

## Singles Organizations

**www.unmarriedamerica.org** Inspiring mission statement, facts, figures, and useful information about living life solo

**www.unmarried.org** Site sponsored by the Alternatives to Marriage Project focuses on cohabitation as well as singles life

**www.singlesonthego.com** National clearinghouse lists information on singles activities, clubs, online dating sites, and travel activities

**www.singlevolunteers.org** An international organization designed to encourage singles to volunteer, with chapters in the United States, Canada, and Australia

## Lifestyle Essentials

**www.astrologyzone.com** Monthly in-depth astrological updates on life, love, and money

**www.colorstrology.com** What are your true colors? Click here to find out how color affects your personality.

**www.eventme.com** Will send invitations to your desktop for some of the hottest parties and events in your town!

**www.filmfestivals.com** Largest database of film festivals around the world

**www.meetup.com** Convenient way to meet others in your neighborhood that share similar interests or avocations or hobbies or passions

**www.RedHatSociety.com** Everything you need to know about joining or opening your own chapter of fun for women over fifty

**www.socialdomain.com** A social, business, and singles calendar for several cities across the country. Bookmark this site and sign up for the weekly event-filled emails

**Having Our Say: The Delany Sisters' First 100 Years** *by Sarah E. Delany and A. Elizabeth Delany with Amy Hill Hearth* Offers the life stories of two never-married twentieth-century lifestyle pioneers in a down-to-earth, mother-wit wisdom kind of way. Book became a must-see Broadway play.

**If the Buddha Dated: A Handbook for Finding Love on a Spiritual Path** *by Charlotte Kasl, PhD* A loving, playful guide on having love in your life with and without a partner

**Love Your Body** *by Louise L. Hay* The perfect bathroom book. Step out of the shower and affirm your body's power and beauty each morning before you begin your day.

**Solo Suppers** *by Joyce Eserksy Goldstein* Collection of good-looking recipes which encourages you to skip takeout or milk-and-cereal dinners for a more satisfying meal. Includes tips on food shopping for one, stocking a basic pantry, and keeping wine.

**101 Ways to Keep Your Soul Alive** *by Frederic Brussat* The perfect inspirational book to carry in your purse or pocket

**100 Simple Secrets of Happy People** *by David Niven, PhD* A page-turner I often loan to my friends

## *Dating Assists*

**www.cuddleparty.com** Need a hug? Get into your pajamas and snuggle up at one of these playful slumber parties across the country.

**www.8minuteDating.com** Speed dating with options. Choose to see someone again for friendship, business, or love.

**www.GreatBoyfriends.com** Here every guy comes with a recommendation—and a commitment rating

**www.HurryDate.com** Warp-speed dating at the hottest lounges in town

**www.lemondate.com** Online daters rating service; members rate past dates

**www.profilehelper.com** Helps online daters create the best profiles

**www.rentmrrightnow.com** Provides dates for evening and wingperson services

**www.wingwomen.com** Makes the first move for men or women daters

## Women & Wealth

**www.FreddieMac.com** Government sponsored website with in-depth home-buying information

**www.myFICO.com** Get your credit score online and sign up for updates on your credit history

**www.NAIC.org** National Association of Investment Clubs; provides information and services for starting your own investment circle

**www.rightonthemoney.org** Sign up for their newsletter offering easy to understand personal financial advice

**Buying Solo** *by Vanessa Summers* Finally a book for us by us on the single biggest investment of our lives

**Girl, Make Your Money Grow!** *by Glinda Bridgforth and Gail Perry-Mason* An emotional and spiritual guide to dealing with complex money issues

**Smart Women Finish Rich: 9 Steps to Achieving Financial Security and Funding Your Dreams (Revised Edition)** *by David Bach* Commonsense guide to wealth building for women

**What's Money Got to Do With It? The Ultimate Guide on How to Make Love and Money Work in Your Relationship** *by Cheryl Broussard and Michael Burns* No-nonsense guide to mixing money and love

## Health & Wellness

**www.bellydancingvideos.com** Beautiful photos and inside look at dancing for fun and profit

**www.covertheuninsured.org** Provides information about free and low-cost health insurance

**www.realage.com** Singles tend to be in better shape! Take the online test and discover if you're as young as you feel!

**www.shira.net** Lots of information how to get the most out of your exotic dance experience

**www.trapezeschool.com** Back to school to learn how not to let go!

**www.trapezearts.com** Brings the circus to your town; offers indoor and outdoor classroom environments

**www.y-me.org** Whose mission is to ensure that no one faces breast cancer alone

**The Stretch Deck** *by Olivia H. Miller* Relieve stress at your desk and on the road with this convenient card deck which allows you to select exercises to relieve tension where you feel it. Stretch your way to success.

**The S Factor: Strip Workouts for Every Woman** *by Sheila Kelley* The ultimate in women's fitness combines yoga, dance, and the sexual expression of stripping for a whole new way to move and view your body.

## *Single Best Shopping*

**www.billiondollarbabes.com** Shop haute finds for less at prive, by-invitation-only sales around the world

**www.bookbyyou.com** Create your own romance novel starring you!

**www.thebodyshop.com** Personalized sensational scents

**www.coco-pink.com** Skip writing your name on a napkin. Hand him or her a personalized calling card from this artsy company.

**www.flashingblinkylights.com** Body lights and brilliant party favors

**www.gotparty.com** More light-up magic for flashy fun

**www.plumparty.com** Fabulous party goods and party planning tips

**www.seatfiller.com** Sign up to fill the seats at big ticket galas and Hollywood parties

**www.smartsco.com** Fun and games that test your knowledge of trivia about chocolates, food, sex, and wine

**www.stubhub.com** eBay-like marketplace for tickets to live sporting events, Broadway musicals, movie premieres, pop concerts and more

**www.warmspirit.com** Upscale home-based spa party

**www.zappos.com** A girl's gotta have shooz!

### Sex and the Single Life

**www.erotica-la.com** Information on the sizzling consumer trade show introducing the newest sensual aids

**www.eroticuniversity.com** Online and offline adult sex education

**www.goodvibes.com** Knowledgeable staff and great events that answer all of your questions about what goes on between the sheets

**www.jimmyjane.com** Upscale sensual aids; "Nice to be naughty"

**www.passionparties.com** Largest sex toy home party business

**www.pureromance.com** Romance quizzes, products, and information

**The Good Vibrations Guide to Sex, Third Edition** *by Cathy Winks and Anne Semans* The best all-around guide to everything you ever wanted ask about being intimately involved with another person

**Our Bodies, Ourselves for the New Century** *by the Boston Women's Health Collective* Classic on the female form, its parts, and what makes it work

**Sex Tips for Straight Women from a Gay Man** *by Dan Anderson and Maggie Berman* Humorous insider's guide to having the best sex with the opposite sex

**Erotic Massage: The Touch of Love** *by Kenneth Ray* Beautiful photos guide your fingers into giving the most pleasurable rubs

**The Best Sex I Ever Had: Real People Recall Their Most Erotic Experiences** *by Steven Finz* The stimulating stories will inspire you to try something new just once.

## *Steal Away Tours & Vacations*

**www.cheapair.com** For those with flexible travel plans, provides access to great fares around the globe

**www.clubgetaway.com** All-inclusive club offering weekend adventures in the Connecticut Berkshires

**www.cstn.org** Connecting Travel Network lists vacations for solo travelers

**www.meetmarketadventures.com** Not a dating service, but a cool way to meet other singles with similar interests

**www.luxurylink.com** Dream travel site auctions off stays at luxury destinations around the world. Accommodations for two but the bid pricing makes it a sensible guilty pleasure for one.

www.TravelZoo.com Subscribe to the weekly newsletter, which offers amazing airline, hotel, and car specials. Great for inspiring last-minute getaways.

www.cadbury.com Cadbury Schweppes Chocolate Factory Toll Free: 1-800-627-367 Tel: (03-62) 490-333 Fax: (03-62) 490 -334 Cadbury Schweppes Chocolate Factory, Cadbury Road, Claremont, Tasmania 7011

www.hersheys.com Hershey's Chocolate World in Hershey, Maison Pralus, Roanne, France,www.chocolats-pralus.com

www.mrchocolate.com Manhattan's Jacques Torres Chocolate Haven,
350 Hudson Street, New York, NY
Telephone: 718-875-9772

www.museumofsex.com Museum of Sex, New York
233 Fifth Avenue, New York, NY
Telephone: 212-689-6337

www.scharffenberger.com Scharffen Berger Chocolates, Berkeley, California
Telephone for groups of five or more: 510-981-4066

## Continue Your Solo Adventure at www.TheLastSingleGirlintheWorld.com!

# About the Author

Jerusha Stewart is the Original Last Single Girl in the World. Not one to shrink from championing self-expression, she encourages single women to revel in being the most sought-after girl at the dance of life. Jerusha believes that on their own, women can realize great personal fulfillment, financial success, and achieve their wildest dreams.

After flaunting the laws of attraction while studying in the library stacks at Stanford University—where she received a BA in international relations and a law degree—Jerusha breezed past the commitments of job and family to explore the power of the one. Today, the sexy singles savant imbues women all over the world with the joy of devouring life in outrageously large doses. She dates globally, but the San Francisco Bay Area is her current playground.

As a perpetually single woman with no children, an irregular dating life, and one divorce under her belt, Jerusha fans the flames of non-conjugal bliss at www.TheLastSingleGirlintheWorld.com.